Murder At Ardaig Castle

ALSO BY DANIEL SELLERS

DCI LOLA HARRIS SERIES
Book 1: Murder In The Gallowgate
Book 2: Murder In Lovers' Lane
Book 3: Murder On The Clyde
Book 4: Murder On Skye
Book 5: Murder At Ardaig Castle

Daniel Sellers
MURDER AT ARDAIG CASTLE

DCI Lola Harris Series Book 5

JOFFE BOOKS

Joffe Books, London
www.joffebooks.com

First published in Great Britain in 2025

© Daniel Sellers

This book is a work of fiction. Names, characters, businesses, organisations, places and events are either the product of the author's imagination or are used fictitiously. Any resemblance to actual persons, living or dead, events or locales is entirely coincidental.
The spelling used is British English except where fidelity to the author's rendering of accent or dialect supersedes this. The right of Daniel Sellers to be identified as author of this work has been asserted in accordance with the Copyright, Designs and Patents Act 1988.

No part of this book may be used or reproduced in any manner for the purpose of training artificial intelligence technologies or systems. In accordance with Article 4(3) of the Digital Single Market Directive 2019/790, Joffe Books expressly reserves this work from the text and data mining exception.

Cover art by Nebojša Zorić

ISBN: 978-1-80573-012-5

For Simon

AUTHOR'S NOTE

Some places in this novel are real, as are some institutions. The characters and the events that unfold are fictional.

Please follow me on X (@djsellersauthor), on Instagram (@danielsellersauthor) and on Facebook (@danielsellersauthor). You can also sign up for my newsletter on my website: www.danielsellers.co.uk

#WhatWouldLolaHarrisDo?

Glasgow Chronicle, *Wednesday 6 January, p. 4*

TROUBLE IN PARADISE? RUMOURS RIFE AT ELITE CASTLE HIDEAWAY

by Jackie Cray, society and fashion

The rumour mill grinds on this week, as more guests take up residence at Ardaig Castle, the Kade Foundation's 'well-being retreat and recovery centre' that opened last autumn near Aberfoyle.

Social media was abuzz at the weekend with speculation that a certain former Scottish Government minister was witnessed being driven, ashen-faced, through the castle gates. A spokesperson for the former minister's party dismissed the rumours as 'speculation'.

It is also rumoured that a former Highland sub-postmistress has checked into Ardaig Castle. Heidi Bryce suffered a reported 'nervous collapse' following her recent campaign to clear her and several colleagues' names after being wrongly convicted of fraud. A family member said Ms Bryce's health was a private matter and refused to comment further.

There can be no denying, however, the identity of at least one of Ardaig's guests. On Monday, reality TV star Josette Daniels — currently battling a self-described 'food addiction' — landed in the castle grounds by helicopter. She live-streamed her own arrival on social media, including footage of her struggling to climb down from the helicopter in Balenciaga heels, resulting in her taking a tumble onto the lawn.

The publicity stunt has irritated Ardaig's management, who already have enough on their plate denying rumours of 'anonymous threats' being received. A castle insider tells me senior staff are worried the threats appear to be escalating.

[Continues]

CHAPTER ONE

Thursday 20 February

6.59 p.m.

Lola started awake as her sister took a hairpin bend far too fast.

'Jeezo, Frankie!' She grabbed the handle over the passenger door.

She peered frantically about. They were outside Glasgow already, somewhere dark and extremely wet. Rain fell like silver rods in the Volvo's headlights.

'Sorry, sorry!' Frankie got the vehicle under control again. 'This road's like a bloody river.'

'Where are we?'

'Coming down the hill into Strathblane. We're about halfway, I reckon. Go back to sleep. And don't worry, I'll take it slower.'

'I think I'll stay awake,' Lola said, trying not to sound grumpy.

She'd offered to drive but Frankie had insisted. 'The weekend's my treat, remember? A chance for you to unwind a wee bit.'

Frankie had been right that Lola needed to unwind. But she also needed time to think — and to make a decision.

Since the start of December she'd been leading a special project, investigating dubious political donations to three of Scotland's political parties, based at the Scottish Crime Campus near Coatbridge. Her team was huge and included analysts, auditors and lawyers. The case was complex and sensitive, requiring not just tactics but tact — which was why she'd been selected for the job, or so she'd been told.

She'd been flattered but cautious, taking her time and discussing it with her boss, Detective Superintendent Elaine Walsh, and with her boyfriend, Sandy, who was ex-police so could understand the pros and cons. Both encouraged her to go for it. Sandy told her she wouldn't be thinking twice about it if she was a bloke. Elaine called it a 'golden opportunity' if Lola was hoping for future promotion.

So she'd said yes.

But after two weeks she knew she'd made the worst decision of her career. There was too much information and the case was insanely complex. Then there were the daily briefings she had to provide to seniors plus continual requests from journalists for updates. Bottom line, the project was dull but plagued with professional risks, including public failure.

A month in, she was exhausted and her confidence low.

'So leave,' Sandy said when she literally cried on his shoulder one night. 'Ask Elaine to take you back to CID. If she won't — or can't — then resign and come and work with me and Ritchie. The work's piling up, and the money's great.'

'You make it sound such an easy choice.'

'It is.'

'To you, maybe.'

It was true Sandy's private investigation firm was overloaded with work. He and his pal Ritchie, another ex-cop, were looking to take on more investigators. But the work didn't always appeal.

'I've told you before,' she'd said, 'I'm not spending my days snooping on cheating husbands.'

At that he'd taken mild offence — though, Sandy being Sandy, he was over it within minutes.

She'd talked to Elaine, but Elaine was adamant. 'I'm not letting you fail at this,' she'd told her. 'Stick it out. Six months at least, or it'll look very bad. Seriously, this is for your own good.'

And so she'd knuckled down, but paid a price: she felt disengaged from her role, anxious in her home life, lethargic at weekends.

In fact, she realised, she had all the early signs of burnout.

When Frankie suggested this weekend away, she'd said no at first, that she had too much reading to get through. Then both her sister and Sandy had ganged up on her and she'd relented, secretly relieved.

A weekend at Rose Cottage, deep in a forested corner of the Trossachs, sounded heavenly. The photos made it look idyllic, not to mention remote. It belonged to a former colleague of Frankie's from the school where she was deputy head. The friend had modernised it and extended it out the back. Both bedrooms were en suite. There was an extensive collection of DVDs — and somewhere they could swim, so Lola should bring her cozzie.

'Why, is it near a loch?'

'Not that kind of swimming! You know I prefer my water above freezing point.'

There was a hotel ten minutes' walk away, Frankie explained, with a heated pool they could use.

It all seemed too good to be true and that made Lola suspicious; with Frankie there tended to be a catch. But she was too tired to pick holes, so decided to trust her sister this time.

The rain was worse now and Frankie had her wipers on full speed. Somewhere north of Drymen they plunged through a flooded section of road and Frankie slowed down some more.

'If this carries on we won't be leaving the cottage all weekend,' Lola said.

The weather had been foul for weeks and was about to get worse. Storm Zebedee was coming in from the south-west and 'intensifying' as it headed for Scotland.

'Maybe we should have checked the roads are open,' Lola said, gazing out at the sodden darkness.

'I'm sure it'll be fine,' Frankie said. 'Catherine said just to watch out on the road that runs along by the river. Part of it got washed away one time, but it's unlikely to happen again.'

'Remind me where I met Catherine again,' Lola said now.

'Oh, I can't remember if you have,' Frankie replied, a little too quickly.

'I thought you said I'd met her once.'

'Did I?' She laughed lightly and not very convincingly. 'It might have been at a school fair.'

'My memory's pretty sound,' Lola had pointed out. 'What did she teach?'

'Business and computing. But only for a few years. She changed careers but we kept in touch.'

'Must be doing okay if she can afford a luxury cottage in the Trossachs.'

Another unconvincing laugh. Lola contemplated her sister's profile. 'You're up to something.'

'Up to—? What? No I'm not.'

'Liar.' But she let it go and instead peered out at the dark, wet night, at the branches of firs caught by the car's lights.

Soon they were through Aberfoyle and following a winding single-lane road past a loch. Lola wasn't sure which one. There'd be time to study maps once she'd caught up on her sleep. She relaxed her limbs and felt pleasantly sleepy.

Past the loch, Frankie slowed for a sharp left turn.

There was a sign on a board. It said: *ARDAIG CASTLE ONLY — PRIVATE.*

And suddenly Lola understood.

'Ardaig Castle?' she said sharply.

'Don't shout at me!' Frankie cried.

'Ardaig Castle, the place where . . .' She stared at her sister in disbelief. 'Frankie—'

'It's not what you think,' Frankie squeaked.

'It better not be.' She fell back in her seat, almost winded as several things quickly made sense. 'Is that where Catherine works?'

'Maybe.'

'So *that's* who she is. She's the friend you asked me about at Christmas — the one who wanted advice about anonymous letters?'

'Maybe . . .'

'You said her name was Rachel.'

'I gave her a pseudonym.'

'Frankie—'

'I was planning to tell you, but—'

'When? When we were there?'

'Yes, well. I wanted you to see how nice it is. Then, when you were settled in—'

'You'd break the news that you'd brought me to your pal's place of work to investigate a loony letter writer? Well, it's not on. Turn round now.'

'I can't. The road's too narrow.'

'I mean it, Frankie. This is too much, even for you.'

'Catherine's so worried. I said I'd see if you'd meet her, even for half an hour. She offered us one of the cottages on the estate. Oh, please, Lola. Say you'll help.'

Lola said nothing. In fact she was too angry to speak. She folded her arms and glared out of the window. The headlights illuminated a low wall and an expanse of fast-running water on the other side. A river, and high by the look of it.

Up ahead was a gatehouse beside a pair of stone pillars. A sign said *PRIVATE PROPERTY*, but the high gates stood open. They slowed as a man in a dark raincoat and cap stepped quickly into view, his shoulders hunched against the rain. Lola started as she got a brief glimpse of a bone-white skull of a face. The man waved them through.

Frankie drove on into wooded grounds and took a left fork at a sign that pointed to *VISITOR ACCOMMODATION*. Then, three or four minutes later, they arrived in front of three little cottages, set against a backdrop of fir trees, resembling the photos Frankie had shown her.

So at least that part had been true.

Frankie stopped the engine. Rain drummed on the car roof. 'I'm sorry,' she whispered. Lola saw she was gripping the steering wheel as if for dear life. 'I should have told you. But we're here now. Please, let's go inside. Just take a look. Okay?'

Lola fell back in the seat. 'Just a look,' she said, hand on the door handle, ready to dash through the rain. 'But if I say so, we're heading straight back to the city. No bones, understood?'

CHAPTER TWO

7.47 p.m.

But the cottage was lovely: quaint outside and luxuriously cosy inside. Lola gazed about the living room, feeling like a spouse who's been duped into viewing a show home but is actually loving it.

'Aye, it's all right.' She took in the pretty green lampshades, the black-beamed low ceiling, the invitingly plump chintzy armchairs (complete with woollen throws) and the log burner in full flame.

A narrow staircase wound up from a corner of the living room. Upstairs, Lola found two small but comfortable-looking bedrooms, each with a tiny but spotless bathroom. She could hear rain on the roof tiles overhead. The bed looked soft, warm and inviting.

'They've done well with the space,' she said, coming back downstairs, her thoughts still on that bed.

'Catherine's given us a welcome basket,' Frankie said from the little kitchen at the back of the cottage. 'How lovely. She said it's something they like to do. These cottages are just for family who are visiting patients. Two bottles of wine — fancy stuff, by the look of it — cheese, pickle, biscuits. Bread too. How nice!' Frankie gave her a winning smile. 'What do you say, sis?'

Lola looked over the goodies, trying not to appear impressed. She took a deep breath, her eyes lingering on the red wine before she lifted them to look hard into Frankie's. 'I say, let's have a cup of tea and a wee chat.'

Frankie nodded sheepishly. 'I'll pop the kettle on.'

Meanwhile, Lola settled into one of the armchairs and took out her phone, ready to text Sandy and inform him what Frankie had done. She had no signal, so set about typing in the Wi-Fi code printed on a laminated card lying on the coffee table.

On the back of the card was a pen-and-ink map of the grounds. It wasn't to scale, so it said, but depicted an imposing Ardaig Castle at the heart of the estate, surrounded by parkland which was in turn ringed round by forest. An 'H' was marked on the grassy area in front of the castle, presumably a helicopter landing pad. Various roads tracked through the woods, including one that forked away from the castle's main driveway towards the cluster of cottages. *Visitor accommodation* said a label. Each of the three cottages was named. This one, Rose Cottage, was the middle of the three, between Hawthorn Cottage and Bluebell Cottage. The drawing showed the river looping round the estate in a horseshoe, so that the whole place was a kind of peninsula cut off on three sides by water. Lola remembered how high and fast that river had been flowing. Behind her, rain pelted against the window and the pane rattled in a gust of wind, making her all the more grateful for the crackling log burner.

'Here we are,' Frankie said, all smiles as she carried a tray in, complete with teapot and china cups and saucers. 'I brought some of those biscuits too. Organic double-chocolate chip.' She set the tray down on the coffee table. 'I'll pour, will I?'

Lola accepted a cup and saucer of black Earl Grey and noted Frankie's evident discomfort as she perched on the edge of the armchair on the other side of the stove. Clearly she was expecting another row.

In fact Lola's ire had subsided somewhat. She liked the cottage — she was even prepared to stay a night — but she wanted to hear Frankie's excuses.

'Go on then,' she prompted.

Frankie winced. 'Okay. First thing: you haven't met Catherine before.'

'I knew that! I do have a functioning memory.'

'She's someone I worked with, just not at Westwood Academy. It was quite a few years ago, when I was in Hamilton.'

Lola sipped her tea and waited.

'She tracked me down online because she was looking for some advice about those anonymous letters. She'd seen you on the TV talking about that crazy business on Skye, and remembered we were sisters.'

'And I told you to get her to ring the police.' Lola remembered the conversation. It had been around Christmastime.

'And I explained she'd already tried that,' Frankie said in a small voice. 'But that they couldn't really help — not without risking things becoming public. Which was why she'd come to me.'

'And I said I couldn't get involved.'

She remembered suggesting to Frankie that the friend, this 'Rachel', might consider using a private investigator — someone like Sandy, in fact. But Frankie said Rachel had already rejected that idea.

'So Rachel — Catherine, whatever her real name is — suggested you might get me out here under false pretences.'

'That's not how it happened.'

'Oh?'

Frankie looked more sheepish still. 'I met her for a coffee in Glasgow a couple of weekends ago. Her suggestion. She told me more about what's been going on here. She'd tried the local police again — honestly, she did — but they wanted to come to the castle and the Kade Foundation wouldn't hear of it. I offered to talk to you again but she said not to.'

Lola made a sceptical face.

'She *did*! So I suggested something else.'

'Oh?'

'I said, what if you and I drove out to the Trossachs one time. We could "bump into her" somewhere. In Callander, say, or the wee garden centre on the way from Drymen. She said that felt deceitful. She said she'd been in half a mind to invite us out for a weekend, to use one of the cottages while they're standing empty. I think she saw my eyes light up. And then I got to thinking — maybe it *would* be nice to have a weekend away, just the two of us. After all, you've been working so hard, so—' she bit her lip — 'I said I thought it would be a wonderful idea. You'll have a lovely weekend, Lola. We both will.'

'And when does my private investigation start, eh? Catherine got the anonymous letters all ready for me along with a magnifying glass and a fingerprint kit?'

'Not at all!' Frankie looked genuinely pained so Lola told herself to back off, just a little. 'She said she hoped we'd have a restful weekend and she'd be pleased to say hello to you if you bumped into each other. No pressure.'

Lola sipped her tea and let the irritation disperse. It was easy enough, that's how tired she was. Tired from her job — not because it was too full on, but because it was draining her soul.

It was another two minutes before either of them spoke. Frankie asked, gingerly, 'Will I start unloading the car, or . . . ?'

'Or what?'

'Or are we going back to Glasgow?'

Lola groaned. 'You can unload the car.'

'Oh!' Frankie clapped her hands and got up. 'You're wonderful. I knew you'd like it once you were here.' She made for the door.

'But Frankie,' Lola said, craning round to eye her sister from the comfort of the chair, 'never, *ever*, do anything like this again — you hear?'

CHAPTER THREE

8.34 p.m.

Frankie had brought homemade veggie lasagne and set about heating it up to have with salad. Meanwhile Lola took a shower, then talked to Sandy on Facetime from her bedroom — the one at the back of the cottage.

'*That* place!' Sandy said when Lola told him where she was.

'Aye, and I'm not happy about it, either. Do you swear you didn't know?'

'Seriously, I didn't have a clue. Bloody Frankie, eh? Roping me in to do her dirty work.' He sounded more amused than annoyed. 'Meant to be an impressive set-up, though. And Frankie's got you there to find out who's sending them nasty letters, has she? Plenty of material for any poison pen writer in that place. You know who was first through the doors, don't you? Smuggled in under the cover of night, according to the *Chronicle*.'

'Let me guess. Lady Gaga?'

'No one so exciting.'

'Well, I don't have time to read the gossip pages, so you'll need to tell me.'

He told her the name of a certain former senior minister at the Scottish Parliament.

'Kieran Fox? Really? Don't they call him something very unkind?'

'The Crazy Fox, aye. After he began claiming the Russians were bugging his brain.'

'Oh, yes . . .'

'It was in the middle of a committee meeting at Holyrood. It was being live-streamed as well. Some kind of manic episode. They had to bundle him out. There'll still be clips online if you care to look.'

'I don't,' Lola said sharply. 'Jeezo, the poor guy.'

'Och, don't "poor guy" him. I'm sure his cupboards are full of skeletons. There's a reality TV star there just now, isn't there? Josette Somebody, the one who wears metallic jumpsuits.'

'What are you? *Hello* magazine or something?'

'Oh, and I know who else was there just after it opened. Ah . . .'

'Who?'

'The woman who was a special advisor to the former Deputy First Minister.'

Lola said a name.

'Aye, her. I'm sure I read she'd checked in. Cocaine addiction, I think.'

'Please tell me she's not still here,' Lola murmured.

The woman in question was one of the many subjects of her special investigation into the dodgy financing of political parties. The last thing she needed was to bump into her.

'I seem to remember she checked in then checked out after a few weeks.'

'Let's hope that's the case.'

'Don't be mad at Frankie,' Sandy said now. 'It sounds like she just wants to help her old pal, and hey, you get a free weekend out of it.'

'Aye, well . . . I'd rather she took me to Benidorm next time. Anywhere that isn't Scotland in February. You should hear the wind. It's screaming through the trees.'

Lola heard a noise from downstairs, the sharp *rat-a-tat-tat* of a door knocker.

So, it's already started.

'Door!' she yelled downstairs.

'I've got it!' Frankie yelled back.

'I'll have to go,' Lola told Sandy. 'I suspect I'm about to be introduced to my hostess.'

Lola was in her PJs so pulled on the complimentary dressing gown she'd found beautifully wrapped on the bed.

She went downstairs as Frankie led a stout hooded figure in a full-length navy-blue mac into the living room. The coat was running with rain and it was dripping on the wooden floor.

'And here's Lola,' Frankie said brightly.

The figure turned and pulled down the hood, freeing a bouncing bob of slightly frizzy, dark-blonde hair. The woman fixed her eyes intently on Lola.

'Lola, this is Catherine Ballantyne,' Frankie said encouragingly. 'Catherine's the general manager of Ardaig Castle. Catherine, meet my sister Lola.'

'Hello,' Catherine said, her intense blue-green eyes filling with tears and her face flushing.

How old was she? Early-fifties, Lola guessed.

'You're really here!' She gave Lola a huge smile and Lola half expected to be pulled into a soggy embrace. 'It means the world to me,' she said, and bit her lip as if to stem an emotional flood.

'Thank you for inviting us,' Lola said, catching Frankie's eye. What on earth had she promised the woman?

As if detecting tension, Catherine glanced nervously at Frankie then back at Lola. 'Of course, this is your weekend to relax,' she said. 'I don't expect anything from you.' She turned her head. 'That's right, isn't it, Frankie?'

'Yes,' Frankie said, clearing her throat, 'we're both in need of the break. And it's very generous of you to give us this place — *isn't it, Lola?*'

'Yes, very,' Lola echoed, and smiled her good-girl smile.

'Of course,' the intense woman said now, looking to Frankie once as if for a prompt, 'it would be lovely to chat to you, Lola, if you have time. Some very, well, *unsettling* things have been happening here. I, erm . . .'

She bit her lip and winced. Lola could see when someone was suffering with stress, and Catherine clearly was.

She heard herself saying, 'I'd love to chat, Catherine.' She even managed a smile.

'Oh, would you?' She put a hand to her face as her features crumpled and she burst into a volley of tears. 'I'm sorry. I'm so emotional. I just—'

'It's okay,' Frankie said.

'I'll put the kettle on, will I?' Lola asked gently.

'No! Not on my account,' Catherine said. 'I'll leave you. But perhaps tomorrow? Or over the weekend?'

'Whenever suits,' Lola said.

'And you're both most welcome at the castle for meals. Lunch and dinner, at least. Both are served buffet style. Perhaps you'll come for lunch tomorrow? Served between twelve thirty and two.'

'We'd love that, wouldn't we Lola?' Frankie said.

Catherine beamed. 'Good, and maybe I could show you a little of the castle as well. It has a fascinating, if not particularly pleasant, history.'

She made to leave, pulling up her hood to contain her voluminous hair. At the door, she said quietly to Frankie, 'You'll remember the forms, won't you?' to which Frankie replied with a nod and a slightly awkward glance back at Lola.

Frankie got the door for her while she turned on a torch. 'Will you be all right getting back in the dark?' Frankie asked.

'Oh, yes. Quite all right. I'm used to it now.' She smiled back at Lola. 'Sleep well, won't you?'

* * *

9.12 p.m.

'I knew you'd come round,' Frankie said. 'She's very sweet, don't you think — Catherine?'

'Seems so,' Lola said neutrally.

'She's been in such a state. I've been quite worried about her. I mean, it's been going on for a good couple of months now.'

It had been just after Hogmanay that Frankie mentioned the letters. They'd been on their way to visit an aunt, their late mother's sister, in a care home in Hamilton. She'd asked it casually, as Lola drove along the expressway.

'Are poison pen letters all that common?'

'Hate mail? No, not particularly.' Lola frowned. 'Why, have you had one?'

'Not me, no. A friend. Someone I worked with years ago. She runs a sort of health and well-being retreat out in the country. She says a few of the staff have had them too. Spite, mainly.'

'Has she reported them?'

'Yes. She said the local police gave her some advice but they wanted to come to the castle, which would have made things awkward. They told her these things are nearly impossible to trace and to try to ignore them.' A heavy pause. 'So I said I'd mention it to you.'

'Frankie . . .' She groaned. 'I can't get involved. You know that.'

Frankie had seemed put out, offended even, but Lola had enough on her plate, without taking on informal investigations for old colleagues of her sister.

'Thank you, Lola,' Frankie said now. 'She'll feel better for being listened to. I think she feels very alone out here.'

'There are other jobs,' Lola said. 'Why doesn't she apply for something else?'

Frankie bridled at that. 'Why should she? Why should anyone be hounded out of a job by some unhinged letter writer?'

Lola had to concede the point.

'What forms was she talking about just now?' she asked.

'Oh, yes.' Frankie bit her lip and eyed Lola cautiously. 'She'd like us to sign a non-disclosure agreement.'

'A *what*?'

'It's because there are a couple of well-known people staying at the castle — as patients, I mean. They don't call them "patients" though. They call them "guests".'

'Show them to me,' Lola said, irritated.

Frankie retrieved the forms.

'I'm not signing this.' Lola refolded the single page and handed it back along with the biro Frankie had handed her.

'It seems reasonable to me.'

'It's a bloody cheek! Catherine invited me here,' she pointed out. 'Rather, she got you to invite me here — under false pretences. Now she wants me to swear I'll be discreet?'

'You will, though, won't you?'

'Of course!'

'So, what's the problem?' Frankie was annoyed now. She marched into the kitchen, ostensibly to check on the lasagne.

Lola went after her. 'She either trusts me or she doesn't. Look, you sign it if you want, but I'm not, and if she doesn't like it, then we can leave.'

Frankie stood up and made a face. They'd fallen out many times in the past over what Frankie called Lola's 'bloody principles'.

'I'm in the police,' Lola pointed out now. 'I'm a senior detective! That should be more than enough for her.'

'It's not just Catherine, though, is it?' Frankie said. 'It's the Foundation. It's their promise to their guests.'

'I can't sign an NDA,' Lola said. 'If there is a future investigation, then I wouldn't be able to give a statement. You can explain it to Catherine tomorrow or I can.'

Frankie said nothing, but set about dressing salad leaves in mutinous silence.

'Now find me a corkscrew,' Lola said.

In the end they had a nice evening, sharing a bottle of the wine and devouring nearly all the biscuits from Catherine's welcome basket while they watched a DVD from the cottage's selection. They'd agreed on *The Bodyguard* with Whitney Houston. Lola had forgotten that anonymous letters featured in the story, particularly nasty ones sent to Whitney Houston's character by a disturbed individual, using cut-up newspaper.

'At least Catherine's never had actual death threats,' Frankie murmured at one point. 'Well, not that she's told me about, anyway.'

CHAPTER FOUR

Friday 21 February

12.23 p.m.

Lola was woken early by the intensifying storm, but she felt rested nonetheless. The bed was one of the comfiest she'd ever slept in, so she lay there quite happily for some time, listening to rain smashing against the window and wind howling through the trees. It was the first time she'd felt properly relaxed in weeks — the first time since she'd taken that bloody job.

No, don't think about that just now.

So she picked up her book — one she'd been meaning to read for ages — and, before she knew it, it was lunchtime.

The weather was so wild when they stepped outside, ripping the breath from their lungs, that they opted to drive the half-mile or so to the castle. There were branches down everywhere, even a fallen tree, and it was as dark as night-time. Frankie drove with her headlights on.

The castle, when it loomed into view, was a sight to behold. Set in the middle of extensive lawns fringed with trees, it was a huge, grey, towered edifice with the asymmetry of an ancient building that has been added to over the centuries. It was like something from a fairy tale — or a Gothic horror story — complete with a large, pillared portico and a round tower that rose to battlements at the right-hand side. The map had shown two additional wings extending from the back of the bulky main tower house. They were invisible from here. Despite the gloomy exterior, the place promised shelter, with lights on in various rooms and smoke emerging from several chimneys.

They parked at the left-hand side of the castle, next to several other cars. Lola realised they were being observed. An unhappy-looking woman with lank dark hair smoked under a shelter beside a pair of industrial-sized bins. Her face was pudgy and blotchy. Lola nodded to her but she merely raised her chin, lifted the cigarette to her lips again and turned away.

'The welcoming party?' she murmured to Frankie.

'Hope not. Ready to run?'

They dashed round to the front of the castle, feeling the full brunt of rain and wind and almost dived into the portico that sheltered the main door.

Frankie tugged on an iron bellpull and they heard a low *bonnnnng* resonate within.

Catherine Ballantyne opened the tall wooden door and met them with a strained smile of greeting.

'This terrible weather,' she said as she pulled the door wider. 'Then again, it is February.' She gave a nervous laugh. 'Do, please, come on in. This is the great hallway.'

Catherine closed the door behind them, replacing the howl of the wind with an echoing bang.

The interior was vast and chilly, with stone floors and a red-carpeted staircase. Heavy oil paintings in chunky gold frames filled the cream walls and a stag's head loomed above a huge fireplace. The hearth beneath it was stacked with logs but not lit. Lola noticed how thick the walls were: at least a metre, judging by the depth of a windowed alcove. The great hallway opened all the way up to the castle's roof, where a skylight showed the grey sky above, and balconied landings spanned the first, second and third floors.

Last night Catherine had seemed upset; this morning she seemed nervy and embarrassed. She certainly didn't seem comfortable making eye contact with Lola.

The awkwardness had to be about the non-disclosure form. A grumpy Frankie had phoned Catherine from the cottage that morning to explain Lola's position, in response to which Catherine had suggested a middle way. Lola could eat lunch in her office and keep away from other parts of the castle.

'Where do you want us?' Frankie asked Catherine brightly now.

'Oh — erm . . .' Catherine bit her lip and looked embarrassed. 'The thing is, Frankie, I wondered if you might like to take lunch in the orangery — while Lola and I have our chat.'

Frankie stared, eyes wide.

'The letters are probably quite sensitive,' Lola pointed out.

Catherine winced.

'Oh.' Frankie seemed briefly off her stride. 'Yes. Yes, of course.' She managed a smile. 'I understand.'

'And here's Senga McCall to show you the way,' Catherine said, putting on a smile and beckoning to a tiny, stick-thin woman in her fifties who'd crept out from behind the great staircase. She wore an apron and a sort of old-fashioned cook's bonnet that suited her pinched face. 'Senga, this is the visitor I mentioned. If you would take her to the dining room so she can get some lunch and then see her safely to the orangery, please. Yes, I think it will be very pleasant there. Oh, and you got my note about the tray that's to come to my office, didn't you, Senga?'

'Yes, yes, I did. This way, miss,' the tiny woman whispered, then beetled off, Frankie following in her wake.

A trim forty-something woman with a pale face and beautifully cut shoulder-length auburn hair was now coming briskly towards them. She wore a trouser suit and carried files under one arm while her eyes were locked on a device in her hand. She stopped when she noticed Catherine and Lola, lowered the device and smiled distractedly.

'Good afternoon,' she said quietly.

'Lola, this is Grace Miller,' Catherine said. 'Grace coordinates the well-being of our guests, contracting yoga teachers, massage therapists and so on to come into the castle. Oh, and she likes to lead walks in the forest, making sure our guests get plenty of fresh air,' she added and gave a forced little laugh.

'That's right,' the woman said. Her eyes were a very pale blue, large and wide set, giving her a startled, wary look. 'Physical fitness is the bedrock of well-being, after all.' She smiled weakly and tucked a strand of copper hair behind one ear.

'And, er, this is Lola,' Catherine said by way of awkward introduction. 'Lola Harris. She's visiting to take a look at the facilities on behalf of a relative.'

Grace gave a nod of discreet acknowledgement. 'I hope you'll be impressed with what you see.'

'I'm sure I shall,' Lola said, playing along.

The woman went on her way, running up the stairs two at a time.

Catherine turned to Lola. 'Let's go through to my office, shall we?'

* * *

12.34 p.m.

Catherine led the way through a low archway, then down three or four steps and along a chilly stone-floored passage with doors on both sides.

'Here we are,' she said, stopping by a door at the end.

She unlocked it and led the way into a circular room with whitewashed walls that seemed to be partly underground, judging by the high barred window. A two-bar electric fire popped and hissed in a corner.

'We're in the basement of the round tower,' Catherine said. 'You have a seat just there.'

She indicated a comfy chair in front of a desk, then set about filling a kettle from a tiny sink, chattering nonsense while Lola waited patiently.

'I've asked the kitchen to send down a selection of bits and pieces,' she said. 'There are usually little quiches and some lovely salads. Now, can I get you tea or coffee?'

Mugs of tea made, Catherine sat at her desk and took a number of deep breaths, apparently to calm her nerves. Finally, she looked at Lola. 'Now, where shall I start? With the first letter?'

'Tell me about this place first,' Lola said. 'What it is, who works here, who comes here, that sort of thing.'

'Yes. Yes, okay, that makes sense. Well, Ardaig Castle opened at the end of November, following six years of renovation. Restoration, really — and a good bit of rejuvenation too.' Lola suspected the words were lifted from marketing spiel. 'The Kade Foundation bought a near-ruin. The part of the castle we're in just now is sixteenth century, though one part is much older, going back to the 1400s. Two wings were added on, though. One that's Victorian, built about 1850, and another in 1905. That's my favourite part of the castle: red sandstone, beautifully carved wood, all Gothic revival and pre-Raphaelite stained glass, and of course there's the orangery too. When the Foundation bought the castle, the Victorian wing was intact. The orangery needed some reglazing, and some of the wooden frame replacing. The old part of the castle was effectively rebuilt.

'Most of us live in. We each have rooms — well, a small flat really: a living room with a tiny kitchen at one end and a bedroom and en-suite bathroom. Most of the staff rooms are in the main part of the castle on the first and second floors, and there's accommodation in the mews as well — the mews extends from the kitchens and sort of encloses a courtyard. The estates, domestic and catering staff live there. Our security manager William Rix lives in the gatehouse.

'Ardaig is a vast place — a Tardis, really. Three storeys in most parts. Four or even five in some, if you count attics and basements. The Foundation put in a couple of lifts, and made the place fit for its purpose as a well-being retreat. A place of health and recovery, a place where people can safely face their personal demons.'

'Meaning drink and drugs?' Lola asked.

'Yes. Or stress or anxiety, or a worn-down spirit. We don't diagnose but we do treat medically where a diagnosis already exists. We also try to treat all our guests in a holistic sense, with a focus on wellness where we can. The Kade Foundation has four such centres now, one in London, another in the Dordogne, one in Tuscany and now this one. All the centres occupy heritage sites. I believe this place is the most historic. We even have a ghost.' She gave a slightly embarrassed smile. 'Two actually. A scullery maid who drowned herself in a well in the grounds when she realised she was pregnant by one of the grooms on the estate. The well is blocked up and the woods have swallowed it up — I don't even know where it is. You're supposed to be able to hear sobbing just before dawn in midwinter. Then there's the monk.'

'The monk?' Lola asked, surprised.

'Yes, this was an abbey for a time, and not that long ago. It was a very devout order. They believed in inflicting pain on themselves — lashing themselves and each other and rolling about on thorny branches. One went completely insane. He tried to escape, but he was caught by two of the brothers. They dragged him screaming back into the castle and shut him in one of the cellars. He found a bottle, broke it and sliced open his wrists and throat.'

'How horrible!'

'I know! A couple of the staff claim they've seen him. Heard him too. Izzy McManus says she saw him one evening, running in the grounds, screaming with his wrists held high and bloody — like this. Then he seemed to vanish into the trees.' She bit her lip. 'Sorry — you probably think this is nonsense.'

Lola thought quickly how to answer. 'I don't think I believe in ghosts,' she said. 'But I'm interested that others do — *and* that they claim to see them. I'm very curious about that.'

'Izzy is a frightened creature, though. The kind to jump at shadows.' Catherine shifted in her chair and looked suddenly very uncomfortable. 'But *I'm* not like that at all.' She looked Lola directly in the eye. 'Yet I've seen him too.'

Lola stared.

'In fact, I'm sure I have. And only the other week.' She gave a little shrug and smiled, letting Lola know it was okay to greet the admission with scepticism. 'Out there on the lawn, in full habit — or cowl or whatever it's called. Crossing the lawn, running for his life, only to vanish into the trees.' She shuddered. 'I can't explain it.'

They sat in slightly embarrassed silence.

'Dr Abbott says it was someone playing a prank. There are a couple of monk's habits, or cowls, in a trunk in one of the attics, he says. Genuine ones. Some wooden jewellery too. Crosses and the like.'

Lola said nothing.

'Anyway, where was I? Yes, back to this place in the here and now.'

'Is it just for the rich and famous?' Lola asked.

'Not in the least. I mean, that's part of it. Very wealthy people can pay to come here, for weeks or months if need be. They live in luxury, with a personalised well-being plan, and a recovery plan too, if that's appropriate. First we have our clinical staff. Then a number of therapists, a couple of whom live in, others who visit part-time. Then there are catering and housekeeping staff. Well, actually we only have one caterer just now — our cook Senga, who took Frankie away just now. She's a little nervy but such a hard worker. We had a chef, but he left at the end of December. We're recruiting, but it's not easy. Senga cooks for the guests. The staff see to themselves. Where was I? Oh, yes, we also have an estates manager and a head of security. We have a gym. A swimming pool too, underneath the Victorian wing — a genuine Victorian swimming pool, with changing cubicles around the sides and the most beautiful tiling. I would show you, but . . .' She stopped, embarrassed, then went quickly on: 'And no, we're not just about the rich and famous. The Foundation makes places available to deserving public servants. People who have dedicated their lives to their country or their communities. Civil servants, politicians, healthcare workers. They don't pay. The wealthy do — and through the nose. So, you can imagine, our community is diverse, to say the least.' She smiled, but then the smile faded. 'But this isn't a happy place, I'm afraid. Since we opened, we've been suffering this . . . this spate of venom.'

'So,' Lola prompted. 'The first letter.'

Catherine took a deep breath. 'It came at the beginning of December, shortly after the castle opened. It was addressed to me. Well, the envelope was. There was no greeting on the letter itself. It was unpleasant and I showed it to a couple of colleagues, but then I tore it up and threw it away, rather in the hope it was a one-off.' She met Lola's gaze. 'But it wasn't. A colleague received a letter the following week. We — the senior management here — decided we should keep it and any others that might follow.'

'Do you remember what the first letter said?' Lola prompted.

'The gist of it, yes.' She shuddered and writhed in her seat with discomfort. 'It said—'

Just then there came a rap at the door.

'Come in,' Catherine called, flustered but also possibly relieved at the interruption.

'Lunch, Miss Ballantyne,' a woman's voice whispered, then the door opened and the little woman they'd met in the hall — the one who'd taken Frankie off — came in with a tray.

Catherine got up to help her. 'Thank you, Senga. Put it here, would you?'

Senga put the tray on the end of Catherine's desk then began to unstack plates and mugs.

'I'll manage quite well, thank you,' Catherine told her. 'You go back to your work.'

The little woman retreated.

Catherine fussed about with plates and cups, inviting Lola to try this quiche or that salad and to help herself to dressing, with a choice of three kinds.

'Oh, and there's some fruit as well. How nice.'

Lola picked at a mini cheese-and-tomato tart, trying to quell her impatience to hear what Catherine Ballantyne's letter had said.

You're not supposed to be interested, remember?

'Now, where was I?' Catherine said with false brightness as she sat back down. She pushed her loaded plate to one side. 'Yes, the first letter — or should I say, the first letter we *know* about. It was nasty.'

'Can you be specific?' Lola asked. She wiped crumbs off her fingers and reached for her tea.

'"You're a fat, ugly old cow who no one likes. You're so pleased with yourself but everyone laughs at you behind your back." Words to that effect. It was all misspelled. All the letters are, though the mistakes aren't consistent: a word might be misspelled in one letter then spelled correctly in the next, which suggests to me the writer is only pretending to be illiterate. I dropped it on my desk when I read it. It felt like something *dirty*. I felt quite ashamed.'

'How long was it?'

'Five or six sentences and no particular connection between them. A selection of insults strung together. At first it was upsetting but after a while I thought it was rather pitiful too. I couldn't help thinking how unhappy this person must be.'

'Was it handwritten or typed?'

'Typed. Well, printed from a computer. All the words were in capitals. As I say, I destroyed it, but it was in the same vein as the letters that followed. I'll show you the ones we have, shall I?'

Catherine rose and went to a filing cabinet and lifted out a box file.

'The paper was always the same,' she said as she brought the box file to her desk. 'Plain white A4. The kind you find in any printer or photocopier.'

'And how did the letters arrive?' Lola asked

'By hand. And I wouldn't say "arrived". It's clear they're the work of someone inside the castle. They were in envelopes — again, the common kind you find in every office — but there was never a stamp. Just the person's name, again typed, and the envelopes left on a sort of stone shelf in the portico outside the front door — just where you came through earlier. Here you go.' She pushed the box file across the desk and resumed her seat.

Lola opened the lid, but just at that moment there was a knock at the door that made Catherine jump. She pulled the box file back across the desk and took it onto her lap.

'Who is it?' she called.

A man's husky voice replied, 'It's Florien, Catherine.'

'Oh.' She glanced at Lola, who shrugged to say she didn't mind the interruption.

'Come in, Florien,' Catherine called.

The door opened and a small man in a dark suit came in. His hair was black, as was his rather theatrical goatee.

'Oh, I am interrupting!' he said.

'It's fine. Florien, this is a lady who's here to see the facilities on behalf of a relative,' Catherine said.

'Lola Harris,' Lola said, turning in her chair and smiling.

'And this is Dr Florien Stenqvist, our clinical psychologist,' Catherine said.

'Pleased to meet you, Miss Harris,' the little man said in a vaguely northern European accent. He beamed and the skin round his eyes crinkled. He put out a hairy-backed, paw-like hand for Lola to take. It was clammy.

His hair was dyed, Lola decided after a moment's study.

'Who is the relative on whose behalf you are here?' he asked now.

'A sort of cousin,' Lola said. 'She's had such a hard time.'

'How interesting,' Stenqvist said, leaning in, his eyes shining as he scratched at his hairy jaw.

'Did you need a word, Florien?' Catherine asked, sounding a little strained.

'Oh, nothing important,' he said. He stopped scratching and moved his eyes from Lola to the box file in Catherine's lap. 'I wondered if you had seen Sister Yorke today, that's all.'

'Amy?' Catherine asked. 'No. Have you tried calling her radio?'

'Indeed I have,' the man said wistfully, 'but she does not answer. Perhaps if you see her, you might tell her I am looking for her.'

'Of course,' Catherine said.

'Then I will leave you ladies.' He studied Lola for a moment. 'If you have any questions about the care we provide here at the castle, I would be more than pleased to speak to you privately.' He scratched at his jaw again, grinning and crinkling his eyes.

'Thank you so much,' Lola said.

Catherine's smile fell away the moment Stenqvist had closed the door after him.

'That was a charade,' she said, 'as I'm sure you realised.'

Lola raised her eyebrows.

'Dr Stenqvist trained in psychology because he likes secrets and adores ferreting them out. I can guarantee that he heard you're here from either Senga or Grace — Senga, probably, as he has her in the palm of his hand — and he came to take a look at you for himself.'

'I think he saw what you were holding,' Lola said. 'Would he know what was in there?'

'Oh, yes,' Catherine said, quietly. 'I've shown it to both him and Dr Abbott — our clinical lead. Well, let him think what he likes. I shan't confirm or deny anything.' She smiled firmly, as if making a conscious choice to put the anxiety aside. 'Now, there you go. Take your time.' And she passed the box file back to Lola.

* * *

12.49 p.m.

Inside the box file, Lola found a bunch of transparent plastic wallets, the kind students used for collating handouts.

'I thought we should protect them in case of fingerprints,' Catherine said. 'Though, of course, each one will have the recipient's prints on it. Here, you can leaf through. They're in date order.'

Lola lifted out a number of the wallets.

'The recipients have given their permission for the contents to be shared with the authorities,' Catherine said. 'Of course, they all deny any specific allegations made in them. Again, these aren't all the letters. Some people destroyed theirs. And, of course, there may be other people who don't want to admit to receiving one!'

Lola leafed through the wallets, her skin prickling as she read snatches of text here and there. She'd seen spiteful letters before, mostly anonymous, some signed, but only ever in their ones and twos. She'd never seen a whole boxful of spite like this.

At a quick count she saw there were around thirty letters in total. Each plastic wallet contained just one letter and bore a label with the name of the addressee and the date the letter had been received. The wallets were stacked in chronological order.

The first was labelled *Dr F. Stenqvist*, with the date *10 Dec 24*.

CREEP, it said. *FORIEGN SCUM. KEEP YOUR DIRTY FORIENG HANDS TO YOUR SELF.*

It went on in a similar vein for several more sentences.

'Dr Stenqvist has his faults,' Catherine murmured, 'but really, he's a very *kind* man. A man of impeccable manners.'

'How did he take it?'

'With great glee!' Catherine said, and chuckled. 'I believe he was rather fascinated. He was keen to share his thoughts on who might have sent it.'

'Oh?'

'The *type* of person who sent it, I mean, not a name, sadly. The psychology was what he was most interested in.'

'And what was his suggestion?'

'That it's a person who has suffered humiliation. A paranoid person. Someone who harbours great resentment, but covers it up well.' She added carefully, eyes on Lola, 'Very probably a woman.'

Lola returned her attention to the stack of letters.

M. Kerr, read the next label. *11 Dec 2024.*

MARGOTS A NO-NO. EVER SO NICE TO EVRYONE, HYPACRITTICLE BITCH.

'Who's Margot?' Lola asked.

'Our art therapist.' Catherine shook her head. 'A nicer woman you couldn't wish to meet. So much dedication to our guests. She was *devastated*. Sat in here with me for over an hour, in bits. I told her Dr Stenqvist and I had had them too, to reassure her she wasn't the only one, but she was still terribly hurt.'

Lola picked through four or five more wallets. Each letter had the same appearance, apparently having been printed on common printer paper. The font looked like Times New Roman and there was consistency in the formatting, with double spaces between each line of ranting spite and each new paragraph beginning with a tab.

'Are they all like these?' Lola asked after reading through six of the letters.

'They're similar, yes, but the later ones were a little different. The ones that came after the meeting.'

Lola raised her eyebrows.

'Yes, a meeting we held with the staff,' Catherine explained. 'It was something the police suggested. I'm not sure it was the best advice, though. Afterwards things only seemed to get worse.'

'Just wind back a bit,' Lola said. 'When did you go to the police?'

'At the start of January,' Catherine said. 'Let me think... Yes, it was Tuesday the seventh. The first real working day after the Christmas holidays — though of course the castle was open throughout. We'd had several letters by then. The most recent had come on Hogmanay, addressed to Dr Abbott, our clinical director. Dr Abbott was very cross indeed. He, Dr Stenqvist and I met and agreed something must be done. I volunteered to go to the police, so I telephoned the local station and asked if I could talk to someone. A community liaison officer rang me back. She was very nice. Her name was PC Moore and she offered to come and see me here, but I declined. We didn't want a police car outside the castle if we could help it. That would be very alarming and some of our guests are already suffering from anxiety, so we made an appointment for the seventh and I went to the station to meet her. I showed her the letters and PC Moore called another colleague in to look. It was all a bit demoralising though. There didn't seem much they could do. They suggested it was more of a personnel issue, and suggested we have an all-staff meeting. That we should show the staff the letters and watch people's reactions.'

'So that's what you did?'

'Yes. The next day. Dr Abbott sent out an email to all staff with a three-line whip to attend, even for the part-timers, and said they'd be paid for coming in after hours. We held the meeting in the orangery. We kept to the facts — we explained that some threatening letters had been received — and it was clearly news to a number of people, judging by their shocked faces. We'd thought people would have heard about it through the grapevine, but apparently not everyone had. We didn't say who had received them, but we showed images of two of the letters on a projector screen. Dr Abbott said we were working on an assumption the letters were an "inside job" and that we wouldn't tolerate such behaviour continuing. We watched for reactions.'

'And?'

'As I say, most people just seemed very shocked, though a couple seemed . . . relieved. It turned out two part-time members of staff had also received letters but hadn't uttered a peep. They'd both ripped their letters up and hadn't told a soul. Neither knew about the other.'

'Any signs of guilt or shiftiness?'

'None that we detected. Florien Stenqvist said the same. I hoped he might spot the guilty party, being a specialist in psychology, but no.'

'And what happened after the meeting?' Lola asked now.

'Well, it had its effect, that's for sure,' Catherine began drily. 'In fact—'

She was interrupted by another knock at the door.

***

1.27 p.m.

Senga was back from the kitchen, this time with a fresh pot of coffee and mugs along with a jug of milk.

'Oh, wonderful,' Catherine cried. 'Just here on the desk, I think. And we've finished with the tray, thank you.'

'Was everything all right with the food, Miss Ballantyne?' the tiny woman asked, anxious eyes on Catherine's untouched plate.

'Oh, yes. I've been talking, that's all. Leave it for now. I'll bring the plate back to the kitchen myself.'

She left the room.

'So, after the meeting?' Lola prompted.

'Things got worse. In fact, they escalated. There were more letters, and more people received them. I got my second one the very next day and a third a few days after that. But, as I said to you before, the later letters seemed . . . *different*.'

'Different how?'

'It's hard to put a finger on it. The phrasing seemed more *poetic*, shall we say? More "hellfire and damnation" too. And the allegations were more specific. Dr Stenqvist had another letter and this time it didn't accuse him of sexual misconduct, but referred to a particular incident where a former patient of his, back in Stockholm, had tried to sue him for malpractice. He confirmed to me himself that that was true. Dr Stenqvist had two further letters, though as I said before, I think he found it rather entertaining.'

'And did these later letters arrive the same way, in the same envelopes, on the stone shelf, with the names written as before?'

'Oh, yes,' Catherine began. 'Though . . . Oh — Oh, now that is interesting.'

Lola waited expectantly.

'The envelopes were the same ones, definitely,' she said slowly, 'but yes, how interesting. Florien Stenqvist's second one — I'm sure it spelled out his first name. And it didn't have his title. The first had said "Dr F. Stenqvist", I'm sure.' She was gazing into a corner of the room now. 'So that ties in, doesn't it?' she murmured.

'What ties in to what, Catherine?'

'Dr Stenqvist's theory,' the woman said simply. 'That a second writer was inspired to get in on the act. It's a possibility, isn't it?'

'It is,' Lola agreed.

'And yet it seems so far-fetched. Oh, but what am I saying? This whole thing is far-fetched!'

'Did you keep the envelopes the letters came in?' Lola asked.

'I'm afraid not.'

'Did you report the escalation of the letters to your police contact?'

'Yes, I phoned the woman I'd spoken to before. Again, she offered to come out and see us, but I said no.'

'You mentioned a security manager.'

'Yes, William Rix. He lives at the gatehouse. He'd have let you and Frankie in last night.'

Lola nodded, recalling the man in the overcoat and cap with the skeletal face.

'Is the security here tight, would you say?'

'The physical security, yes. The gates are kept locked and the estate is in the loop of the river, which is wide and fast-flowing even when the weather is dry. The woods are thick and there are thorn bushes everywhere. It would be hard for someone to get in.'

'What about CCTV?'

'No. Well, there's a camera on the road up to the castle, but none within the estate itself. It's a stipulation of the Kade Foundation. Privacy is the number-one concern.'

'Prized over security?' Lola asked drily. 'Over safety?'

Catherine lowered her gaze.

'Surely you've made efforts to see who's been leaving the letters?'

'Yes, but not using technology. William spent a miserable couple of nights in December staking out the portico from the flower beds to the right of the door. He didn't see a soul, and no letter was left either night. Should we have persisted?'

'Maybe,' Lola said. 'I would have advised it.'

She considered the box of letters in her lap.

'Dr Stenqvist was the second person to receive a letter, after you?' she checked.

'Yes.'

'Had Dr Stenqvist upset anyone in particular?' Lola asked. 'Offended them?'

'Not that we know. He couldn't think who would do such a thing!' Catherine smiled sadly. 'And there you have it — our sorry situation.'

'Who do you think is doing this?' Lola asked.

'Honestly?' Catherine lifted her chin. 'I have no idea.'

'There must be talk. Speculation.'

'Oh, that!'

'Tell me what's been said,' Lola pressed.

'There's talk among the clinical staff that it must be one of the part-timers. Perhaps one of the domestics. Because of the poor spelling. Except, it seems clear to me the misspelling is a smokescreen.

'Senga's name has been suggested.' Catherine nodded in the direction of the door. 'But honestly, she's a good person. Timid, but very kind. Others have suggested Izzy McManus. She's a very strange individual. Domestic supervisor. Not very tidy herself, I'm afraid to say, but she came as one of a married couple. Her husband Rory is the estates manager.'

'What does she look like, Izzy?'

'Dark hair, blotchy pale face, rather unhealthy-looking. Often to be found smoking by the bins.'

'I think I've already seen her,' Lola said. 'And what do you think about that theory — that it's Izzy McManus?'

'I don't know. She's dour enough — the way she looks at you. You get the feeling she's sitting on her real feelings. But, then again, how could Izzy know so many things about so many people? The later letters have been so specific.'

'But you've never challenged anyone directly?'

'Goodness, no!'

'Nor searched their living quarters?'

'Absolutely not! Trust would be completely destroyed. Besides, what's going on here is clearly more complicated than just an aggrieved member of staff blowing off steam. I think Florien Stenqvist's theory is correct: there are two writers. The first is an unhappy individual throwing out poison to make herself feel better — and yes, I agree with Florien that a woman is behind those letters. And then, after our meeting with the staff, I think a second person decided to use the opportunity to torment individuals and to make more specific allegations. That person could be male or female, a domestic or . . . or someone more senior. Someone with a specific goal.'

'That goal being . . .' Lola prompted.

Catherine took a deep breath. 'I suspect it's someone with a grievance against this whole place, against Ardaig Castle, or against the Kade Foundation.' She fell silent and chewed her lip.

Lola leaned in and studied Catherine carefully. 'What haven't you told me?'

Catherine looked up. 'There's one more letter,' she said in a quiet voice. 'I received it two weeks ago. It wasn't put on the stone shelf but pushed under the door of this office. It's not in that box file and no one else has seen it except me — and the writer, of course.'

Lola waited.

'It's the reason I'm so disturbed,' Catherine said, and Lola could see the tension in her eyes. 'The reason I contacted Frankie again and begged her to bring you here.' Her voice wobbled. 'I know I shouldn't have done that, but you're here now, and I'm so grateful.'

'Show me the letter,' Lola said.

Catherine got up and went to a second filing cabinet, unlocked it and lifted out a buff A4 envelope.

'In there,' she said, handing the envelope to Lola at arm's length, as though she couldn't wait to be rid of it.

She remained standing while Lola unpicked the flap.

Inside was a plastic wallet, folded in half. Lola flattened it, heart beating fast as she readied herself for whatever was inside.

It was the shortest letter so far. It asked simply:

WHY HAVE YOU EMPLOYED A KILLER AMONG YOUR STAFF?

CHAPTER FIVE

1.35 p.m.

'It's horrible, isn't it?'

'Yes, it is,' Lola said. 'And have you — employed a killer, I mean?'

'No! It's a wicked lie, based on gossip.'

Lola looked at the single line of text again.

'Spelled perfectly,' she murmured. 'Well punctuated too.'

She read and reread that single bald question.

'And you've shown this to no one?' Lola double-checked. 'Why, if it's not true? Why keep it back?'

'Because it's so cruel.'

'"Cruel"? Who to? A moment ago you said it was "wicked gossip", or words to that effect.'

'It is. It's . . .'

'Gossip about a member of staff? Is that what you mean? I need you to tell me, Catherine.'

Catherine was staring at her with wide eyes. Two red dots had appeared on her cheeks.

Lola consciously softened her tone. 'Please,' she said.

Catherine's expression changed to one of reluctant defeat.

'I'll tell you,' she said. 'But this can't get out.'

Lola raised her eyebrows. 'It might have to,' she warned. 'If we want to find out who's doing this.'

Catherine watched her again, assessing. 'Very well,' she said. 'It's a sad story, I'm afraid. It was a scandal at the time. An international one. The kind someone might never move on from, no matter how innocent they were.' She took a long breath through her nose. 'Do you remember the case of Vivien Wray?'

Lola scanned her memory. The name did seem familiar...

'It was about twenty-five years ago, in Australia. A toddler...'

It took Lola a moment, but then she placed the name. 'I remember.'

In her mind she saw an image of a young woman — still in her teens — in a courtroom on TV, crying, mascara smeared down her face. She saw newspaper headlines calling this woman vicious names. *EVIL MURDERER. COLD-BLOODED KILLER.* She recalled images of crowds of people outside the courtroom, awaiting a verdict. Then, amazingly, she was found not guilty. Images of the same young woman standing wearily propped between her lawyer and an older woman — her mother, Lola seemed to think — as the press took photographs.

'Vivien Wray was tried for the murder of a baby in her care,' Catherine said quietly. 'She was an au pair to a wealthy family in Sydney — the Grimshaws. One night the child's parents came back from a party to find the child, Alex, dead in his cot. A doctor said he'd been shaken to death and the finger of blame pointed directly at the au pair. The media were against her from the start, the public too, probably thanks to the media. She was charged and the case went to court. It was on the nightly news across the world for weeks. But the defence was strong. Medical specialists gave evidence on her behalf. The child had not been shaken. His death had been from natural causes. Vivien Wray was found not guilty.

'The Grimshaw family wouldn't accept it, though. They hired the best lawyers in the country and a PR firm to boot. They hounded Vivien. In the end she was given a new identity and she and her family moved to a new area outside Sydney.

'You have to understand,' Catherine said, those points on her cheeks scarlet now, 'that she was innocent and that she had every right to start a new life. To study for a career and to fulfil her ambitions.'

'And she's here at the castle?'

Catherine nodded. 'Yes.'

'Employed here, you mean?'

'Yes,' Catherine said. 'You met her in the great hallway earlier.'

Lola stared. The woman with the pale face and auburn hair, but with wide and wary eyes . . .

'You said her name was . . . Grace something?'

'Grace Miller,' Catherine said. 'She is our head of guest well-being. In a past life, she was Vivien Wray. Oh, she's been very open about it with me and the other senior staff — Dr Abbott and Dr Stenqvist. She laid her cards on the table before she took the job. She is deeply committed to her patients and loyal to Ardaig Castle and the Kade Foundation. She is a friend as well as a colleague.'

Lola tried hard to recall the girl on the TV news all those years ago. Her face had been pale and lightly freckled, her auburn hair cut in a neat bob, but it was those big blue eyes that confirmed for her that Grace Miller and Vivien Wray were the same person. *The Blue-Eyed Baby Killer*, one tabloid had dubbed her, quickly changing their tune and painting her as a wronged, vulnerable girl once the verdict was returned — before moving on to fresh scandals elsewhere in the world.

'Above all,' Catherine went on, 'Grace is innocent of the crime she was tried for. But she is also human, Lola. She feels things very deeply. She is a very empathetic person, but she suffers with anxiety, and I'm very afraid for her.'

'Afraid she'll be exposed, you mean?'

'Exposed, vilified all over again, her career destroyed. All of that. I'm afraid for this institution too. And for myself, if I'm absolutely honest. Is that selfish of me?'

'It's entirely natural, I'd say,' Lola murmured. She asked, 'Has Grace Miller seen the letter?'

'No,' Catherine said. 'I thought about showing it to her but I decided not to. But I do wonder if she's had letters of her own. Most members of staff have received multiple letters, but the only one Grace has admitted to receiving came in December, and it was very general. It's there in the box file. I can't imagine she hasn't had further letters — from our second writer, I mean. She's seemed so jumpy lately. I've asked her if she's okay, and she says yes, but she's extremely defensive.'

Lola's brain was now racing. She raked quickly through her thoughts and came back to the key question:

'A few minutes ago, when we agreed there is likely to be a second letter writer at work, I asked you what that second writer's goal might be.'

'And now you understand.'

'But I'm not sure I do,' Lola said. 'The writer *might*, as you say, wish to destroy Ardaig Castle — in which case, we need to ask, why? But it might be more personal. The writer might be targeting Grace Miller.'

'Out of spite?'

'Perhaps. Or revenge. It could be that a member of the castle's staff — or even one of the guests — has come here deliberately to find her.'

The twin red dots were back on Catherine's cheeks. 'But how could we possibly find out who that is?'

'I think, first of all, we need to look for patterns.'

'Patterns?'

'In the letters themselves: who they were sent to, when, in what numbers, and what they say.'

'Well, everything is in that box, apart from the few that were destroyed.'

'I'd like to see a timeline,' Lola said. 'A table showing who received what letters on what dates. That will help me to spot anomalies. Could you put something like that together?'

'I could do it today and bring it to you at the cottage.'

'Good. Have any guests received letters?' Lola asked now.

'No,' Catherine said. 'I'm confident we'd know. Besides, we've only had five guests to date. One came before Christmas and has left. Just now we have four in residence. We have capacity for twenty-four and plan to be at that number by the late spring.'

Lola sat quietly for a few seconds, thinking.

'Could you also include in the table a note of any member of staff who *hasn't* received a letter?'

Catherine chewed her lip. 'I *could*, but of course, people may have received letters but are unwilling to say so. They might open up to you, though. Perhaps if you talked to them — oh . . .' She stopped when she saw Lola's expression.

'I'm not here officially, remember,' Lola said gently. 'I can't investigate this for you. I'll look at the evidence and make some suggestions, but it's for you to take things forward. You might have to bring in the local police after all.'

'Really?' Catherine said with dismay.

'It could help. The merest glimpse of a uniform around the place might do the trick. There are other options too. A private investigator, for example.'

She thought of Sandy. How he and his colleague might love to get their teeth into a case like this. And at the edge of that thought was another, tantalising one: what if she, Lola, was a private investigator, working the case with Sandy . . .

'Of course,' Catherine said, failing to mask her disappointment. Lola felt a surge of pity.

'You said this place is funded by the Kade Foundation,' Lola said now. 'Have you informed them about this business?'

'I . . . spoke to Stefan Kade's private secretary about it in December. He relayed it to Mr Kade and the trustees. A rather blunt message came back that we were to "contain matters".'

'Ah.'

'Mr Kade hasn't always enjoyed the best publicity, as you might be aware. It's important to him that the Foundation's work is celebrated. Any negative PR could be disastrous. There have been hints in a couple of the tabloids, suggesting a poison pen letter writer is at work, though of course we denied it.' She paused and furrowed her brow. 'There might be an opportunity to bring it more directly to Mr Kade's attention, however.'

'Oh?'

'He happens to be paying us a visit this weekend,' Catherine said. 'He and his new wife, the American actress Maya McArthur. A flying visit — literally, because they're arriving by helicopter — providing there's a window in the weather. Cocktails in the orangery, dinner and staying the night — at least, that was the idea. I'm very worried about it, if I'm honest. I said to Mr Kade's PA, it's all very well him coming in by air, but if the storm gets any worse, the part-time staff might not be able to get here from Aberfoyle — and even if they could, they might not want to risk getting cut off here. A couple of them have very young families. I said, if he's intent on coming, then he'll need to accept we'll probably be running on a skeleton staff. There'll be only the simplest of catering. Lasagne and salad probably. The PA said Mr Kade was determined to come and that I could explain any staffing problems to him in person.' She looked sick at the prospect. 'But you never know, it might be a blessing that he's here. A chance for me to get him on his own and show him the letters. To try to make him understand. What do you say?'

'I think perhaps you should,' Lola said.

They watched each other for several seconds.

'Prepare the timeline and I'll look through everything,' Lola said. 'Then we can talk again.'

'Do what you can and I'll be eternally grateful.'

'I'll do my best,' Lola said.

CHAPTER SIX

2.25 p.m.

Catherine led Lola back along the chilly passage, up the stairs to ground level and back into the great hallway. The wind was howling round the castle's lantern roof. The great wooden door creaked in its frame as if the storm was trying to get in.

Catherine had called Senga on a kind of radio to fetch Frankie, and now the two appeared from a passage to the right of the grand staircase.

'Everything okay?' Frankie enquired.

'Lola has been wonderful, Frankie,' Catherine said. 'I'm so grateful to you both.'

'I'm pleased,' Frankie said.

Back in the car, Lola said, 'You wanted a look at the letters, didn't you?'

'Well, I did hope for a peek, yes. Were they horrible?'

'Pretty much,' Lola said. 'Tedious in their way too.'

'Anyway, our cover's blown,' Frankie said, slowing to go round a large branch that lay across the road. 'A strange man found me in the orangery and interrogated me.'

'Oh?'

'Black beard, pink suit. Stenhouse or something.'

'Stenqvist,' Lola said. 'I met him too.'

'Psychiatrist or psychologist, one of those. I never know the difference. You know I'm always wary of psychiatrists. He wanted to know all about this relative you and I are here on behalf of. He said it seemed odd that you were meeting Catherine on your own. I said, yes it was, wasn't it? Bit of a creep. Sat down next to me on a sofa and kept edging up, till I stood up and told him not to let me keep him back from his work. Ha!'

She slowed again, this time to skirt a large puddle in the road.

'You should see the orangery, though,' Frankie said now. 'There are fountains, palm trees in huge pots. Statues too.'

'Sounds great,' Lola murmured.

'Maybe you could let me have a wee peek at the letters later,' Frankie said now in a winsome voice. 'Just a quick glance through.'

'Not gonnae happen. Sorry.'

'You're no fun.' Frankie put her foot down and they careered through the driving rain.

Back at the cottage, Frankie made coffee while Lola loaded logs into the burner and lit them.

The coffee poured, Frankie curled up on the sofa with an Agatha Christie, while Lola settled down to think. Rain lashed the window while the wind whistled in the chimney, making the flames in the stove leap and dance.

Someone might be fooled into thinking this was a cosy idyll, free of stress. But a troubled mind, driven by spite and malice, was at work here. Perhaps more than one troubled mind. Lola watched the flames and imagined how it might be to be here officially, working with Sandy on a private investigation, where the pair of them could bring their joint years of police experience to bear for their clients. Ones who were willing to pay for peace of mind and a job well, and discreetly, done. Everything would be on their shoulders, with no police force behind them, but they'd make a success of it. She knew they would.

It would beat the tedium of managing analysts and their mountains of data. And it would be a lot less stressful and joyless than those endless meetings with corporate comms colleagues constantly wanting to 'manage the messaging'.

And how nice it would be to work beside the man she loved every day. Just the thought of it provoked a pang in her chest. She wished Sandy was here right now. She smiled to herself, recognising that was a good sign.

Sandy had emailed her that morning with the draft business plan he and Ritchie had put together. *We've noted in red where you could support the business,* he'd written in the email. *We're envisaging a full-time role, but everything's negotiable. Check out the estimated first-year salary — that's if we make 75% of our target. Could be substantially more!! Have a read and tell me what you think.*

She opened the document, but then closed it again. Seeing words and figures, laid out in black and white, made it very real.

She'd read it quickly later, perhaps with a glass of wine in her hand to ease her nerves. She could study the detail another time.

Either way, she knew she had to make a decision, and soon. As Sandy had said, repeatedly, the work was piling up. They'd be recruiting soon, and if it wasn't her, it would be someone else. And she'd be stuck in an office with only her analysts to keep her company.

The door knocker sounded. Lola went to get it.

It was Catherine, once more in her mac and wellie boots, having dashed from the estate van she'd left a few metres from the door. She came into the living room, dripping wet, a supermarket bag-for-life in hand.

'Everything's in here,' she told Lola. 'The box file, plus an envelope containing that other letter. I've also done you a table showing the names and roles of all the staff at the castle, with dates they received letters, and a brief note about the subject matter. And I've noted whether letters were received before or after the all-staff meeting. I think you'll recognise a shift in tone. As I said earlier, there are probably letters we don't even know about, but this should give you a start.'

Frankie watched with avid interest from the sofa as Lola led the way into the kitchen.

Lola emptied the contents of the bag onto the kitchen table and began to look it over.

'Thanks for this,' she said to Catherine.

'No — thank you! Now, with regard to dinner this evening,' Catherine said, more brightly, 'I'd invite you to dine at the castle, but . . . you know.'

Lola knew. The form.

'The thing is, we've had word from the local police that there are trees down by the river,' Catherine went on. 'The road's still passable, but I wouldn't risk going into Aberfoyle if I were you. What if I send down a tray from the kitchen? I could email you the menu so you can both choose. We have a very good wine cellar, as well. I could send a bottle, depending on what you order.'

'That sounds very nice,' Lola said. 'I'm sure we'll both be very grateful.'

Catherine passed the time of day with Frankie, repeating again her gratitude for Lola's kindness. Then she was on her way. Lola watched from the living room window as the van's tail lights disappeared into the grey mist. She realised how isolated this strange community was. She certainly didn't relish the thought of being trapped here, even for a single night.

* * *

3.07 p.m.

Lola made more coffee then settled down to study Catherine's table, while Frankie read on the sofa. She began to detect patterns almost at once and felt adrenaline kick in. She never got this buzz in her current job.

At the same time she knew she couldn't get too absorbed in the problem of the letters. This wasn't her investigation and it certainly wasn't official. She would spend one hour with the letters and no more. She'd make notes and try to draw some conclusions. Then tomorrow morning she'd meet Catherine again and give her what advice she could.

And that would be that.

KEY DATES AND FACTS:
7 December — first letter received (C. Ballantyne)
7 January — meeting with local police
8 January — meeting with all staff
7 February — letter received by Catherine asking, 'Why have you employed a killer among your staff?'

Number of letters known about received PRIOR TO all-staff meeting: 19
Number of letters known about received AFTER all-staff meeting: 11
Number of further letters we now know about that were not declared at the time (all destroyed): 3

LETTERS RECEIVED BY CLINICAL AND THERAPEUTIC STAFF:

Dr Tom Abbott, clinical director
Before meeting: 2 letters (14 Dec, 31 Dec) — unpleasant remarks about his competence as a doctor
After meeting: 1 letter (11 Jan) — accusation of prescribing opiates for his own use, also misdiagnosing a patient in previous job with serious consequences

Dr Florien Stenqvist, clinical psychologist
Before meeting: 2 letters (10 and 15 Dec) — inappropriate (sexual) behaviour and not respecting personal boundaries

After meeting: 3 letters (11 and 20 Jan, 2 Feb) — malpractice (letters becoming more detailed over time)

Sister Amy Yorke, psychiatric nurse
Before meeting: 1 letter (22 Dec) — unpleasant personal remarks, including about her 'snippy' manner with others
After meeting: 1 letter (9 Jan) — allegation of spiteful behaviour and gossiping

Grace Miller, head of guest well-being
Before meeting: 1 letter (19 Dec) — generalised allegations of lack of attention to detail in her work
After meeting: no letters received

Margot Kerr, art therapist
Before meeting: 3 letters (11, 14 and 24 Dec) — unpleasant remarks about her personality
After meeting: 1 letter (10 Jan) — untidy personal appearance

LETTERS RECEIVED BY OPERATIONS, ESTATES AND FACILITIES STAFF:

Catherine Ballantyne, castle manager
Before meeting: 1 letter (7 Dec, destroyed) — personal insults, including allegations of incompetence
After meeting: 3 letters (9 and 12 Jan, 7 Feb) — allegations of financial corruption, most recent letter contained an accusation of having 'employed a killer'

Rory McManus, estates manager
Before meeting: 1 letter (15 Dec) — unpleasant personal remarks, including about his ability to understand instructions
After meeting: nothing received

Izzy McManus, domestic supervisor
Before meeting: 4 letters (11, 13, 16 and 20 Dec) — allegations of stealing and laziness, strange manners and poor personal grooming
After meeting: 1 letter (11 Jan) — comments about poor personal presentation

Davey Foster, chef — left role end of December (recruitment currently underway)
Before meeting: 2 letters (13 and 16 Dec) — unpleasant remarks, some specifics re how he did his job; also an allegation relating to poor personal hygiene

Senga McCall, kitchen assistant
Before meeting: 1 letter (12 Dec) — unpleasant remarks, including an allegation she drinks during work hours
After meeting: 1 letter (12 Jan) — allegation of being slapdash and clumsy

William Rix, head of security
Before meeting: 1 letter (20 Dec) — comments about his attitude to his job
After meeting: 1 letter (14 Jan) — allegation he had looked at pornography on the computer in his office

Other staff (live off-site, including part-time domestic staff and therapists)
3 letters declared but all destroyed by recipients

Lola read the table, circling dates and underlining some words. Occasionally she made notes on the table itself. Then she leafed through the letters in the box file, reading them to check she agreed with Catherine's brief descriptions. She also compared the formatting of the letters received before the all-staff meeting with those received afterwards. Almost an hour later — and within the time she had permitted herself — she came back to that final letter, the one that had come under Catherine's door a week ago. She stared at the nine-word question again:

WHY HAVE YOU EMPLOYED A KILLER AMONG YOUR STAFF?

Your staff. Not *our staff.* Not *the staff.*
Your staff.

Did that suggest the writer was not a member of staff after all, but an outsider? Or was that just the impression they were trying to give?

She put the table and the letters aside and took up her phone.

She typed *Vivien Wray trial* into the search bar. In seconds the screen was full of links, some to contemporary reports of the trial itself, others to retrospective pieces, a link to a Wikipedia entry, then links to various online forums.

She clicked on images, and a selection popped up: the young Vivien in her school uniform, smiling through braces. Then Vivien sketched in court in pastels, head hanging, her face shielded by a wing of auburn hair. There were photos taken of her entering court and leaving during the trial, flanked by her parents, occasionally her sister: another pretty, auburn-haired child — and always with a lawyer or two in tow.

The image that occurred most frequently in the search results was of Vivien, mother on one side, a lawyer on the other, then her sister and father flanking the group, standing before a crowd of reporters, cameras and microphones, smiling under some strain on the courthouse steps. Straplines below the images read: *Vivien Acquitted, Innocent, Vivien Walks Free, Months of Speculation End in Shock Jury Ruling.*

Lola studied Vivien Wray's young, bewildered face, and saw the similarity with the woman she'd met briefly at Ardaig Castle earlier in the afternoon — a shy, dignified woman, who seemed as far from anyone's idea of a murderer as could be. The hair of the girl in the photograph was the same colour as Grace's now, and there were her big blue eyes. Where were her family now, Lola wondered, and how had the trial impacted them?

She went into the Wikipedia article and scrolled to the section headed *Aftermath of the trial*, but there wasn't much text and the detail was thin. The family moved, it said, to a different suburb, north of Sydney. Vivien's father changed his job, the mother left her work as a teacher and took up sewing. The younger sister was home-schooled by her mother. The father died a few years later, the mother shortly after that. Vivien suffered continued harassment from some quarters, the article said, including once being attacked in public. Eventually she changed her name. The sisters stayed close, even living together. Tragically, the sister was killed in a road accident four years ago, leaving Vivien — or Grace as she now was — alone in the world.

Lola put down her phone and took up an A4 pad. She stared into the flames, listening to the wind, and thought . . .

Finally, she began to write, her pen moving fast over the page, occasionally returning to scratch out a word or underline another.

A page filled, she picked up her phone and went into her email app. She found a message from Catherine attaching a menu for the evening's dinner. She replied, thanking her, and adding: *I have a few ideas to share with you. Shall we meet tomorrow?*

Catherine's reply came seconds later. *Wonderful*, she said. *Come to the castle. Shall we say 9.30?*

CHAPTER SEVEN

Saturday 22 February

9.29 a.m.

Lola left Frankie at the cottage, now onto a second Agatha Christie. They'd had a very nice evening, dining on excellent food sent down from the castle, brought by Catherine in carefully labelled cartons. They'd watched another DVD from the cottage's collection: this time a black-and-white comedy thriller starring Bob Hope, set in an old house cut off in a Louisiana swamp. No anonymous letters in this one — just an escaped lunatic using the old house's secret passages to launch attacks on the residents.

There were branches down everywhere in the estate, and the sky was low and heavy. Lola parked at the side of the castle once more and then hurried through the rain to the portico at the front.

Catherine opened the door and took Lola's raincoat from her before leading the way to her office once more. There was coffee waiting in a pot and Lola accepted a mug.

'Bear in mind, for me this was a purely academic exercise,' she began, her A4 pad open in her lap. 'I don't know any of these people, or their backgrounds. To me they're just names. *But*, going by the letters, and the information you provided in the table, I think you and Dr Stenqvist are quite right. A second writer got in on the act after the meeting.'

'So it was a mistake to hold it?' Dismay flashed in Catherine's eyes. 'But your colleagues suggested it. They—'

'No, I don't think it was a mistake,' Lola said quickly. 'In fact, I think it did the trick.'

'Meaning what?'

'It stopped the first writer dead in his or her tracks.'

Catherine stared.

'Yes,' Lola went on, 'I really think so, going by the patterns.'

'What patterns?'

Lola consulted her notes. 'First, throughout December, letters were received at a rate of one or two per day, from the seventh until the sixteenth, again on the nineteenth, twentieth, twenty-second and twenty-fourth. A total of nineteen that we know about, fairly evenly distributed throughout the month. Things died down over Christmas, which may in itself be significant. After the all-staff meeting on the eighth of January, eleven more letters were received — that we know about — but nine of them were received within five days of the meeting. After the fourteenth of January, there are only two further letters that we know about: one received by Dr Stenqvist on the second of February, and the one that was pushed under the door to this room on the seventh, the one alleging you had employed a killer.'

'But what does that mean?' Catherine looked mystified.

Lola forestalled her with a hand. 'Second, there's another pattern that I think is significant. In the December letters that we know about, there is a clear targeting of two individuals, suggesting an antipathy from the writer to those people.'

'Margot Kerr and Izzy McManus,' Catherine said.

'Exactly. Margot Kerr received three letters, Izzy McManus four. Another couple of individuals received two letters each, so they may be special targets for the writer too. After the all-staff meeting, during the five-day flurry of activity, there was a fairly even distribution of recipients, though Dr Stenqvist received three letters, spelling out allegations about sexual misconduct, and so did you, though one was the allegation of having employed a killer. Grace Miller supposedly received no letters after the staff meeting, but I suspect she did and just hasn't admitted it.'

Lola watched Catherine's face as she processed the information.

'So the first letter writer,' Catherine said, 'who apparently had it in for Izzy McManus and Margot Kerr, stopped after the meeting, and the second writer had a particular objection to Dr Stenqvist.'

'It does seem that way. And I think the flurry of letters — the nine sent in the five days after the meeting — I think they were simply a smokescreen to hide a bigger purpose: namely, tormenting Dr Stenqvist, and exposing Grace Miller's past.'

'You know, I cannot imagine anyone having it in for dear Margot,' Catherine said. 'The person writing the letters must be particularly spiteful.'

Neither spoke. Rain battered the high window behind Catherine Ballantyne's desk. Very little light came in, the morning was so dark.

'So, who are they?' Catherine asked at last. 'Who are our two writers, and why are they doing this? Are they in league?'

'I don't think so, no,' Lola said. 'I think they're probably very different people, in terms of psychology and motivation. The first writer is an unhappy and repressed person — probably a woman, as Dr Stenqvist has suggested — who harbours great resentment against a number of people, and against two in particular. That person's letters are an outlet for spite. The second writer is playing a very different game, emulating a deranged person with that initial slew of letters right after the meeting. The second writer's goal is specific and . . . altogether more dangerous.'

'Another woman?'

'This is a person using a disguise. So it could be anyone. I would suggest, though, that the first writer is one of the operational staff. There's a possibility it's someone in a low-paid role with little power, though that's not a given. The second writer could be anyone, at any level of the institution.'

Catherine took it in, blinking and pale. Her lips parted as if she was about to say more, but then she closed her mouth.

'What are you thinking?' Lola asked gently.

Catherine met Lola's gaze and she bit her lip. 'I shan't say. Not yet. Let me think about how to handle this. As for the second writer, it's someone with antipathy towards Dr Stenqvist and Grace.'

'Towards Dr Stenqvist, yes. To Grace Miller, possibly, but it could just be someone with an overblown moral sense, who wants to expose her, or perhaps take vengeance for what she was accused of doing long ago.'

'And that could be anyone here at the castle,' Catherine murmured.

'Yes. But most likely someone who plays by the rules, who harbours grudges, who might be fearful about being identified as the source of the information about Grace. And on that subject, I do think it would be sensible for you to talk to Grace again. To ask her if she received any letters after the meeting. I feel sure she must have, though she may have destroyed them. But it would be good to know, to get a sense of the second writer's motivation.'

'And what then?' Catherine asked. 'Go back to the local police?'

'You could. But I'd be inclined to treat this as a human resources issue.'

'So it's down to me, you mean?'

'No. If I were you I would speak to Stefan Kade when he's here later today. Be assertive. Ask for twenty minutes of his time. Show him the box file. Tell him you're worried for the institution. Say that you have taken informal advice from a police detective who has advised that the Foundation should hire a specialist HR consultancy to deal with the matter — one that's discreet and efficient. It will probably be expensive, running to tens of thousands of pounds.'

'I see.'

'This can't carry on, Catherine. What's happening here could get out of hand. I think the findings of an investigation by a specialist agency could put a lid on the situation.'

'And what if Mr Kade says no?' Catherine asked now.

'If I were in your shoes? I'd leave. For my own safety and sanity.'

But as the words came out of her mouth, Lola knew it was a lie. She'd stay. Of course she would. She'd find out who was doing this and stop them in their tracks. But that was her, and she was resilient. Catherine was less so, and she was suffering for it.

Catherine stared. 'Yes,' she said. 'Beyond that I can't control anything, can I? So I'm best just to go.' She gave Lola a sad smile. 'I can't tell you how much this means to me. To have you take this seriously. It confirms things for me. It makes me realise I need to act.'

'You do.'

Lola got up and reached for her raincoat, currently hanging on the back of the door.

'I'd like to apologise to you,' Catherine said now. 'I shouldn't have asked you to sign a non-disclosure form. You've been so generous. I ought to have trusted you.'

'It's fine,' Lola said.

'I'd like to invite you and Frankie to dine with us this evening. To hell with that form. There'll be a group of us dining with Mr Kade. His new wife too. You may know he's married an American actress recently. Maya McArthur. She was in one of those *Ocean's* films. It's cocktails in the orangery from six, dinner at seven thirty. Please say you will.'

'It's very kind of you,' Lola said, 'but I don't think we should. I'm happy if you feel I've helped you but I think Frankie and I would love another quiet evening on our own.'

'Then what about an afternoon in the pool? We have a sauna and steam room, a jacuzzi bath too. Please say you will, then I'll feel I've given you something for your trouble.' Catherine smiled winningly.

'I don't think so. But I appreciate the offer.'

But as they made their way back along the chilly passage, Lola itched to take a better look around the castle, to get a glimpse of the orangery with its palms, fountains and statuary, not to mention the Victorian swimming pool and sauna. And more: she wanted to see the people, to talk to them, to see if she could detect the source of the poison. But no, she'd done what she could here, and to go further would be inappropriate. For once she would contain her natural curiosity and let others resolve the problems here at Ardaig Castle, problems she suspected extended beyond the letters.

They said their goodbyes in the high, echoing great hallway and Lola dashed out into the pummelling rain and round to where she'd left Frankie's car.

The automatic wipers kicked in as soon as she started the engine.

The woman she and Frankie had spotted smoking in the bin shed yesterday was there again, only metres in front of the car. She scowled across at her; then, as Lola watched, she was joined by a thin, pale-faced young woman in a blue nurse's uniform, complete with old-fashioned cap cape over her shoulders. The nurse, who Lola thought might well be Sister Yorke, as identified in Catherine's table, muttered something close to the smoking woman's ear. The smoking woman's eyes widened, then she nodded towards Lola's car as if to warn the nurse they were being watched. The nurse turned startled eyes towards them, appeared to hiss something further to the smoking woman, before quickly turning heel and vanishing through a low archway.

* * *

10.43 a.m.

'Dinner with Maya McArthur?' Frankie stared in openmouthed astonishment. '*The* Maya McArthur? And you said, "No, thanks"?'

'It was nice of her to invite us, but I shouldn't get more involved than I am already.'

Frankie gave Lola a curious look. 'You were tempted though, weren't you?'

'Tempted?'

They were in the kitchen, waiting for the kettle to boil.

'You're intrigued,' Frankie went on. 'Don't lie to me. I saw you with those letters yesterday afternoon. You were *riveted*.'

'I took it seriously, if that's what you mean. I've given Catherine my thoughts, but that's the end of it. Let's just make the most of this place, shall we?'

'Stuck inside because of the weather?'

'Actually, no. Sandy texted just now. The BBC are saying the rain's due to finish around lunchtime, though it'll return this evening and it's going to be heavier than ever.'

'So we could maybe get a walk in, that what you mean?' Frankie said hopefully.

The kettle clicked off and she poured.

'Not quite . . .'

Frankie stopped mid-pour and gave her a look.

'I think we should take the opportunity to head off. We don't want to risk getting trapped here. If the weather gets worse the road out might close, and you and me are both back at work on Monday, whether we like it or not.'

Frankie looked dismayed.

Just then there was loud rapping on the front door. Lola went and Frankie followed.

It was the gloomy, bone-faced security manager, shielding himself with an umbrella.

'Name's Rix,' he said.

'Is everything all right?' she asked him.

'Not exactly,' he said with a note of almost salacious glee. 'Not if you ever want to leave this place. The riverbank's fallen in a few miles upstream. They're worried it might take the road with it, so they've closed it. I've shut the gates — just in case you thought you were being kept prisoner. It's for your own good.'

'Is it a precaution, or do they think the road's in real danger?' Lola asked.

'Who knows? Any excuse to close a road these days, if you ask me. But there's definitely a few trees down too. Thought you'd like to know.'

CHAPTER EIGHT

12.15 p.m.

A quick google confirmed they were indeed stuck there, so Lola phoned Sandy. He seemed to think it was exciting, an adventure. Lola wasn't so sure.

'It'd be different if you were here,' she told him.

'I'll be there in spirit,' he told her.

Catherine phoned a short time after William Rix had delivered his news. She explained they'd been cut off once before, in mid-January, but that the road had reopened within twenty-four hours. She tried to persuade Lola to accept her invitation to drinks and dinner but again Lola refused. Frankie had come round to another quiet evening in the cottage.

'I'll organise for food to be sent to you in that case,' Catherine said. 'Oh, and I've arranged for sandwiches to be prepared for your lunch. Someone will pop over with them. Try not to be too anxious about all this. As I say, it shouldn't be for too long.'

In the end Catherine brought the sandwiches herself, wrapped in foil and packed in a paper bag, along with fruit and a couple of the mini quiches Lola had had the day before.

She seemed excited, the red points on her cheeks almost scarlet, and readily accepted Frankie's offer of tea.

'I've spoken to Grace Miller in the past hour,' she confided to Lola while Frankie was in the kitchen. 'You were right. She has received two letters we didn't know about. She became tearful, but I think she felt better for telling me.'

'Did she show you the letters?'

'No. She'd destroyed them but she remembered the contents. Horrible stuff, I'm afraid: "You murdered that little baby. Don't think you can hide away forever. Justice is coming." So it seems the second writer has their targets firmly set on Grace.'

'Does she have any inkling as to who it is?'

'She says not.' Catherine's tone brightened. 'I sent an email to Mr Kade this morning. Direct to him, rather than to his office. I said I wanted to make him personally aware of a potential reputational risk to Ardaig Castle and the work of the Foundation. He replied personally and straight away. He's agreed to meet me tomorrow morning at eight thirty.'

'That's good,' Lola said. 'Do you feel reassured?'

'I think so. I'm going to follow your suggestion and recommend we bring in a discreet HR consultancy to try to get to the bottom of things.'

Frankie was back with their teas and so Catherine turned to other subjects.

Frankie wanted to know about Maya McArthur and Catherine told her about meeting the actress once before at an event in London, and how charming she'd been.

'They're due to land at three,' Catherine said. 'The weather's going to be fine until five-ish, according to all the reports. You could watch them arrive, but it's best to keep a distance — to protect your eardrums for one thing.'

'We could go for a walk, couldn't we, Lola?' Frankie piped up.

'Oh, and just so you know, the Kades are coming without their usual entourage of assistants, but Mr Kade *is* being shadowed by a journalist,' Catherine said. 'She's writing about him and the work of the Foundation.'

'A journalist!' Lola commented. 'Won't that compromise the privacy of the guests?'

'Well . . .' Catherine bit her lip. 'We did point that out to Mr Kade's office but apparently he's insistent on bringing her along. He's keen for all the positive publicity he can get. We've made the guests aware that a journalist will be visiting. A couple of them are quite pleased, I think. One is a reality TV star — rather enjoys attention, between you and me. The other was imprisoned during the post office IT scandal. She relishes every opportunity to talk to the press, as you can imagine. As for the other two guests — well, let's just say that they've expressed a wish to steer clear of the party this weekend.'

'What's her name, this journalist?' Lola asked.

Catherine frowned. 'I did know it. She works for one of the big Glasgow papers. I can't recall it right now, but anyway—' she gave Lola a rueful smile — 'let's hope she doesn't get wind of the letters while she's here, eh?'

* * *

3.14 p.m.

The rain stayed off and the wind had died down to a breeze. A few rips in the gunmetal clouds revealed the blue sky beyond.

Lola and Frankie made the most of it, pulling on boots and cagoules and setting off into the castle grounds. They walked in the sodden wood and found the river that encircled the estate, though they couldn't get close thanks to a wall of spiny bushes between them and the water. Lola was happy to keep back because the river appeared to be in full and ferocious spate.

They really were cut off here. Even if they could cross the fast-flowing water, there was dense fir forest on the opposite side, then a ridge of mountains. Lola wouldn't fancy their chances. All it would take would be a slip leading to a broken ankle, and you would be dead from exposure within a day or two.

Following the curve of the river, they emerged from the trees behind the castle, with a view of both of the newer wings: the Victorian in gloomy grey stone, with a flat, crenellated roof; the Edwardian in red sandstone, and altogether more fairy-tale, with its stained-glass windows in tall Gothic arches, and a peaked roof complete with pointed finials and even a gargoyle or two. They walked to the right and a great glass structure came into view.

'That's the orangery,' Frankie said. 'It's fabulous inside.'

The structure was appended to one side of the sandstone wing, at least three storeys high, with pavilion-like domes. Golden light glowed from lanterns suspended from the roof. Lola could see palm leaves, and one or two people moving about inside.

'Stunning,' she said.

'That's where they'll be having pre-dinner cocktails,' Frankie suggested wistfully. 'Go on, sis. What do you say?'

'I say no thanks.'

They crossed a soggy expanse of lawn, heading for the main driveway, so they could wend their way back to the cottage, when Lola detected a rumbling from beyond the trees. Her first thought was thunder, and a return of the storm, but as the clamour grew she realised it was mechanical. And then, seconds later, they saw the black shape of a helicopter materialise from the clouds like a giant predatory insect.

Frankie screamed with delight in Lola's ear, but she heard nothing as the aircraft's racket ricocheted back off the buildings and the trees. With an almost stately grandeur, it relaxed onto the large H in front of the castle.

Its engine died and its blades drooped, and figures emerged from the castle's main door. Lola saw Catherine Ballantyne in a dark jacket and skirt, and the black-bearded Dr Stenqvist in a garish stripy suit. The pair were joined by a third man, tall and thin, with a head of blond curls. The three walked across the gravel to the edge of the grassy area.

The sisters remained by the trees.

'There she is!' Frankie cried, as a willowy woman with ice-blonde hair descended a short flight of steps from the chopper onto the grass. She was casual in tapered jeans, tailored leather jacket and boots. Lola was reminded of Princess Diana when she wore casuals but still turned every head.

'Isn't she beautiful?' Frankie demanded.

'She's certainly got presence,' Lola agreed

At the foot of the steps, Ms McArthur lifted a gracious hand in greeting to the three waiting people, then turned as a dark-suited man with short, slicked-back dark hair appeared in the aircraft's doorway and began to descend. The actress lifted a hand for him to take, and now he was down at her side. He too waved to the waiting group.

'That must be Stefan Kade,' Frankie said.

'I expect so.'

It was him all right. Lola had done her research, looking for information online after lunch and making mental notes.

Kade was fifty-two, darkly sleek and slender in photographs, with fine cheekbones and very widely spaced grey eyes that looked almost silver in some images. He was often pictured in black or charcoal suits, posing on high-end furniture, looking coolly into the camera as if he was a model for older men's designer clothes.

He'd come from wealth, the only son of Jonathan Kade — who had made a fortune expanding his own father's building firm — and starting growing a rental company that was now worth billions. Kade had inherited land from his parents — half of Galloway and a good chunk of Ayrshire by the look of it — but had transferred much of it to local communities via his charitable trust, the Kade Foundation.

So far, so good and worthy. But there were rumours too.

Stefan Kade had invested in medical technology companies, including some who were developing tiny robots that could 'edit incorrect genes'. He'd also made forays into political lobbying, apparently pressing leaders in some developing countries to invite his Foundation to undertake 'population research and management'.

Kade Foundation Behind Eugenics Agenda? one US newspaper headline asked. A British medical journal described him as 'seemingly obsessed with lineage and racial purity'.

The Foundation appeared to have pushed back with some clever comms activity, showcasing Kade's charitable work in African countries, and launched a programme to 'promote social good', called the Better Social Outcomes Scheme. It appeared Ardaig Castle and its sister 'well-being centres' were part of this scheme, which aimed to provide the 'finest personalised care to social, cultural and political leaders'. The emphasis appeared to be on the political, with hints in some parts of the media that Kade had political ambitions which again leaned towards racial purity and what was termed — sinisterly, in Lola's view — 'genetic health and well-being'.

Kade Procuring Political Favour? a headline in a London broadsheet had asked only last month, specifically referring to Ardaig Castle. The article implied that Kade was hoping to use his Scottish retreat to woo international leaders with his own agenda. It was no secret, the article pointed out, that Kade had personally invited the new US president to spend time at the castle, should the presidential schedule permit . . .

Lola and Frankie watched as the couple picked their way across the lawn, two male lackies following with cases held high above the sodden grass, and a third figure behind them, a woman in a trouser suit, a rucksack on her back and a laptop case in her hand.

Lola stared, mouth open in disbelief. The woman was Shuna Frain, news editor of the *Glasgow Daily Chronicle*, an old sparring partner of Lola's, someone she'd clashed with on numerous occasions, but who'd also been helpful at times . . .

'Of all the journalists in all the world,' Lola murmured to herself.

'What's that?' Frankie shouted over the roar of the chopper's engine.

'Nothing,' Lola said.

She shrugged the collar of her jacket higher. Shuna hadn't noticed her and she hoped to continue unspotted.

The three members of the greeting party came forward to the edge of the lawn.

As they watched, a fourth figure slipped out of the castle's front door. It was the thin woman Lola had seen earlier wearing an old-fashioned nurse's uniform and talking to the smoker in the bin shelter. Now she was without the cap, revealing dark hair in a neat bob, and wearing an ankle-length raincoat. She strode purposefully forward, raincoat flapping, and gave her colleagues a wide berth, marching out onto the grass, heading straight for Kade and his wife.

Catherine Ballantyne seemed to realise what was happening. She looked briefly frozen, then turned to Dr Stenqvist on her right, then to the other man on her left. Taking a cue from the second man, she called something out then ran across the lawn after the nurse and stopped her, a hand on her arm. Kade's wife, Maya McArthur, pulled away as if instinctively.

'What on earth—?' Frankie began, but Lola shushed her.

Dr Stenqvist and the other man were on the grass now too. Dr Stenqvist had the nurse by the other arm, while Catherine seemed to be making rapid excuses to the new arrivals.

The nurse turned on Dr Stenqvist, said something that made him recoil, then pulled herself free and ran, fast as a hare, back across the lawn towards the castle, making not for the front door this time, but the side where Lola had been parked. She disappeared from view.

'Some new drama?' Frankie asked.

'Place is full of it,' Lola murmured. She looked up at the sky. There was no blue to be seen now. The grey had congealed.

'Come on, let's go back and get the fire on.'

They were walking along the road to the cottage when a cacophony filled the amphitheatre made by the trees. The chopper was airborne again. They turned to see it tilt, turn and rush towards them, so low both Lola and Frankie ducked, shielding their faces from the blast — then it rose and was swallowed by the louring, pewter sky.

Back at the cottage a few minutes later, Lola was thoughtful, standing in the living room, her jacket still on.

'What's the matter?' Frankie wanted to know.

'That business back at the castle just now,' Lola said.

'Trouble, do you think?'

'I don't know.' She watched her sister, her skin creeping.

She knew what she had to do. It would mean dealing with Shuna Frain, who would want to know exactly what Lola was doing here, but that didn't bother her.

She turned to Frankie. 'Why don't you ring Catherine?' she said. 'Tell her we'd be pleased to accept her invitation to dine after all.'

Frankie's eyes bulged with glee. She went to the phone, only to find the line dead. Lola checked her mobile and saw there was no Wi-Fi either.

Against the windowpane, she heard the renewed rattle of rain.

CHAPTER NINE

4.45 p.m.

They had just over an hour to get ready. Frankie drove up to the castle to accept Catherine's invitation to dinner — and with an important question for Catherine from Lola. While she was gone, Lola went into her phone's camera reel and looked over the photos she'd taken of Catherine's table, trying to commit to memory who had received which letters and when. No doubt she would meet several of these people this evening, and it would be good to try to make sense of what she already knew of them. She'd take her phone with her and, if need be, sneak a look or two to remind herself.

Frankie was back within fifteen minutes. Lola rose to meet her. 'Well?'

'All systems go,' Frankie said, barely able to contain her excitement. 'Our story is that we're scouting out the place for our cousin, a top neuroscientist who's in need of a rest cure. Catherine and I came up with that.'

Lola raised her eyebrows. 'She sounds impressive, this cousin of ours. Does she have a name?'

Frankie stared. 'Oh. Do you think she needs one?'

'Best not. If anyone asks, we can just say how private she is. And did you ask Catherine about the guests?'

'I did. She said two of the guests are coming for the dinner. One of the others doesn't want to attend and the other is . . . uh . . . too ill.' Something in Frankie's expression caught Lola's attention.

'Why are you saying it like that?' Lola asked.

'The thing is . . . Catherine said you probably know him — the one who's in a bad way. He's just retired from the police. He was a detective in Glasgow. Pretty senior.'

'Right . . .'

'She thinks you might have interacted with him on a recent case, based on her own googling. She didn't tell me his name. She said he'd had a "complete mental collapse". That can't be good, can it?'

'Dear me.'

Lola felt her cheeks reddening a little as she raked through her memory. She'd 'interacted' with several colleagues in recent months, and not every 'interaction' had been positive — to put it mildly. She hoped she'd had nothing to do with this former colleague's current sorry state . . .

'Time for a shower,' Frankie said briskly. 'Have you decided what you're wearing?'

'Aye. My black trousers and my red cashmere sweater,' Lola said dismally. 'Choice is a wee bit limited. If I'd known we'd be dining with billionaires and Hollywood actresses I'd have packed a dress.'

'Your sweater'll be fine. You can wear that cream-and-gold silk scarf of mine too. You want a lend of some eyeliner?'

'Aye, go on,' Lola said, and climbed the stairs after her sister.

* * *

6.06 p.m.

'Is it Lola?' the woman who answered the door said cheerfully.

'That's right,' Lola said. 'And this is my sister Frances.'

'Frankie,' Frankie corrected.

The woman, whose solid frame filled the doorway, beamed all over her large face and shuffled aside to let them in. She was wearing an unusual brown-and-green dress, something that would have been glamorous in the 1970s. Her nut-brown hair was piled up on her head in an oddly old-fashioned way too.

'You drove up from the cottage, did you? Very sensible. Of course, drinking and driving laws don't apply on private grounds, do they?'

'We'll be walking home,' Lola told her.

The woman pushed the door firmly shut, and the echo boomed for a second or two in the towering space. Wall lights lit the space beautifully and a log fire blazed in the grate, spitting out sparks.

'Now, I'm Margot Kerr,' the woman said, and offered her hand first to Lola then to Frankie. 'I'm the art therapist here. You're both very welcome. Your cousin is *so* lucky to have you looking out for her.' She inclined her head and beamed some more.

'Oh, she is,' Lola said with a broad smile of her own.

'Our guests are, each and every one, special to us and we care *very* deeply for their well-being. Please be assured of that.'

'Thank you,' Lola said.

'Catherine is with Mr Kade and Ms McArthur just now. They're taking a tour of the upstairs. She said to take you through to the orangery and introduce you to a couple of our colleagues. If you'd follow me.'

Proceeding with pained, almost shuffling steps, Margot Kerr led the way slowly under an archway to the right of the staircase and into a gloomy passage.

Margot Kerr, Lola reminded herself. *Three letters in December, unpleasantly personal. One letter following the all-staff meeting. Something unflattering about her appearance.* What had Catherine said about the woman's reaction to the first letter she'd received? *She'd been in bits in her office.* Yes, that was it.

They made a dog-leg turn into another, brighter passage with parquet flooring and doors along one wall. The walls here were papered and bore occasional framed paintings with all the usual Scottish scenes: lochs, mountains, stags and forests.

Lola was tense, not just because she expected to come face to face with Shuna Frain at any moment, but because she'd persuaded herself a storm was coming — a different kind of storm to the one that was once more battering the castle. It was something to do with the young nurse, the one who'd made a failed beeline for Stefan Kade.

'The orangery is built onto the Edwardian part of the castle,' Margot Kerr said to them over her shoulder, breathing hard now. 'It's a bit of a trek, I'm afraid, but this is the quickest way.'

'I was in there yesterday,' Frankie told her.

'Well, the bar is open tonight!' Margot said, and laughed. 'Usually it's kept firmly locked, for obvious reasons! Just along here.' She led them round to the left.

Lola gauged they were at the back of the castle's main building now. The decor changed, as if they'd moved into a different period — arts and crafts, perhaps. The floor was dark burnished wood that gleamed, reflecting beautiful glass wall lights. The ceiling was higher here, vaulted with wood beams. The sound of voices came from up ahead, and Lola heard the splash of water. Not rain this time, but the ornamental fountains Frankie had mentioned.

'And here we are.' Margot stopped and sighed as they entered a lobby area from where a wide, tall archway gave onto a huge glassed-in space.

The orangery was vast, wood framed and towering: the kind of palatial greenhouse you found in botanic gardens. Except this had very few plants — just four or five palms and a couple of giant ferns standing about in huge pots, and a huge vine that climbed the wall of the castle to their left then crept out across the frame of the structure. The place was beautifully lit, high lanterns giving the place the look of a cathedral at winter evensong. In the middle of the orangery was a free-standing, art-deco-style bar, complete with a fan of mirrors and gold and teal tiles. Outside was only darkness, and the glass sides and roof became black mirrors reflecting the gold shining interior — but mirrors that shimmered with the rain pouring over them. The whole frame creaked in a gust of wind then settled again.

The voices stopped and Lola saw they'd been spotted. A man and a woman rose to their feet from low, pink cocktail chairs, drinks in hand, and gazed across at them. The man was holding what looked like a gin and tonic, complete with a slice of lime.

She recognised both of them. The man was the psychologist Dr Florien Stenqvist, flamboyant in a pink jacket, complete with a yellow cravat poking from the collar of his white shirt. The woman was the auburn-haired Grace Miller, who was more conservatively dressed in dark trousers and a cream blouse.

Margot Kerr made cheerful introductions. 'These ladies are here to see the place for a relative. Lola Harris and her sister Frances.'

'Both ladies I have already encountered, though briefly,' Dr Stenqvist said, and gave a theatrical little bow.

'Hello, again,' Grace Miller said to Lola. She smiled but it went nowhere near her eyes. 'Nice to meet you,' she said to Frankie. She tucked a strand of her copper hair behind one ear, a nervous gesture if ever Lola saw one.

Dr Stenqvist spoke. 'You are both most welcome to Ardaig Castle.' He gave another bow then raised his eyebrows to Margot Kerr. 'A drink for these ladies, perhaps?'

'Yes,' Margot said. 'I don't have the key for the bar. I'll go find Izzy. I see you've already begun, Florien.' There was disapproval in her voice. 'Please,' she said to Lola and Frankie, 'won't you take a seat? I'm sure Florien and Grace will be happy to tell you about their work here. Now, please excuse me for two minutes.'

Florien Stenqvist found them seats — a pair of peacock-blue cocktail chairs with gold, splayed legs — and the four sat in a rough square.

Lola gazed around at the towering wood-and-glass structure, feeling oddly nervous, as if this was the set of a play and she was expected to perform. She put on a smile and said brightly to Grace Miller, 'This is a beautiful building, isn't it?'

The woman managed her own attempt at a smile and nodded. 'It really is,' she said. Her darting, fast-blinking eyes told Lola she'd rather be anywhere than here right now.

Lola smiled, while her thoughts picked over what she knew of Grace.

Grace Miller, a.k.a. Vivien Wray. Put on trial for murdering a child, but found not guilty. Recipient of one of the first batch of letters, accusing her of poor decision making. Claimed to get no letters after the staff meeting, but today admitted to receiving two more, both referencing the child's death.

The woman was studying her pale hands, folded in her lap. Lola saw in her mind a pencil-drawn image of a teenaged girl sitting in a dock in an Australian courtroom.

Frankie was asking Dr Stenqvist about his work. Lola made herself pay attention.

'Our approach here is psychodynamic therapy,' he told her with enthusiasm — actually rubbing his palms together. 'It is found to be most effective for treating numerous complaints, from anxiety and depression to eating disorders and — yes! — even addictions.'

Frankie had a friend who had benefited from such a course of treatment, and began to regale Dr Stenqvist with the details. The doctor sat forward and peered hard at Frankie as he listened, his amber eyes beady with interest.

Lola began to ask Grace about her work, when Grace was suddenly distracted. 'Here's Margot, back with Izzy,' she said.

Lola turned. Margot Kerr shuffled cheerfully in, but slouching in her wake was the gloomy, blotchy-faced woman Lola had seen smoking in the bin shed. She looked just as miserable this evening, and barely fit for an evening of entertaining, with her untidy clothes and lank dark hair. Lola noticed there was food spattered on her black shirt.

'Izzy will get drinks,' Margot beamed. 'I must now go and make sure Senga is all right in the kitchen. She's on her own, the poor little thing.' She shuffled away.

'What do you want?' Izzy asked glumly, eyes down.

To serve ourselves, ideally, Lola wanted to reply, eyes on the grubby shirt.

'G and T, please,' Frankie said. 'And if you've got any crisps or nuts . . .'

'I'll have to look in the box,' the woman told her. 'Can't promise.'

'Coke, please,' Lola said. 'Diet if you've got it, but it doesn't matter.'

Izzy shook her head and slunk off to the art deco bar. Lola heard the chink of keys as she unlocked fridges.

'Izzy is catering staff, is she?' Lola enquired of Grace.

Grace met her gaze and winced, as if embarrassed.

'Domestic supervisor,' Florien Stenqvist replied for her. 'Though not especially well domesticated herself.'

'Oh, Florien,' Grace said.

'Pah!' He dismissed her reprimand with a wave. 'Her husband is the estates manager, Rory. All the catering staff will be tied up preparing our banquet.' He beamed at Lola, and his small amber eyes seemed to flash hungrily at the mention of the dinner to come.

Dr Stenqvist had received five letters in total, Lola recalled. The same score as Izzy McManus. There'd been a few specific allegations in Dr Stenqvist's letters — ranging from sexual misconduct to medical malpractice. He could have destroyed them, but had handed them over — which suggested he was either innocent or didn't care.

Lola smiled pleasantly back at him, wondering which it had been.

From the bar there came the tinkle of bottle tops and the clink of glasses. Izzy did not look happy in her work. As if she sensed she was being watched, she stopped and glowered across at Lola. Lola smiled and the woman's eyes widened fearfully before she flinched away.

Stenqvist was asking Frankie about their fictional cousin, scratching his beard and leaning forward with intense interest, and Frankie seemed ready to regale him with a made-up tale of woe.

'Let's not discuss her situation informally like this,' Lola interrupted, touching Frankie's arm.

'Oh. Yes, okay.' Frankie looked disappointed.

Lola brightened her expression. 'You must feel isolated working here sometimes,' she said, looking from Stenqvist to Grace Miller. 'So far from the nearest village.'

'Oh, but we relish it, don't we, Grace?' Stenqvist said.

'It's very peaceful,' Grace said, sounding unconvinced.

Izzy was coming their way bearing a tray of drinks. She groaned as she set it down on a low table before Lola's seat.

'Thank you so much,' Lola said, and got a whiff of sweat and unwashed hair.

'Mm.' Izzy went into the pocket of her trousers, took out two small packets of nuts and tossed them down beside the drinks. 'Salted,' she said, then turned heel and went back to the bar. 'They're in date. I checked.'

'Dear Izzy,' Dr Stenqvist murmured, eyes fixed contemplatively on the retreating woman's back.

Footsteps sounded on the floorboards behind Lola. Grace Miller craned her neck to see, then gave a sharp intake of breath.

'And here is Sister Yorke,' Dr Stenqvist commented. There was something dour and disapproving in his tone. He gave a tiny sigh.

Lola half turned in her chair. It was the same thin, pale woman she'd seen talking to Izzy in the bin shed and who'd run to speak to Stefan Kade as he left the helicopter. She strode, chin imperiously high, into the orangery, eyes fixed on the bar as if she was completely unaware that four people were seated to one side, all of them watching her. Lola sensed the exact opposite was true. This was a performance.

Izzy, who'd been arranging glasses, now stood rigidly to attention, eyes wide and fearful. Sister Yorke put both hands on the edge of the bar and leaned across it to utter some request. Izzy nodded and set quickly to it. At which, Sister Yorke spun round and glared daggers at the little group, as if she'd caught them in the act of spying on her. Lola smiled, but the woman turned again and strode quickly, head held high, to another group of seats at the other side of the orangery.

Lola heard Grace give an audible sigh of relief.

Dr Stenqvist began talking about his former practice in Sweden, scratching away at his beard. Lola pretended to pay attention, while concentrating instead on Sister Yorke. According to Catherine's notes, Amy Yorke had received just two letters, one before the staff meeting and one after. The first contained unflattering personal remarks, the second alleged she'd mistreated domestic staff.

Lola smiled pleasantly at Dr Stenqvist. 'Do you think Sister Yorke might like to join us?'

Dr Stenqvist made a thoughtful face, while Grace looked at her hands. 'Amy is somewhat shy,' Stenqvist said diplomatically.

'I might say hello, nonetheless,' Lola said, not to be foiled. She shot a brief glance at Frankie then rose, drink in hand.

If the nurse saw Lola coming she didn't let it show, and feigned surprise when Lola said brightly, 'Hello, there! I'm Lola Harris.'

She put out a hand, which Sister Yorke peered at for a moment before reluctantly taking it.

'I'm here with my sister on behalf of an unwell relative,' she said. 'I understand you're a nurse here.'

Sister Yorke sat up, clearly realising she had to make an effort. 'Yes,' she said, clearing her throat. 'Yes, that's right.'

She introduced herself and even managed a small smile, which Lola chose to take as an invitation to sit down and make herself comfortable.

'And how long have you been here yourself?' Lola asked now, all smiles.

'Since November,' the nurse said, barely making eye contact. 'The week before we opened.'

'How lovely,' Lola cooed. 'You must feel part of the place, then?'

'Hmm.'

'A very happy community here in the forest,' she went merrily on, watching the woman carefully. 'Though I imagine things can sometimes feel a little . . . hemmed in, perhaps.'

'There's plenty of room for everybody.'

'Yes, I'm sure. The place is huge, isn't it?'

Izzy appeared, carrying a tray with a glass containing ice, a tiny mixer bottle of tomato juice and another of Worcestershire sauce. She put it down with trembling hands and the sauce bottle toppled over.

'*Be careful,*' the nurse snapped, jumping up before she realised the top was on the bottle. She snarled at the cringing Izzy, teeth actually bared. 'That stuff *stains.*'

'I'm very sorry,' Izzy said, her features crumpling as if she was about to cry.

Sister Yorke righted the bottle. 'I'll mix it,' she said, more calmly. 'Just . . . take a little more care, especially when we have guests with us like—' she waved at Lola — 'this lady.'

Izzy backed nervously away, then turned heel and almost ran back to the safety of the bar.

Sister Yorke poured her drink and tipped a few drops of sauce into the blood-red juice. She stirred it with a stirrer Izzy had provided, then raised the glass to her lips and sipped, eyes roving round the orangery.

'My sister and I watched Mr Kade's helicopter arrive earlier,' Lola said, keen to keep some kind of conversation going. 'What a noise!'

'Indeed.' No eye contact at all. Her expression was blank, but her lips were pursed with resentment.

'I think you tried to speak to Mr Kade, didn't you?'

Sister Yorke's whole body seemed to go rigid at Lola's words, only her nostrils contracting and expanding as she tried to control what Lola suspected was rising panic.

Then the quiet eruption came. She turned sharply on Lola, teeth bared in a snarl. 'Who are you?' she spat. 'Why are you really here?'

Lola made a show of wide-eyed bafflement and said nothing.

'You're nobody's relative. You're here undercover. *Don't lie to me.*'

Still Lola didn't speak, but tilted her head to show she was listening. To any external observer, they would look like two women having a slightly intense chat over drinks. Lola glanced over at Dr Stenqvist, Grace Miller and Frankie. All three were looking this way, but the doctor was scratching his chin and watching with unashamed interest.

'You're here about the letters, aren't you?'

'What letters would those be?' Lola's fingers were tingling now.

'You know damned well.' She leaned in, holding the glass of tomato juice high against her chest, as if she might be about to dash it in Lola's face. 'But it isn't the letters that are the problem,' she went on quietly. 'There are bad things going on here. And it's not a letter writer you should be looking for.'

Senga, the cook, hurried into the orangery, followed by a much slower Margot Kerr. Senga made her way quickly to the bar, where she spoke to Izzy McManus. Izzy said something and Senga turned to where Lola sat with Sister Yorke. She looked fearful.

Margot reached the bar now and was saying something to the little woman, who nodded and clutched her apron.

Margot spoke some more then left the bar and headed for Lola and Sister Yorke.

'Do forgive my interrupting,' she said to Lola. 'Amy, dear, there has been a small error made in the kitchen.'

'What now?' Yorke snapped, making Margot bridle somewhat.

Margot glanced, embarrassed, at Lola. 'Maybe we could speak away from here?'

'Just say what you've got to say,' Yorke said.

Margot flushed and took a moment to gather herself. 'Oh, well. Okay. Well, I'm afraid it's like this. Senga has made two lasagnes. They smell delicious.'

'Do they?' It was said with a sneer.

'Yes. One vegetarian, the other with beef. I'm afraid she's put a little chilli into both.'

'*Idiot*,' Sister Yorke said.

Margot looked mortified at Lola. Lola made a quick reassuring gesture with her hand.

'She's very upset—'

'Hmm.'

'She's seeing if Izzy can fetch some cans of tomatoes and some olives so she can make you a special pasta.'

'Tell her to forget it,' the nurse said, nose in the air. 'I shall eat in my room.' She turned to Margot. 'But I shan't forget this. I shall speak to her about it, *one to one.*'

The threat made Margot gasp. 'I'm so sorry,' she said to Lola. And with that she took off out of the orangery.

Senga came away from the bar, followed by a mutinous-looking Izzy, and the two left the orangery as well.

Lola sat for a moment, while the nurse sipped her drink and scowled. 'A moment ago,' she said, 'you told me that it wasn't a letter writer I should be looking for. What did you mean by that?'

The woman chuckled darkly to herself. She took another mouthful of her drink then put down her glass, leaving a red half-moon on her top lip.

'Talk to me, Amy,' Lola said quickly. 'Not here, not now. Later, back at Rose Cottage, tonight or tomorrow morning — whichever you prefer. You can trust me.'

Sister Yorke turned sharply on her again. 'I don't trust *anybody*,' she hissed.

Voices sounded through the archway. They both looked up and Lola heard the nurse gasp. Catherine Ballantyne came into the orangery accompanied by another woman, one whose fast-roving gaze landed on Lola. Shuna Frain made a theatrical expression of amazement, then shook her head.

Lola got up. The nurse rose with her. But while Lola stood, readying herself to meet her old foe, Sister Yorke pushed past her and bolted out through the archway, leaving the castle manager and Shuna Frain looking stunned.

***

7.08 p.m.

Shuna allowed Catherine to lead her over to Dr Stenqvist, though her questioning eyes kept drifting back to Lola. It was five minutes before Shuna managed to get away. She drew Lola into a quiet corner.

'How lovely to find you here, of all people,' she said with a toothy grin. 'They said I might recognise one or two of the patients — "guests", sorry — but you were the *last* person I expected to come across.' She took a sip of her fizz and smirked.

'We're here to scope the place out for a relative who's having a hard time,' Lola said.

'Sorry, "we"?'

'My sister and I.' Lola indicated Frankie.

Shuna peered briefly across the room, then returned her gaze to Lola.

'Nice story. Now tell me why you're really here,' she said, echoing Sister Yorke's demand of a few minutes ago. 'Come on, Lola. Spill.'

'That's the God's honest truth,' Lola said. 'What I don't understand,' she added, with a smirk of her own, 'is what the *Chronicle*'s news editor is doing tailing a billionaire and an actress on a PR jaunt. Unless you've been demoted to gossip columnist, that is.'

Shuna smiled and her eyes were avid. 'What if I told you I wanted an "in", so I made one?'

'An "in"?'

'I wanted the inside story on this place.' She took another sip of fizz and peered around the orangery. 'To find out if certain rumours were true.'

'Oh? What rumours are those?'

'About some . . . "correspondence", shall we say?'

'"Correspondence"?'

'Cut the crap, Lola. The poison pen letters. That's why you're here too, isn't it?'

'I don't know what you're referring to, Shuna. I reckon the only poison pen around here is the one in your handbag.'

'Very funny.' Shuna lowered her voice. 'That woman you were talking to when Catherine and I appeared — the one who ran out. Having an interesting chat, were you?'

Lola gave the journalist a weary look. 'Shuna . . .'

'She's the same one who came tearing across the lawn to try to get to Stefan Kade earlier, isn't she?'

'Nothing gets by you, does it?'

'Not much. Sister Yorke, isn't it?'

Lola narrowed her eyes.

'Now why would you—'

'Oh, oh,' Shuna interrupted.

There was a hush of excitement. Lola turned to see a dark-suited, cool-expressioned Stefan Kade materialise into the orangery, his wife towering beside him on very high heels, looking impossibly glamorous in a kingfisher silk dress with long sleeves. Catherine went to meet them.

'Stunning, isn't she?' Shuna murmured, as they watched Catherine introduce the pair to Dr Stenqvist and Margot Kerr. 'And really, a genuinely nice woman. Bright too. You don't expect that with actresses, do you? You know she's twenty years younger than him? He's fifty-two, though he doesn't look it. Of course, thirty is old in Hollywood. She probably jumped at the chance of a rich husband.'

Lola rolled her eyes. 'Not everyone's so cold-blooded, Shuna.'

'You know how they met, don't you? The real, unofficial story, I mean.'

'No?'

'She was a patient — sorry, "guest" — at the Foundation's London clinic. She was in there for *months*. Bouncing off the walls to begin with. I suppose they got her on a load of pills and — well, look at her now!'

Lola looked. Maya McArthur appeared every inch the successful modern woman, completely in control of herself and her career.

'There's a reason the dress has sleeves, so I hear,' Shuna said nastily in Lola's ear. Then, before Lola could reply, Shuna dropped her a wink and said, 'Better go schmooze. You and I can chat again later,' she added. '*Properly.*'

Lola smiled nicely, though her thoughts were racing. So, Shuna knew about the letters. Catherine had said there'd been hints in some of the tabloids . . .

More people were in the orangery now, including a pair of women, whom Lola suspected might be two of the castle's 'guests'. One was a large woman in her late twenties or early thirties, encased in a metallic purple jumpsuit like something from a sci-fi film and chunky yellow shoes with blocky heels. Her dark hair was piled high and held up with shiny clips. She gazed about, pouting and batting her eyelashes, as if waiting to be noticed, or even photographed. Lola felt sure this was the TV star Sandy had mentioned. The woman with her was almost comically plain by comparison, middle-aged, with short grey hair, a grey blouse, blue woolly cardigan and darker trousers over sensible shoes. She looked excited, if nervy, peering excitedly about, chattering all the while to her glamorous companion, who said nothing and was possibly not even listening. Lola decided the second woman must be the sub-postmistress who'd been wrongfully jailed over the post office's software scandal. Catherine had said the other two guests currently in residence were keeping away from the party. One of them, according to Sandy, was Kieran Fox, the politician who'd thought the Russians had access to his thoughts. Then there was the fourth guest, the former colleague of Lola's, whose path she had likely crossed and who had had a 'complete nervous collapse' . . . Now who was that?

Dr Stenqvist was suddenly at Lola's side and, with slightly drunken glee, escorted her to meet Maya McArthur in person.

'How nice to meet you,' the actress said, all smiles.

'Likewise,' Lola said.

They fell into easy, shallow conversation, but Dr Stenqvist couldn't help himself and began to tell stories about actors he had treated at his clinic in Stockholm. He didn't name any names, but gleefully listed their neuroses and personality disorders, saying at one point, 'Of course, most actors suffer from a narcissistic personality disorder. Some of them really are quite malignant, with a violence of the mind!'

'Present company excepted, I'm sure,' Lola said, eyes on Maya McArthur, who took it gracefully and was clearly every bit the excellent actress people said she was.

Then Catherine appeared and drew Lola away to introduce her to Dr Abbott. 'Our clinical director and my boss!' Catherine said, beaming away.

'Call me Tom,' the man said, smiling haughtily down from a great height. 'I do hope you and your sister are impressed by what you've seen here.'

'Oh, very much so,' Lola told him, busily trying to recall his entry in Catherine's notes.

Dr Tom Abbott, clinical director. Three letters, two with personal insults in December, another received shortly after the staff meeting, this containing a screed of allegations. Misuse of drugs — opiates, wasn't it? — and something about a misdiagnosis.

Abbott had the kind of blond curls you saw on carved baby angels in churches. His eyes were pale blue and he blinked quickly as he chattered on about his career history. Lola wished she was as good an actress as the charming Ms McArthur.

They had to move when a cloth-covered table was carried in by two men. Lola recognised one as the man from the gatehouse, the skeleton-faced security manager, William Rix, who'd come to the cottage to tell them the road was closed. The other she hadn't seen before. He was very tall and had thinning fair hair, a hooked nose and downturned mouth, and seemed deeply uncomfortable in the presence of so many people. Rix and the second man vanished, then the little kitchen assistant Senga appeared, bonnet still pinned on, steering a trolley bearing trays of canapés. She arranged the trays at lightning speed, peeling off plastic film, then zipped off with her now-empty trolley.

'We haven't met,' a smooth, slightly clipped voice said.

Lola turned to find herself facing Stefan Kade, hand out, a snake's smile on his lips, his grey eyes like flint.

'Lola Harris,' she said, giving him her warmest possible smile and taking his cool, dry hand in hers.

'Here on behalf of a relative, I believe,' Kade said, leaning in, his eyes narrowing slightly and scanning her face, as if he was running a quick audit.

'That's right. It's a very impressive set-up,' she said.

'You'll be looking for a funded place, I imagine,' Kade said, eyes on Lola's less-than-luxury jumper.

'Yes, and such a generous offer. We hope we'll be successful.'

'Yes.' The snake smile broadened slightly to reveal not fangs but a row of perfectly even, brilliantly white little teeth. 'Not the best weather to see the castle,' Kade said now. 'Indeed, in the infancy of its operations.'

'And yet you're here, Mr Kade,' Lola said pleasantly.

He blinked and the smile, though still in place, seemed to set. 'My time is so short, and my life minutely programmed for so many months in advance,' he said. 'We return to America in two days' time. I want to know that everything is in order here.'

'"In order"? Is there something you were concerned about?'

'Good lord, no!' Kade made a face of shocked amusement. 'A mere turn of phrase, I assure you.' And the complacent smile was back.

His eyes were on his wife now. She seemed to be signalling something. Kade sent a tiny nod back. 'If you'll excuse me,' he said, and Lola was treated to a final glint of his flat grey stare.

Catherine was passing. Lola reached out and touched her arm and motioned for a private word.

'Do you know where Sister Yorke went?' she asked.

'Oh, Amy?' Catherine said. 'I'm not sure. She doesn't do well in company, I'm afraid. She might be checking on the guests who have stayed in their rooms. She makes a round between seven and eight every evening — to make sure they've taken their medication and to do a bit of a welfare check on anyone who seems out of sorts.'

'She was upset,' Lola said bluntly. 'She talked about "bad things" happening here.'

'Did she . . . ?' Catherine winced and bit her lip. 'Oh dear.'

'I tried to get her to talk to me, but then when you and Shuna Frain came in, she just ran out.'

'I'll nip upstairs and see if I can find her,' Catherine said. 'She's supposed to be eating with us, after all.' She made to leave the orangery, but was caught by Stefan Kade, who appeared to have a question.

More champagne came round, poured by Izzy McManus, now changed from her grubby outfit into a skirt and blouse, but still wearing the same gloomy expression. 'Help yourselves to nibbles,' she said balefully before moving on.

At last Lola was on her own. She took the opportunity to vanish for a few minutes, and found a corner away from the throng by a grand piano that was tinkling away under its own steam, the keys bobbing up and down as if it was being played by one of the castle's ghosts. She settled onto its stool, suddenly very tired.

She found parties wearing at the best of times, but it was worse when she was playing a part. She watched people through the fronds of a giant potted fern. Frankie was clearly having a great time, laughing and joking with the jolly Margot Kerr.

Lola peered around, ticking off the other people she now recognised. There was Grace Miller, looking uncomfortable and fiddling with her hair, while an over-animated Dr Stenqvist chattered away to her. Stefan Kade, Maya at his side, was in conversation with the towering Tom Abbott, while Shuna listened in. Izzy McManus slunk about, collecting empty glasses, and at the canapés table Senga came and went, busying herself as if she had too much nervous energy, arranging plates, filling gaps and removing empty trays. There was no sign of Sister Yorke, nor of Catherine, who might well be off looking for her.

There was chatter and laughter and people were smiling, but Lola detected tension everywhere, as if the air crackled with dangerous energy.

* * *

7.47 p.m.

'Catherine? No, I haven't seen her for ages,' Frankie said when Lola got her attention. 'Why, what's wrong?'

'Nothing.'

Frankie shrugged and turned back to Margot Kerr.

Just then, Lola spotted Catherine standing beyond the archway, with a stricken expression on her face, as if she was building up her nerve to enter the orangery. Lola hurried through, making Catherine jump when she saw her. Her face was white, but for two scarlet spots on her cheeks.

'Can you come?' she asked Lola in a small, frightened voice.

'Where to? What's happened?'

'To my office,' the woman said, and bit her lip hard. 'Please come.'

They half ran there, Catherine going ahead, panting hard, pushing through doors until they were finally at her room. Her hand shook as she tried to get the key in the lock.

'Let me,' Lola said, and Catherine surrendered the key.

Lola turned the lock and pushed open the door.

'You go first,' Catherine urged.

She went into the room and Catherine followed, shutting the door quietly behind her.

'Oh, Catherine,' Lola said, gazing about in horror.

The room was in disarray. Papers covered the floor. Cardboard wallets were ripped open, their contents scattered wide. Books and files had been swept from shelves, and the top of Catherine's desk, so neatly ordered before, was clear, but for two sheets of paper that must have floated there. The kettle had been pulled from the wall and two mugs lay broken on the floor. The filing cabinet stood open. A wrench lay on top of it, possibly the tool used to jack it open. More files lay about.

'I came in here five minutes ago,' Catherine said, sniffing a little. 'I didn't touch anything — apart from the door handle. I was trying to find Amy. I'd looked everywhere, then Dr Abbott suggested the old nursery in one of the attics. So I came for the key but — I found *this*. They even went through my bag.'

Catherine pointed and Lola saw a handbag, open and upturned on the floor, its contents strewn pathetically about: a lipstick, a mobile phone, a packet of hankies, a scarf, mints, a purse.

'And look at the mirror above the sink,' Catherine said, and it sounded like a sob. 'It's so wicked.'

Lola looked. Someone had scrawled six words on the mirror in what looked like lipstick, then underlined them:

HOW MANY KILLERS UNDER ONE ROOF?

CHAPTER TEN

7.55 p.m.

'The box file's missing,' Catherine pointed out. 'That must be it, mustn't it? Someone wanted the letters.' She paused and frowned. 'But why do all this? Why write on the mirror like that?' She began to sob. 'Who could despise me so much?'

'I don't think it's personal,' Lola said.

'What?' Catherine cried, incredulous. 'How can it be anything else?'

'Are you sure the box file is missing?' Lola asked now, eyes raking the room. 'Pass me one of those tissues,' she said, pointing to a box of Kleenex.

Catherine whipped one from the box and handed it to Lola, who used it to pull open the drawers of the filing cabinet, one by one. Then she went into a cupboard and finally the drawer in Catherine's desk.

'See?' Catherine said miserably.

'We need support,' Lola said. 'I want the local police here as soon as possible.'

'But the road!'

'They closed it as a precaution. I'm hoping they'll still be able to get through.'

'We can't have the police here. Not tonight! Stefan Kade . . . the Foundation. That journalist is here. We can't say this has happened. Oh, I wish I'd never come in here.'

There was a quick rap at the door.

Lola went to the door and opened it a crack.

Tom Abbott peered in and down at her. 'Is Catherine all right?' he demanded in a high, alarmed voice.

Lola turned her head. 'It's Dr Abbott,' she said quietly.

Catherine looked momentarily stricken, but then her shoulders dropped. 'Let him in,' she said.

Lola opened the door and stepped aside. She said, 'Please don't touch anything.'

'Oh, Catherine!' The doctor gaped as he took in the damage. 'What's happened?'

'Look at the mirror, Tom.'

'My God.' He sounded genuinely shaken. 'This has to stop. But . . .' He looked at Lola with sudden interest. 'Why are you here? I mean—'

'She's a police officer, Tom,' Catherine said with weary resignation. 'A detective.'

'What?' He frowned. 'I'm sorry, I don't understand.'

'She isn't here about a relative. That was a cover story. Lola is a friend.' Her voice broke with emotion. 'I asked her here for the weekend to advise me what to do about the letters. None of you took it seriously, you see! And the local police couldn't help. I've been so frightened!'

'Catherine—' the doctor began.

'And just look!' Catherine continued, her cheeks bright pink. 'Look at my things — my personal things, my work files.' She waved an arm. 'And yet the door was locked. So someone had a key.' She stopped and took deep breaths. 'I'm sorry,' she said to Lola. 'I'm in such a tizz. Tell me what to do.'

'We need the local police here as soon as possible,' Lola said.

'Oh, surely not,' Abbott protested. 'A ransacked office is hardly a crime. Look, I'd really rather we—'

'The letters have gone,' Catherine said bluntly. 'Someone took them.'

'The anonymous ones?' Abbott asked, sounding strained. 'But they're hardly valuable.'

'They could be to someone,' Lola pointed out.

Abbott ignored her. 'Well, it's hardly a break-in if the person had a key, is it?'

'Still a theft, Dr Abbott,' Lola said.

'The phone lines are down in any case,' Catherine said quietly. 'And there's no mobile signal here at the best of times.' She added, a little peevishly, 'I've said for some time that we should invest in a satellite internet link, given how remote we are. But nobody agreed with me, so—'

'We can try the emergency services network,' Abbott said.

Lola stared in surprise. 'Is this a pilot area?'

'Yes. We're just on the edge of the Highland testing region.'

The emergency services network had been planned for years and was now in its testing stage before roll-out. If all other communications channels were down, the ESN's special masts enabled emergency services to talk to one another in even the remotest parts of the country.

'The device is in my office,' Abbott went on. 'It should be fully charged. At least it was when I locked it away, though that was some weeks ago.'

'I'll come with you,' Lola said.

'Very well,' he said, barely disguising his displeasure.

Somewhere in the castle a gong sounded once.

Abbott sighed with exasperation and rolled his eyes. 'That means half an hour until dinner.'

'Then we'd better make the call as quickly as possible,' Lola said.

'Should I come?' Catherine asked.

Lola looked to Abbott to answer.

'Better not,' he said. 'You go back to the party. I don't want Stefan getting wind of any of this.'

'Don't you think Mr Kade should be told?' Lola asked.

'No, I do not!' He closed his eyes and seemed to deflate. 'I'm sorry. I didn't mean to snap. Of course he should know. But after dinner.'

* * *

8.07 p.m.

'How many keys are there to this office?' Lola asked as Catherine locked her office from the outside.

'There are two that I know of,' Catherine said. 'This one and a spare I keep in my flat upstairs.'

Lola thought for a moment. 'Give me your key now, and go upstairs and collect the spare and bring it to me.'

'Very well.' Then she winced as if remembering something. 'We still don't know where Amy is. I was supposed to get the key to the old nursery.' She glanced back at the office door. 'Should I collect it now?'

'Amy has a habit of going missing,' Abbott said testily. 'She always turns up. Forget the nursery key. Ms Harris — follow me.'

Catherine hurried off in one direction, Abbott in the other. Lola endeavoured to keep pace with his long-legged strides. He stalked towards the back of the main building then turned right into the Victorian wing. Lola hadn't been in this part of the castle before. She followed him down three steps and through a door.

Lola detected the faint smell of chlorine, then saw a glass door with the words *SWIMMING POOL* stencilled on it. Beyond the glass door, steps led down.

'This way,' Abbott said, irritated that she wasn't keeping up.

She followed him along a chilly passage with walls covered in red and yellow tiles, then through another door. Then they emerged in a wide, marble-floored hallway, as big as a room, with settees and low tables set about, lit by wall and table lamps but which felt even colder than the passage they'd come from. Above the sitting area was a dark space, and Lola saw that they were effectively in a covered courtyard, with galleried landings running round the space on each of three levels above them, and a skylight in the high ceiling.

'The castle has so much space,' she said, gazing up.

'Yes, indeed. And largely unused as yet. We have our consulting rooms here on the ground floor: Grace Miller, Dr Stenqvist and myself. The higher floors are all locked up, but we'll open them as we take in more guests. Now, my office is along here.'

They skirted around two sides of the hallway. Abbott came to a halt by a door and pulled a bunch of keys from his pocket. His hand was shaking and he dropped them before trying again.

He'd turned the lock when the door of the next room opened, making both of them jump guiltily. A face peered out. It was Grace Miller, looking surprised, then concerned.

'Dr Abbott! Is everything all right?' She eyed Lola with caution.

'Yes, quite all right, Grace.'

'It's nearly time to eat,' she pointed out. 'The gong went and I realised I didn't have my EpiPen.'

'Thank you, Grace. We heard it too. And we aim to be at dinner on time.'

Grace frowned slightly but withdrew into her room.

Abbott tutted as he closed the door. 'That's the bugbear with this place. Everybody is in everybody else's business the whole time! You can't get away from it. Sit down while I find the phone.'

Lola did as she was told while Dr Abbott crouched before a wooden cabinet and began searching in a drawer. He was clearly cross and upset, not just at the vandalism but at Catherine's deception at having brought Lola onto the premises. She could hear him chuntering under his breath, but decided to let the man's grumpiness wash over her and gazed about the room. It was bigger than Catherine's, with a proper window too, currently covered by a blind. It was a man's room: spartan, neutral, functional in every way. There was an impressively large empty desk, a black leather couch and floor-to-ceiling bookshelves filling one wall, complete with carefully arranged books. A trailing ivy sat in a pot on one of the higher shelves, its leaves like green webbed hands feeling their way over the books. On a small table there was a shallow dish with keys in it — a key to a Mercedes, going by the key ring. There was a torch too: a black, long-handled, sturdy kind. Framed qualification certificates covered the wall by the door.

Abbott was back on his feet, peering at a smartphone in one hand. 'It's on and seems to be connected,' he said after a moment. 'Yes, full 4G signal. Remarkable.'

'I'll make the call,' Lola said, hand out to take the device.

'Yes, well . . .' He looked at her, barely concealing his irritation. 'As you wish. You might want to hold onto the charger too in case it runs out.'

He sat heavily in his desk chair, making the leather sigh.

'The phone number is printed on the label on the back,' he pointed out.

Lola dialled 101 and waited. A woman answered. 'Hello. This is DCI Lola Harris, off duty but present at the scene of a crime. Address is Ardaig Castle, by Aberfoyle, which is possibly inaccessible by road due to the storm. I'd like a local officer to call me back on this number.' She read out the device's number. 'There's been a theft and vandalism, but there's a threat of further problems, so I need local officers informed.'

She rang off and made sure the phone's ringer wasn't muted before setting it on the desk.

'What "further problems"?' Abbott demanded, looking appalled.

'The writing on the mirror,' Lola said simply. 'The fact the letters have been taken.'

Abbott watched her, nostrils flaring as he clearly controlled his temper.

'I'm not happy about your being here without my knowing,' he said coolly.

'Too bad, I'm afraid,' Lola said brightly. 'Perhaps you should have given Catherine more support.'

'Catherine knows where I am if she needs me. Good grief, what a mess this is.'

A thought occurred to Lola. 'Why did you come to Catherine's office just now?'

'I was looking for her,' he said, bridling a little.

'What for?'

'To find out if she'd tracked Amy down. She'd asked me if I'd seen her. I suggested places she might try. I thought I'd check. Is that a problem?'

'Not at all.'

The device began to ring and buzzed into life. Lola grabbed it up.

'Lola Harris speaking.'

'Is that . . . DCI Harris?' a woman's voice asked.

'Speaking. Who's this?'

'My name's PC Stephanie Moore,' she went on shyly, and Lola could hear how young she was. 'I'm one of the constables at the station here in Aberfoyle. You've got some trouble over at the castle, I hear?'

'You could say. Vandalism, theft of "certain letters" — does that mean anything to you?'

There was a brief but indicative pause.

'It does. Are you there in a personal capacity, or . . . ?'

'Entirely personal. Things are escalating fast here and I think they're about to get out of hand. I'd like some officers to come out here. Now, I know the road's closed, but I'm hoping it's precautionary.'

'Oh, I see . . .' the constable said, sounding worried. 'Give me one minute to talk to colleagues.'

She was back within seconds.

'The Ardaig road is impassable,' she said. 'The river's high, but there are trees down — they're the real problem.'

'Well, it needs to be cleared. This is Stirlingshire, isn't it? Get onto whoever looks after resilience in the local authority and say it's urgent the road gets cleared.'

'"Resilience". Right . . .'

'Look, it's very important. If you get pushback, ask whoever it is to phone me. Can I leave this with you and ask you to call me back in twenty minutes whether you've had any joy or not?'

'Yes, of course.'

'And give me your direct number in case I need to call you.'

The constable gave it. Lola hung up.

'I need to go join the dinner,' Abbott said. He shook his head despondently. 'I'm going to have to tell Stefan Kade, aren't I? *God.*'

'I think that's wise,' Lola said. 'We'll talk to him together, but it could probably wait till after the meal.' She held up the phone. 'Now, will I get a reception on this thing in the dining room?'

'I expect so.' He began to get up. 'We'll need to—'

He was interrupted by a high-pitched scream — more of a squeal — from out in the hallway. Abbott froze and gaped at Lola, who wheeled round to face the door. The scream stopped and there was a great crash, like the sound of smashing glass.

'My God,' Abbott said, and leaped round his desk.

Lola was up and at his side. 'Let me,' she said.

She opened the door, holding her breath and her nerve.

Grace Miller stood in the middle of the hallway, amid the settees, hands clamping her horror-stricken face as she gazed at something on the floor before her. Lola stepped gingerly forward and saw what Grace was gaping at: a woman's splayed form, half on the stone-flagged floor, half on a rug, limbs twisted at all angles, her head wrenched to one side. It was Amy Yorke. She was facing towards Lola and her eyes were wide and staring. Dead. There were pottery shards everywhere, white and blue, shining in the lamplight of the hallway.

Grace turned and saw Abbott and Lola. She opened her mouth but her jaw trembled and no words came out.

'It's Amy,' Abbott said on Lola's right.

Grace returned her eyes to the splayed form and let out a wail. 'Oh! Oh, Amy!' She knelt, as if to reach out and touch the twisted woman.

'Let me,' Abbott snapped, taking the words from Lola's mouth. He turned his ashen face to Lola. 'That's all right, isn't it?'

'Yes,' Lola said.

Abbott hurried round a pair of settees set in an L-shape. He knelt by Amy and put a hand out to her twisted throat.

'She's dead,' he told the two watching women. 'Still warm.' He sprang back to his feet, then lifted his eyes to the high ceiling. 'She must have fallen.' He took a few steps to one side and looked up.

'I'll turn the lights on,' Grace said. She hurried round two sides of the hallway to a panel on the wall and began to throw switches, flooding the landings above them with light.

Lola checked the time on her phone. It was 8.21 p.m. They'd heard the scream and the smashing vase a minute ago.

'Look, there!' Abbott cried and pointed.

Lola joined him, careful not to step near the body. She looked where Abbott was pointing.

There were blue-and-white vases on plinths spaced around the top landing. One plinth was empty.

Grace was at Abbott's other side now, standing very close.

'The vase must have fallen with her,' Grace said in a quiet, frightened voice. 'Oh God . . .'

'It's all right, Grace,' Abbott told her, and put his arm round her shoulders, a gesture that Grace seemed eager to respond to. He turned her so she was facing away from the scene of devastation.

'I heard the scream,' Grace said in a small voice. 'The vase smashing. I ran out of my office . . .' She began to cry.

'It's okay,' Abbott said.

'Did she do it on purpose? I know she was never happy.'

'I don't know,' Abbott said. He added, in a distracted murmur, 'Then she was in the old nursery after all . . .'

'I need to sit down,' Grace said now. There was a high note of panic in her voice, Lola noticed.

'Go into Dr Abbott's office and sit there,' Lola suggested. 'Leave the door open. We'll be right here.'

The woman nodded weakly. Abbott led her, arm still round her shoulders, round the edge of the hallway to his office and took her inside.

A minute later he was back, breathing hard.

'Those balustrades are waist high,' he said, gazing up once more. 'It could have been an accident, couldn't it?'

'It's hard to say.' Lola peered at him. 'You said something just now about the old nursery — that Amy "was in the old nursery after all".'

He swallowed. 'Catherine was looking for her earlier. Amy can — *could* be strange. She'd go missing. Catherine always worried. She came to me to ask if I'd seen her. I could see she was in a state. She said she'd looked everywhere and I said maybe check the attic. There's an old nursery up there. I was only half serious.' He closed his eyes and put a trembling hand to his brow.

Lola stepped away from him to look at the body from different angles, then she peered up to the high balcony once more, her mind racing. An accident seemed unlikely but suicide was a possibility. Grace Miller's words echoed in her ear: *she was never happy*. Murder? But who? And why? *There are bad things going on here*, Amy had said.

'The nursery,' she said to Dr Abbott. 'How big is it?'

'Oh, gosh. I've only been in there once. It's a long room under the roof. There's a bathroom at the far end. Sloping ceilings, a few windows — the dormer kind. Bars on them — to stop children falling out, I imagine.'

'What other rooms are up there?'

He licked his lips, eyes away in a corner of the hallway as he thought about it. 'There's another door across the landing.

It goes into a kind of storeroom. There are spare roof tiles in there, flashing and tools. Another door leads out of it onto the flat part of the roof. That's all.'

She should go up there and take a look. Try to work out what had happened. But if Sister Yorke's death was at someone else's hand, then that person could still be up there.

'There was a torch in your room,' she said to Abbott. 'Could I borrow it?'

'The torch? Yes, of course.'

He darted off to his room and returned with it seconds later.

'Stay here,' she said, 'just where you're standing. I'm going up to the balcony to take a look. Please don't touch anything.'

'I understand.'

The stairs were shallow and carpeted and the only sound was Lola's breathing as she climbed. That and the steady drum of rain on the skylight over her head.

Her heart raced with the exertion, and the stress.

Keep calm, seal the scene, make sure the right people know. The road will reopen and the local police can take over.

Within two minutes she was on the highest landing, which ran round three sides of the floor. She peered over the banister and saw Tom Abbott exactly where she'd left him, looking up, his face as white as his pale curls. There were nine plinths surrounding the well of the hallway, evenly spaced, three per side. Eight of the plinths bore a large, antique-looking vase. One, on the next landing round, stood empty. Nearby was a door that stood ajar, the room beyond it in darkness. Steeling her nerve, she turned on the torch and pointed it, then pushed the door further open.

Seeing no one inside, she felt on the wall and found a switch. She flicked it and two dim bulbs, bare of shades, came on, illuminating a long, low room with a sloping ceiling. She made out a child's cot and a rocking horse. There were piles of blankets in one corner, cushions too, and teddy bears and dolls stacked high. There was a train set and a folding screen behind them, painted with animals and birds, with soft toys piled against it, some with eyes that caught her torchlight and glinted. It was a veritable menagerie. She saw monkeys, a sparkling dragonfly, colourful parrots and white swans. Peering about, the torch held like a weapon, she made her way through the room to a door in the far wall. She grabbed the door handle, turned it and yanked it open — to reveal a small, empty bathroom. One that hadn't been used in decades, judging by the state of it. A cupboard stood open, displaying empty shelves.

She released a breath. No one was here.

Back on the landing, she made her way round the next two sides, to a second door. This one was locked. She peered through the keyhole. No key on the inside. Just darkness.

She returned to the empty plinth and scanned for clues as to what had happened.

The plinth was an elongated cuboid of white-painted wood, dusty, as were the ones on either side of it. This one had a large ring mark in its centre, maybe thirty centimetres in diameter, where the now-broken vase had sat. The plinth, like the others, stood about twenty centimetres back from the white wooden balustrade, its top beam at waist height, with uprights every ten centimetres or so. Just to the left of the plinth the paint of the balustrade was scuffed. Lola came close to examine the mark and saw it was deep — that paint had been scraped off. Something had caught it. What? The heel of a shoe?

She stood right at the edge of the balustrade and peered directly down into the well of the hallway. Dr Abbott remained where she'd left him. He gazed back up at her. Sister Yorke's body lay sprawled only a metre and a half away from him, right in the centre of the space. Lola tried to envisage her fall. Yes, the angle seemed right. If she'd tumbled over the balustrade here, she could have landed just like that, with her feet pointing this way, her head the other.

Her feet . . .

She only had one shoe on. How had Lola missed that when she was looking at the body?

She peered about and spotted a single black pump, wedged between the plinth and the balustrade. It must have come off just before — or as — she fell.

So what had happened here?

Not an accident. Surely not that. She tried to envisage Sister Yorke standing. The woman hadn't been taller than Lola, who was five foot four. The balustrade was higher than Lola's hip. Lola knew that even if she tripped, she'd merely bounce off it.

Suicide, then?

She peered over the edge again, down to Abbott and the body. It was high, but it wasn't *that* high. And there were rugs all over the floor, not to mention three sofas. What if you threw yourself over and landed on a sofa? You would hurt yourself badly, but death was far from guaranteed.

Then there was the vase. If Sister Yorke had thrown herself off the landing, Lola simply couldn't see how she could have taken the vase down with her. If she'd climbed up onto the balustrade, she would then have had to reach back for the vase — but why would she do that? What, then? A running jump? Had she flown down the landing, perhaps having burst through the attic door, leaving it open, then barged into the vase and carried it over with her?

She was nervous now. Nervous of that locked door to the roof. Someone could be behind it, could perhaps unlock it and come tearing out after her in a flash. And she couldn't be sure, either, that she'd checked every possible hiding place in the attic.

She took a last good look at the landing, at the plinth, the fallen shoe, the scuffed balustrade—

And then she saw it, and couldn't believe she hadn't spotted it before. She turned on the torch, bent and pointed the beam at one of the wooden uprights, three along from the scuff mark.

A tiny but unmistakeable splash of red — blood, quite possibly, which suggested the victim had been struck and her flesh torn before she fell. Could a vase have done that?

She headed for the stairs. The first flight down from the top floor passed a window — and there it was, lying innocently on the sill: a claw hammer.

Lola peered closely, inspecting not only the hammer's claw, but the white-painted wood — and another smear of red.

* * *

8.29 p.m.

The emergency-networked phone buzzed into life as she was hurrying down the stairs between the second- and first-floor landings. She stopped and pressed it to her ear.

'DCI Harris? It's PC Moore,' the voice said, beautifully crisp and clear despite the raging storm. 'Just to say I've been onto the resilience team and they've got a unit just near Aberfoyle so they're heading down your way.'

'Good,' Lola said, 'because it's now urgent. There's been a death here, and it's suspicious.'

A slightly stunned pause. 'But we only spoke a few minutes—'

'I need you to text me your contact's name and number and I'll ring him myself. And ask the local DCI to contact me ASAP.'

She rang off and hurried down the remaining flights of stairs. She put the torch down on a side table.

'Well?' Abbott asked, his worried eyes trying to read her expression.

'It's about as serious as it can be,' she told him.

'Oh God.' His eyes returned to the splayed corpse and a hand went to his forehead. 'This is a disaster.'

'I'm hopeful help is on its way,' Lola went on, determinedly calm. 'But meantime, we need to take some steps.'

'Yes.' He swallowed. 'Yes, of course. Just — just tell me what we need to do.'

'How is this wing connected to the rest of the castle?'

Abbott took his time before answering. 'Erm. There's the passage on this floor — the way we came. There's one on the first floor as well. Both have doors at the point where the wing connects to the main building. The second and third floors are only accessible from within the wing itself. Catherine will know where the keys to the connecting doors are. I'll radio her from my office. The radio system's local to the castle, so it should still work.'

Lola let the information sink in. It was possible for someone to have been up there on the third floor, done the deed, then hurried down to the first floor and escaped back into the main building from there.

'What about doors to the outside?'

Again he hesitated. 'There's a fire exit at the end of this corridor, round to the right. You can get out that way but not in. I think that's it, apart from the way out onto the roof. There's an external staircase — a fire escape. Of course, all our offices have windows, and they can be opened wide, but I expect they'd all be shut, given the weather.'

The phone buzzed again. It was a text message with the name of a contact for one of the local authority's resilience team. She pressed on the number and put the phone to her ear, but the line was busy.

'What do we do about Amy's body?' Abbott asked.

'We leave her where she is,' Lola said simply.

'Can't we cover her up? Surely we can't just leave her like this.'

'I'm sorry. We have to preserve evidence. I'll take a few photos on my phone, but it's really important my forensics colleagues see the scene as it is.'

Abbott seemed to pale even more. 'You think she was killed, don't you?'

She considered him for a moment and reminded herself he was just about the only person in the castle who couldn't be responsible for pushing Sister Yorke to her death.

'I do,' she said.

He stared at her aghast, seeming to process the possibility.

'I'll need to tell the others. I mean — tell them something.'

'I'd suggest telling Stefan Kade first,' Lola said gently. 'And I think we'll need to tell him what else has been going on here.'

'Yes,' he said miserably. 'Okay. But first I'll go radio Catherine.'

CHAPTER ELEVEN

8.38 p.m.

Catherine arrived quickly, face flushed.

'What's happened?' she cried as she hurried down the passage from the main building. 'Tom said someone's been hurt.'

Lola went to meet her and blocked her way.

Catherine's mouth was drawn with panic.

'Amy Yorke has fallen from one of the balconies,' Lola said. 'I'm afraid she's dead.'

Catherine gave a little cry and stepped backwards, eyes widening. 'Amy, oh no . . .'

'Help is on its way,' Lola said.

'You said she fell,' Catherine said now, eyes on Abbott. 'So she was up there, in the nursery?' She put a hand to her forehead. 'Then I could have stopped her. I should have ignored the mess in my office and taken the key and gone straight up there to find her. Oh God, I could have stopped her!'

'We need to seal off this whole wing,' Lola said. 'I understand there are keys for the doors that connect to the main castle.'

'Yes, in the general office. I'll get them for you.'

'Could you bring a plastic bag?' Lola asked. 'The kind you put in any waste bin, with tie handles, if possible. And if you could find gloves too. Disposable ones. Several pairs, please.'

Abbott chipped in: 'There should be some in the first-aid room.'

Catherine hurried off.

Lola took the opportunity of the wait to get as close a look at the body as she could, stepping carefully between the broken shards of pot. Amy had landed on her front, but her neck was twisted, so she seemed to be looking over her shoulder.

Lola crouched and peered closer, wondering if it was the light that was creating the shadow, or . . .

She rose and made her way back through the pottery minefield.

'What is it?' Abbott asked.

'I'm not sure,' she said honestly. She retrieved the torch from the table by the wall and returned to the body, where she shone the beam into the narrow space between the stone floor and Amy's cheekbone. There was a bruise and a cut too, crusted with blood.

Catherine was back, breathing heavily. 'I've got the keys and some gloves.'

Lola jumped up. 'Keep back!' she ordered as Catherine picked her way back through the shards.

But it was too late.

'Oh!' Catherine cried, eyes on the body.

'Let's move back a little,' Lola said gently but firmly, taking one of Catherine's arms and leading her back towards the passage.

Catherine's cry had brought Grace from Dr Abbott's office. She looked ashen but calm.

'Grace!' Catherine said. 'Isn't it terrible?'

'I heard her fall,' Grace said, coming towards them. 'I heard it all. I heard her body hit the — hit the floor.'

Abbott went to her again and pulled her into an embrace. It was such an understated move, one that Grace responded to so naturally, that Lola couldn't help conclude she was right about her earlier instinct that the two were close.

'The keys,' Lola said to Catherine and held out her hand. 'I'll lock the doors. Just tell me which key is which.'

Catherine gave Lola two keys. 'That one's for this floor, and that one is for the first floor. Oh, and here's the spare to my office. You're the only one with keys to that room now.'

'And the gloves?' Lola checked. 'And a bag, if you found one.'

'Yes, here you go.' She passed Lola a bundle of blue disposable gloves along with a rolled-up bin bag.

'You said help was coming,' Catherine said now. 'But the road . . .'

'A team's gone to see about clearing it. If they can get through, they will.' She hoped she sounded more confident than she felt.

'We'll need to tell Amy's family,' Catherine said, eyes darting. 'Though I seem to remember she was all alone in the world. Or was there a sister?' She bit her lip. 'I have the next-of-kin information in her file — that is, so long as her file hasn't been tampered with. I'll try to find it.'

'Catherine,' Lola said now, 'is it possible for me to stay here tonight? In the castle, I mean.'

Catherine stared, but then nodded quickly. 'Yes, of course.' She sounded pleased — relieved too. 'There are spare bedrooms ready for guests on the third floor of the main building. Mr and Mrs Kade are in the suite on that floor too. The beds in the guest rooms are made up, though they mightn't have been cleaned or aired for a few weeks.'

'That doesn't matter. I'd be happier if I was here on the spot.'

'What about Frankie? I could give you adjoining rooms if you like.'

Lola thought about it. 'She might prefer to be at the cottage. I'll ask her. I can fetch a few things from the cottage and bring them back later on. Right now I'd like to talk to Stefan Kade alone, please.'

'Stefan? Yes, but the second gong went some time ago. He'll be at dinner now.'

'It's important,' Lola said. 'Call him away. I can talk to him in the orangery.'

'Yes, all right.'

Catherine was frowning past Lola, seemingly distracted by something at the far side of the hallway. Lola turned to look.

'What is it?' Lola asked.

'It's nothing,' she said, eyes still distracted. 'Nothing at all.' She looked back at Lola and put on a weak smile. 'I'll go find Mr Kade.'

She hurried off, and Lola darted upstairs to the first landing. She found the passage that led from that floor back into the castle and the door between the two wings. She locked it. From there she dashed up two more floors to retrieve the hammer from the windowsill, lifting it with a hand that was inside the bin bag, then drawing the bag over it. She tied the handle. Then she took out her phone and snapped a photo of the tiny blood smear.

Rounding the landing, she found the blood splash on the balustrade and photographed that too. Then she went to the nearest plinth that bore a vase. After snapping on a pair of disposable gloves, she lifted the vase in both hands. Though it was large it was unusually light, as if it was made of very fine porcelain. Lola could have carried it a good distance before getting tired. It would have taken very little force to knock it and send it flying over the balustrade.

A scenario was crystallising in her mind. In it, Sister Yorke had been on the landing and an attacker had emerged from the attic and launched at her with the hammer, catching her on the cheekbone and tearing the skin. Amy had then staggered towards the balustrade and gone over, unbalancing the vase and taking it over with her. Her shoe had come off. Then the attacker had fled down the stairs, leaving the hammer on the windowsill, perhaps abandoning hope of taking it away to get rid of it.

She grabbed the bagged hammer and hurried back downstairs.

Dr Abbott and Grace Miller were where she'd left them, standing very close. She placed the bagged hammer on the console table and stepped between the shards again, trying to take the same path as before. She reached Amy's body. Then, controlling her own distaste, she began to feel in each of the dead woman's trouser pockets. She found a tissue, folded and clean, a stick of chewing gum, and a key on a simple key ring bearing the words: NURSERY ATTIC, V. WING. No phone, no other keys.

She rose and turned to face the embracing couple, both of whom looked shattered and slightly embarrassed. Grace saw Lola and moved discreetly apart.

'We need to leave this area,' she told them. 'Fetch anything personal from your offices. I doubt you'll be able to come back this way for at least a day or two.'

CHAPTER TWELVE

9.05 p.m.

Stefan Kade marched through the archway into the orangery, Catherine hurrying after him. Lola had found a table and two chairs at the far end, beyond the piano. The bagged hammer was stashed under her chair, out of sight. The rain lashed the panes on all sides, and the structure creaked as wind tormented it. Lola turned to meet him as he drew near.

'What's happened?' Kade demanded.

'I'm Detective Chief Inspector Lola Harris of Police Scotland,' Lola said. 'I'm afraid there's been a suspicious death.'

'A *suspicious death*?' He stared and seemed to pale. 'And what did you say — you're a *detective chief inspector*?' He whirled round to Catherine. 'What's going on?'

Catherine began to speak but Lola cut across her. 'Quite a lot, or so it seems.'

'Who's dead?'

'Sister Amy Yorke.'

'Amy Yorke . . .' He turned to Catherine. 'Did I meet her?'

'Briefly, Mr Kade,' Catherine said, embarrassed.

Lola spoke up. 'Sister Yorke is the woman who ran from the castle to meet you and your wife as you came from the helicopter earlier today.'

She sensed Catherine cringing beside her.

'Oh, yes.' He turned sharply to Catherine. 'You stopped her.'

Catherine dropped her gaze.

'Did Amy Yorke say anything to you?' Lola asked. 'Then or later in the day?'

'No,' he said. 'But she looked very agitated when she came out to meet us. What happened to her?'

'It seems she fell from a high balcony in the Victorian wing, Mr Kade.' Lola added pointedly, 'I believe she may have been attacked and possibly pushed to her death.'

He stared, then gave a sharp laugh. 'You mean—'

'I think it's possible she was deliberately killed. I've found a potential weapon.'

'Weapon?'

'Yes.' She wasn't going to be drawn just yet.

'But who would do such a thing?'

'I don't know, sir. I've sealed the wing and no one can go in there until the authorities arrive.'

'Authorities? For God's sake!' He looked away into a corner of the orangery. 'This is going to be all over the press, isn't it? They'll have a field day!'

'The police must attend,' Lola said curtly. 'Paramedics too, to remove the body.'

Kade lifted his eyes to the watery glass roof over their heads. 'Well, they'll have a struggle in this weather, won't they?' he said. 'No helicopter can land in this.'

'Colleagues are trying to clear the road as we speak,' Lola said.

'"Colleagues",' he muttered. 'You said "quite a lot" has been going on here. I think it's about time I heard about it.'

'It's what I wanted to talk to you about,' Catherine said. 'We were due to meet in the morning.'

'I suggest,' Lola said, 'that we're joined by Dr Abbott. We can explain everything then. Is there a room we can use, Catherine?'

'The library,' Catherine said. 'It'll be warm in there and it's very private. I'll go find Dr Abbott.'

* * *

9.21 p.m.

Lola tried the resilience team again while they made their way to the library, but the line was still busy. She paused to type a text message: *This is DCI Harris at Ardaig Castle. Please call me ASAP.* She sent it, then hurried to catch up with the others.

Catherine had found Abbott in the dining room with Grace. He was trying to get her to eat something, while fending off questions from his colleagues.

The library was on the ground floor of the main building, accessed through a doorway to the left of the staircase. It was a long room with windows at one end and books on every wall. Some — presumably rare or valuable — sat behind glass. Catherine went about turning on lamps.

'We can use the table,' she said, a little breathlessly, and pointed at a boardroom-style table by the window.

Stefan Kade went first, then Dr Abbott. Lola sat opposite the two men.

Catherine drew the red velvet curtains then sat too.

'Well,' Kade began, gazing contemptuously at the faces round the table, breathing hard through his nose as if he was just about containing his temper. 'Who's going to explain?'

'I think Catherine should provide some brief background,' Lola said quickly, before Abbott could speak.

'Then please proceed,' Kade said, eyes on Catherine.

'Horrible letters,' the castle manager said in a small voice, eyes on the table top.

Kade frowned. 'Yes, but . . . I thought that was dealt with.'

'We tried our best, Mr Kade. We took advice from the police too. But things continued. In fact, they got quite a bit worse.'

He stared in disbelief. 'You're telling me this woman's death is linked to "nasty letters"?'

'It's possible,' Lola said. 'Yes.'

Catherine said, 'The letters are the reason I asked to speak to you tomorrow morning, Mr Kade.'

'I see.' He scowled at her. 'But you thought you would call the police in ahead of that?'

'I called on Lola because I was desperate,' Catherine said, sniffing a little. 'I asked her to advise me what to do. She suggested I should talk to you, sir — only now things have overtaken us. This evening, my office was vandalised. I'd kept the letters in a box file. Someone went into the office — apparently someone with their own key — and took them. They broke into my locked filing cabinet and took a further letter I'd been keeping in there — one making a very specific allegation. And then Amy . . . She was upset earlier in the evening. Then she went missing.'

She fell silent.

Lola stayed quiet herself, wondering who would speak first.

Kade asked, 'What specific allegation was in this letter you had locked away?'

Catherine peered at Abbott. Abbott waited, his face a blank.

'It was addressed to me,' she said. 'At least it was my name on the envelope. It said I'd employed a killer.'

Kade stared in disbelief.

'Are you suggesting Sister Yorke was the one writing the letters? That she'd discovered one of her colleagues was a murderer, and that that person broke into your office to get the letter back, then went and killed Sister Yorke? But that's insane!'

'I'm not saying that, Mr Kade,' Catherine said quietly. She looked appealingly towards Dr Abbott, as if willing him to step in and rescue her.

Lola said, 'Whoever broke into Catherine's office left her a message there too.'

Kade's eyebrows rose and he looked to Catherine for more information.

'It said, "How many killers under one roof?"' Catherine murmured.

'"How many—"?'

'"*Killers*",' she said more loudly.

'Meaning what exactly?' Kade demanded, eyes on Lola.

'We don't know,' Lola said. 'Yet.'

Kade lowered his eyes and seemed to be processing the news.

'Anonymous letters, a woman dead,' he said at last, 'accusations of murder. This is supposed to be a place of well-being and recovery. An *asset*. One I want to invite the world's most senior leaders to visit.'

Abbott cleared his throat, but before he could speak the phone buzzed into life.

Lola grabbed it and rose from her seat, going instinctively to the window — anything to ensure a signal.

'DCI Harris?' a man's small voice asked.

'Speaking.' Lola could hear the wind buffeting the microphone.

'My name's Neil Forbes,' he said. 'I lead one of the road teams. We're on the road to Ardaig Castle.'

'Go on.' Every muscle of her body felt locked with tension.

'There are two trees down. They're not the problem. I'm afraid part of the riverbank's collapsed and taken a chunk of the road with it. There's a chance the whole road could go.'

Lola felt as if she'd been drenched in icy water. 'What are you saying?'

'We can't get through to you, certainly not with vehicles. It's too dangerous. We'll scope the possibility of someone coming in on foot. As for everyone at the castle, you're going to be stuck there some time.'

* * *

9.45 p.m.

The people round the table listened in silence as Lola related the news. All eyes turned on Kade, waiting for his response.

'So we're trapped here with a dead body and a murderer?'

'It would seem so, sir,' Lola replied blankly.

'And I expect you propose to assume some sort of authority here in the meantime?' he asked.

Lola sat up. 'There's been a suspicious death, sir, following a series of suspicious incidents. I may be off duty, but I do have a duty of care, first to protect life, then to protect evidence. If that means setting some rules and making sure people abide by them, I hope you'll support me in that.'

Kade sniffed. 'That bloody woman,' he muttered.

'I'm sorry, sir?'

'Shuna Whatever-her-name-is, the journalist who's been trailing after me. She's supposed to be writing an article about me and the work of my family's foundation — specifically, our work here at Ardaig.'

Lola said nothing.

'Constant questions, constant challenges. It's clear to me she has an agenda of her own.'

'Perhaps she simply wants to report truthfully,' Lola said mildly.

Who would have thought she'd one day be defending Shuna Frain . . .

Kade softened into weariness. 'It's going to be a long night. We should speak to the staff and guests.'

'I plan to talk to the local DCI first,' Lola said. 'We can talk to everyone later.'

He eyed her with something that might be a modicum of respect, manicured eyebrows slightly raised.

'Very well,' he said, then rose and gave a curt bow before departing.

* * *

9.56 p.m.

It took a couple of calls and then a wait of a few minutes, but at last Lola got to speak to the local DCI, a grumpy-sounding man who clearly didn't welcome this development on his patch one bit. She talked through protocols, double-checking she'd done everything properly so far — not that there was a book for this kind of situation. She explained she'd taken photos of the scene, including a close-up of the bruise and cut on Amy's cheek, and of the smashed vase and the now-empty plinth on the third landing, together with snaps of the scuff mark on the balustrade and that tiny splash of blood. She told him about the claw hammer and how it was now secure in the office safe, then detailed how she'd sealed the crime scene, and taken charge of any keys that were known about. All that was correct, the DCI agreed.

'As for next steps,' Lola went on, 'I've asked for a list of who should be on the estate, and then I'm going to talk to everyone together. I'll ask everyone to write down their movements and try to narrow down who was unaccounted for at the time Sister Yorke fell to her death. I'll appeal for anyone with information to come and see me. Oh, and I plan to stay here in the castle tonight. I want to keep as close an eye on things as possible.'

'In other words, you've unilaterally decided to lead an investigation,' the man said, making adrenaline spark in Lola's chest.

'I'm doing what I can,' she told him after a moment's hesitation. 'Time is of the essence, after all.'

'That comes with risks,' he growled. 'I suggest you step back and limit your involvement to a watching brief.'

'But what if the killer plans to strike again?' she asked him now.

'You're going to stop him single-handed, are you?'

'I note your concern,' she said coldly. 'I need to go.'

Lola took a few moments to sit in silence, her eyes closed as she tried to disperse some of the stress of the past hour. She was disturbed by a knock at the door.

She called to come in, expecting Catherine with a list of names. But it wasn't Catherine.

'Well, well, well,' Shuna Frain said. She closed the door behind her and sauntered down the library, smirking.

'Hello, Shuna.'

'So, the shit's really hit the fan, hasn't it? And you're here, all on your tod!'

'No need to gloat.'

'I'm not gloating. I'd just like a line on what's going on here. Off the record for now, if you prefer. Besides, I can hardly "phone it in", given we're all but cut off here.' Her eyes focused hungrily on the device in Lola's hand. 'Does that thing have a signal?'

'Yes,' Lola said, and instinctively moved the phone out of reach, as if Shuna might snatch it from her. 'And I can't tell you anything—'

'It was the nurse, wasn't it? Sister Yorke.'

Lola didn't reply.

'Someone did for her, didn't they?' Shuna went on. 'One of the people here tonight. One of those nice folk glugging cocktails earlier or picking at their dinner in the dining room right now. Which reminds me — you won't have eaten anything. Want me to fetch you a plate? I could ask you questions while you eat and you could nod or shake your head.'

'I'm fine, thank you.'

'Going to be a long night,' Shuna said. 'Sure you wouldn't appreciate a wee hand — especially from someone who might already know some interesting stuff?'

'What "stuff"?'

'Stuff about the letters. I reckon I know who sent them. And I know why.'

'Shuna . . .'

Shuna tilted her head. 'It was lasagne — I'm sure there'll be some left in the kitchen. Plus some nice salady things. Now, tell me what you fancy and I'll be back in a jiffy.'

* * *

10.12 p.m.

Catherine appeared while Shuna was away.

'The list of names,' she said, holding out a sheet of paper with neat handwriting on it.

Lola folded it over without looking and put it on the table beside the phone.

'How are you holding up, Catherine?'

'Not very well, I'm afraid.'

Lola invited her to sit down.

'Word's got round,' Catherine said gloomily. 'I suspect Grace told Margot when Margot was comforting her, and that was it. People want to know what's going on. Mr Kade is telling people you're going to make an address to all the staff. Is that right?'

'Yes, but not quite yet.'

'And, of course, there are the guests too,' Catherine went on. 'Two of them at dinner just now. Goodness only knows what they're thinking.'

'Keep people fed and watered and in the dining room. If you could keep people away from the alcohol that might be helpful. Maybe put on some fresh coffee.'

'What if someone needs to, well, you know — *step out*?'

'For the loo, you mean? That's fine. Don't let people go up to their rooms. Talking of which, I'd like to see inside Amy's flat. Can you arrange that?'

'It'll be locked, but I think William Rix will have a key. He keeps spares for the flats. I expect Amy would have had her own key with her.'

'She didn't,' Lola said. 'At least, it wasn't in any of her pockets.'

'Of course. You'd have checked.' Catherine blanched slightly as if visualising Lola rummaging through the dead woman's clothes. 'In that case, it's probably in her locker. Those are in a changing area in the Edwardian wing, next to the first-aid room. The codes on those lockers are digital. I wouldn't know her code. Anyway—' she got up to go — 'let me go find William for you.'

'Thank you.'

'Oh, one thing to note,' Catherine said, 'I put the names of the four guests on the list too. The fourth is the one I think you'll recognise, but I know you'll be discreet.'

'I will,' Lola said, and reached for the paper, readying herself.

A quick rap at the door and Shuna let herself in, balancing a plate and a glass of water.

'Oh, Shuna, isn't that nice of you?' Catherine said, eyes on the food as she made to leave.

Lola fixed a smile.

If only you knew, Catherine. If only you knew . . .

* * *

10.20 p.m.

'Give me a minute,' Lola said as Shuna pulled out a chair.

'Of course.'

Lola scanned Catherine's list of names, holding her breath. She reached the bottom and the names of the four guests. And there it was . . .

Angus Wilde.

A name Lola knew very well, and from her recent past: Detective Superintendent Angus Wilde, a man with whom she'd clashed horribly during her hunt for the murderer known as the Clyde Pusher. They'd made their peace at the end of the case, but it had been an uncomfortable one. His wife had been ill, Lola remembered — terminally so.

And now he was here. She remembered Catherine's words, as reported to her by Frankie: 'complete mental collapse'.

Oh dear . . .

She chewed her lip as she anticipated meeting him again, and when he was so vulnerable.

'Something you want to share?' Shuna asked slyly, and Lola realised she must have sighed aloud.

'No,' Lola said smartly. She folded the paper and pushed it across the table, then turned her attention to the food.

'So,' she said, cutting a slice of lasagne, 'you had something to tell me?'

'Amy Yorke contacted me three weeks ago,' Shuna said.

Lola was glad she hadn't taken a mouthful because she would have spat it out.

'Thought you'd be interested.' Shuna smiled. 'It was in confidence, obviously, but that hardly matters now, does it? We only ever spoke on the phone. She certainly had no idea I'd be here this weekend — probably explains why she took fright when I came into the orangery with Catherine Ballantyne earlier this evening.'

'That's assuming she knew your face,' Lola pointed out.

'Oh, she knew,' Shuna said. 'She'd done her research on me. Kept saying the story was "right up my street".'

'Tell me everything,' Lola said, abandoning the food and turning to face Shuna.

'She sent me an email. Said she was a nurse at this place and that she had evidence of criminality. That it was being covered up. She said she wanted to meet. I replied, saying my time was too limited and it'd have to be on the phone, so she agreed to that. We spoke on a Sunday afternoon. She was out and about and quite alone, calling from a mobile. She said there was a murderer working at the castle. She said she'd tried to blow the whistle but was told to keep quiet.'

'What did she want from you?' Lola asked.

'A promise to take her seriously, and to write about it: an exposé of this person and the castle management. Oh, and to swear I'd protect my source.'

'Did you believe her?'

'No, if I'm honest.' Shuna gave a rueful smile. 'I thought she was a very unhappy person trying to cause trouble for a colleague — and for her employer. Seems I was wrong.'

'When did you say this was?'

'We spoke two Sundays ago.'

'Did she tell you the name of the person she thought was a murderer?'

'Yes. She's here this evening. In fact, I had a lovely chat with her. She's the "head of guest well-being", whatever that means. Name of Grace Miller — or, rather, that's her name now.'

Lola nodded but said nothing.

'You already know about it?' Shuna asked.

'Grace Miller has been open about her past with the castle management. She took a new identity after the trial but she hasn't lied about who she is. She was found not guilty.'

'Wrongly, according to Amy. She claimed to have proof of her guilt. I said, "What proof?" She said she'd reveal it in time. So I pushed her, and she admitted she didn't have anything concrete. Just rumours she'd found in chatrooms online. But she said "proof was coming her way" and that it was just "a matter of time". I said that wasn't good enough. She got shirty then and hung up. I tried to call her back, then realised she'd blocked my number.'

'If you didn't take her seriously,' Lola asked, 'why on earth are you here this weekend? I assume this is the real reason you're here — that the puff piece on Stefan Kade is a ruse?'

'Too right.' Shuna smiled. 'The call intrigued me, so I started looking into the whole Vivien Wray thing. There's lots of conjecture online: Did she do it? Didn't she? That doesn't necessarily mean anything — these cases always lead to speculation. Then there are the amateur detectives determined to find her. "Where is Vivien Wray now?" Couple of answers were right too. Well, right in that they knew she was living in Scotland and working in healthcare.

'I put out some feelers of my own,' Shuna went on. 'Asked a couple of contacts down under to do some digging. And within a day or two I had a *very* interesting piece of news indeed.'

'Oh?'

Shuna gave one of her cat-like grins.

But before she could speak, she was interrupted by a knock at the door. Catherine was back. She signalled to Lola and Lola came across.

'That's William with the key to Amy's rooms,' Catherine said quietly. Lola spotted the gloomy security man skulking in the great hallway over Catherine's shoulder. 'Do you want to come upstairs now or are you busy?'

Lola looked over her shoulder. 'Shuna, can you give me ten minutes?'

'Sure thing,' Shuna said, getting up from the chair. 'I'll go back to the dining room. See what I can overhear.' She dropped Lola a wink and beamed as if they were the best of mates.

* * *

10.36 p.m.

They climbed the grand staircase, William Rix going first, Catherine struggling to keep up with him. Lola took her time, pausing to snap on a pair of disposable gloves as she went.

The wind was high again, whistling and moaning round the lantern at the top of the great hallway. Hail clattered against the high windows like a volley of shot.

'Is that the only spare key?' Lola asked, when they were on the second floor.

'Only one I know about,' Rix said without looking round at her.

'Amy may have made a spare,' Catherine pointed out.

'Did someone clean her flat?'

'No. No, she didn't want them to. The domestics will clean our rooms once a week, but Amy declined the opportunity. She was private like that. Plus, she had the most *terrific* standards. I doubt anyone else could have met them.'

Rix pushed through a pair of swinging fire doors and they were in a short, dimly lit passage with doors on both sides and a window at the far end.

'Who else lives on this floor?' Lola asked Catherine.

'Margot Kerr's rooms are here on the right. Grace Miller's are at the far end. Amy's rooms are here on the left.'

Rix had stopped by the door, which had a brass sign screwed to it with the words *Private — A. Yorke*. He had a key out, ready.

'I'll take that,' Lola said and wrested it from him, earning herself a scowl.

'Thank you, William,' Catherine said. 'Lola, do you want me to come in with you?'

Lola eyed the nervous woman and decided she should have a witness to corroborate any finds. 'Follow me in but don't touch anything.' She looked at Rix. 'You wait out here. Don't let anyone else in.'

He lifted his chin and glared.

Ignoring him, she unlocked the door and stepped inside Amy's flat.

The place was in darkness. She found a light switch and turned it on to see a small entrance lobby, with shoes on a rack and coats, scarves and a couple of hats on a stand. A doorway to the left was open. Again, she felt for the light switch and illuminated a small, neutrally decorated, dingy living space, with a dark-green armchair, a fold-out dining table with two upright chairs, and a television and DVD player. There was a tiny kitchen area in a corner by the window, little more than a sink, with a kettle, a cupboard over it and a small fridge underneath. Green curtains were pulled across the window. There were paperback books here and there, and an oldish laptop on a table beside the armchair, but there was no personality here. It was a clean, tidy, joyless space.

'This flat is at the front of the castle, isn't it?' Lola asked Catherine.

'Yes. That window looks out over the driveway.'

Lola went to it and peered down and to the left, making out the pointed roof of the portico through the rain.

A second door led from the living room into a bedroom.

This too was tidy, clean and neutral. A neatly made single bed stood against one wall, a narrow wardrobe at its foot.

Lola sensed Catherine in the doorway of the bedroom behind her, watching.

'What are you looking for?' she asked quietly.

'I don't know,' Lola said truthfully.

She opened the drawer of a bedside unit and found a bible, a packet of tissues and a very old paperback of a P. D. James detective novel, the cover of which showed a sinister gloved hand holding a syringe.

The wardrobe contained blouses, skirts, trousers, jackets, mostly in plain, earthy tones. There were four pairs of shoes at the bottom, flat heeled, plain, functional — and a yellow cardboard wallet slid in beside them.

Lola crouched for it then turned her back to Catherine and opened the flap to look at the contents. A4 paper, some blank, some printed on, with familiar paragraph spacing and tabbing. And envelopes.

Everyday stationery, put to extraordinary — now deadly — use.

CHAPTER THIRTEEN

10.52 p.m.

The stationery and pre-printed correspondence could have been planted there, but Lola doubted it. Amy Yorke was surely the letter writer — the second one, at least.

'What is it?' Catherine asked in a small, shaky voice.

Lola closed the flap and turned.

'I'm going to need a secure place to store some items,' she said.

'It's the letters, isn't it?' Catherine said, eyes on the wallet. 'Amy...'

'A safe, ideally,' Lola went on, determined to stay focused, 'but a lockable filing cabinet would do.'

'There's a safe in the general office,' Catherine said. 'I keep one or two personal items in there. Work papers I keep in the lockable cabinet in my own office, but obviously that's been broken into.'

'Who knows the passcode to the safe?'

'Only me. But it's digital. You can change the number if you like, then you're the only one with access to it.'

'I think that would be best. I need to look at this first.' She patted the wallet. 'I'll let you know when I need access. In the meantime, please say nothing about this.'

'Of course.'

She took a last glance around the neutral rooms. 'I think I've seen enough here.'

They left Amy's flat in silence. Lola locked the outer door then removed the key from William Rix's ring and pocketed it.

Kade was waiting for them at the foot of the staircase, a pale hand holding the newel post. His knuckles showed white.

'We can't keep people waiting any longer,' he said.

'I agree,' Lola said.

'Everybody's in the dining room. Some people moved into the orangery but it started to hail and it was terrifically noisy. I say "everybody", but that's not quite true. That Swedish doctor has insisted on packing the two guests back off to their rooms. One of them — the older one — is quite distressed.'

'I'll still want to speak to the guests,' Lola said. 'All four of them. I can do that individually, if need be.' She turned to Catherine. 'Could you find some paper for me and some pens? Enough so everyone in the dining room can have a pen and a sheet each?'

'Yes. That's no problem.'

'It's this way,' Kade said impatiently, while Catherine scurried off.

Lola briefly contemplated the yellow card wallet she was carrying. She didn't want the staff to see it, but at the same time she was reluctant to leave it in the library, even if the door was locked. She took off her scarf and carefully wrapped it round the folder, then tucked it under one arm.

There was a way to cut through from the great hallway to the dining room, through an archway to the left of the staircase, along a short passage then through a door, which

Kade threw open. The thrum of voices ceased as he strode in. Some people were sitting, others standing. Every head turned.

Kade stopped at the head of a long shiny table, still bearing empty plates and half-drunk glasses of wine, and looked out at the sea of faces, some anxious, others merely apprehensive. Lola stood deliberately apart from him and took in the room, which had the air of a banqueting hall, with dark green fleur-de-lis wallpaper and heavy red curtains and carpet. The rich aroma of food and wine lingered in the air.

Lola stepped forward and scanned the audience. Shuna Frain was nearest, Frankie beside her. Frankie eyed Lola cautiously — a little guiltily, maybe. A tense-looking Tom Abbott was next, then a pale and frightened-looking Grace Miller. Margot Kerr was at the far end of the table, then beside her a beadily curious, even amused, Dr Stenqvist. Next to him was Izzy McManus and beside her the tall man with the thinning black hair and hooked nose Lola had seen briefly in the orangery, moving tables with William Rix. She recalled Catherine saying Izzy lived here with her husband, who was something to do with the management of the estate. Next to the thin man was tiny, nervous Senga McCall from the kitchen, at last without her bonnet, revealing a head of thin reddish-brown hair. Next was William Rix, looking more bone white than ever, and finally, Maya McArthur, looking gaunt with strain.

Catherine appeared through the door, a sheaf of printer paper in her hand and a number of pens held together with rubber bands.

Kade cleared his throat and said, in a stiff, stentorian voice, 'This is Detective Chief Inspector Lola Harris of Police Scotland. *Not* a relative of a prospective guest as we had all been led to believe.' He paused for effect. 'She wishes to address you about a most serious matter.'

All eyes were on Lola. Expressions ranged from confusion to outright astonishment. Lola stepped forward, taking time to meet people's eyes. Maya McArthur left her position at the back of the dining room and came forward to stand beside her husband, eyes down. He barely seemed to notice she was there.

'As Mr Kade says,' Lola said in a loud, clear voice, 'I am a police detective. Though I want to stress that I was here in a personal capacity. I am still not here officially, but because of my experience I have a duty to take charge of the situation.'

She paused, observing Senga McCall wiping a tear from her eye, William Rix's dark eyes shifting about the room, and Margot Kerr patting Grace Miller's arm. Lola had no doubt they all already knew what she was going to tell them.

'I'm sorry to confirm that your colleague Amy Yorke died tonight. Based on the evidence I've found, I believe her death to be suspicious.'

A sob from Senga. Murmuring from others.

'The road in and out of here is blocked,' she went calmly on, 'and the weather is too bad for a helicopter to land. So, until local detectives can get here, it's my job to protect evidence, and to protect you. If *anyone* here knows *anything at all* about Amy's death — or about the series of unpleasant letters that have been circulating for the past three months, then I ask you to find me and speak to me direct. Come straight to me. I'll be in the library. If I'm already talking to someone, please wait. I'll stay up for as long as I need to, and I'll be spending the night here in the castle, so I'm on hand.'

She caught Frankie's surprised stare, then remained quiet for a few moments to let the words sink in and stole a glance to her right at Kade and his wife. Kade's expression was stony but she detected a weary resignation. Maya McArthur eyed Lola anxiously.

'Now, I know it's already very late, but I need information from each of you. Shortly I'm going to ask you to note down your movements, as precisely as you can remember them, between six p.m. this evening and now.'

She saw perplexed frowns and sheepish glances.

'This will help me to understand whether anyone might have a deeper insight into what happened here tonight. I ask that you do this before you leave the room again, but once you've written your note and brought it personally to me, you can retire for the night.'

Catherine rose and began to hand out pens and pieces of paper.

'Now, any questions?'

Remarkably, there were none.

* * *

11.20 p.m.

Lola took Catherine with her back to the library, using the passage under the stairs.

'We should have a few minutes before anyone comes along,' Lola said when she'd closed the door. It was just the two of them alone in the long, book-lined room. The only sounds were the ticking of a clock and the wind moaning outside. 'I'd like to ask you some questions.'

'Yes, yes, of course,' Catherine said, twittery and nervous now. 'And I'm happy to write everything down like the others.'

'Yes, and that will be helpful,' Lola said as they took their seats at a corner of the table by the window. 'But I'd like to pin down the sequence of events just now.'

Catherine nodded in meek understanding.

Lola had brought a pen and paper back from the dining room and wrote Catherine's name at the top of the first sheet.

'I want to ask you about your office,' she began. 'Did you note the time you discovered it had been vandalised?'

'It was . . . it must have been seven forty.'

'Talk me through what you did next.'

'Erm . . .' Catherine frowned. 'I was frozen for, I don't know, maybe a minute. Then I made myself take stock of what had been done. I saw the message on the mirror, then I looked in the drawers — I mean, they were already standing open — to check what had been taken. I saw the box file was gone. Then I came away. I locked the door and came to the orangery, and found you were looking for me. I'd run there, so I was out of breath. I was very upset.'

'And that was at seven forty-five,' Lola said.

'It must have been, yes.'

'And when had you *last* been in your office before it was vandalised?'

'Earlier in the evening. I'd popped in for some headache tablets.' She bit her lip. 'That must have been just after six. I'd been with the Kades. I went straight to my office, got the tablets from my bag and locked up again.'

'You're sure you locked the door?'

'Yes. I always lock it. The filing cabinet where I keep all the financial and personnel papers has its own lock, but I like to make doubly sure.'

Lola pondered how to ask the next question. 'Was anyone else in your office at any time today, for any reason?'

'Only Dr Stenqvist. He came to report that the blinds in his office are broken. He's forever running them up and down and getting them in a tangle. I was in there working and he knocked and came in. He was only with me a minute or two.'

'And when was this?'

Catherine blinked and frowned. 'I had the radio on. Yes, I'd just listened to the news. A little after three, I'd say. You could check with Florien, though time isn't really his thing. He comes and goes when he likes.'

Lola made a note. Catherine hadn't asked why she'd wanted to know, and she didn't feel the need to explain.

'You told me you were looking for Amy,' she said now. 'That you'd gone to your office for the key to the old nursery at the top of the castle's Victorian wing.'

'That's right.'

'Why were you looking for Amy?'

'Why was I . . . ? Well, I'd seen her earlier leaving the orangery in rather a hurry. She'd been with you and I'd just arrived with Shuna. I was anxious she might be upset and . . . well, if I'm honest, I was concerned after her behaviour earlier in the day, when she tried to intercept Mr Kade. I had an idea she might be about to disrupt the dinner. I wanted to talk to her, to see what state she was in, except I couldn't find her anywhere.'

'You looked all over?'

'Yes. Well, not in the Victorian wing. But then I saw Dr Abbott coming from his flat — that's here in the main building, on the first floor. He'd been with the Kades and had nipped back for something. I asked him if he'd seen Amy and he said he hadn't. He could see I was anxious and he suggested the old nursery.'

Lola nodded slowly.

'It was a good idea. And of course, it turned out he was right! I went straight down to my office — and that's when I found it in the state it was in.'

'But Dr Abbott didn't come with you?'

'No. I assumed he was on his way to the orangery to join everyone else.'

Lola wrote.

'Was there anything else?' Catherine asked with a sigh. 'I'm so tired. I don't intend to go to bed, but I would love a coffee.' She gave Lola a small smile. 'I expect you would too.'

'I would, as it happens,' Lola said. 'Just one more thing, though. I need to understand the castle a little better. Could you find me a map of the place? And I wonder if someone could give me a tour round. I want to understand how the different wings fit together and how you can go between them. Perhaps William Rix could do that.'

'I'm sure he would. And, yes, I can find you a plan. There's one in the general office, in the health and safety folder. It shows all the fire exits, that sort of thing. I'll go do that now and I'll talk to William too.' She got up. 'And I'll ask Senga to make us a fresh pot of coffee.'

* * *

11.46 p.m.

Left on her own, Lola turned her notes into a neat table, with timings as close as she could get them.

> *6.10 p.m. — Time Catherine says she last saw her office unvandalised (note: last time anyone can corroborate this is Dr Stenqvist at 3.05 p.m.)*
> *7.05 p.m. — Sister Yorke runs out of orangery upset (as Catherine and Shuna arrive)*
> *7.40 p.m. — Catherine finds office in a state*
> *7.45 p.m. — Catherine tells LH about vandalism to her office*
> *7.55 p.m. — Dr Abbott arrives at Catherine's office and joins LH and Catherine*
> *8.05 p.m. — 1st gong for dinner heard*
> *8.07 p.m. — (Time checked by LH) Catherine's office locked, LH and Dr Abbott head to his office (speak to Grace Miller briefly a few mins after this — 8.09 p.m.?)*
> *8.20 p.m. — Scream and smashing vase heard*
> *8.21 p.m. — Sister Yorke's body discovered by Grace Miller, very quickly joined by LH and Dr Abbott*
> *8.37 p.m. — 2nd gong for dinner*

She made two further notes, based on what the table indicated:

> *Catherine's office was vandalised between 6.10 p.m. and 7.40 p.m. (providing Catherine is telling the truth — NB Dr Stenqvist may corroborate that the office was unvandalised when he visited at 3.05 p.m., but apart from that I'm relying on Catherine's word).*

> *Sister Amy Yorke was killed at 8.20 p.m. Whoever killed her would be unable to account for their whereabouts between roughly 8.15 and 8.25 p.m. Who?*

CHAPTER FOURTEEN

Sunday 23 February

12.01 a.m.

Catherine came back to the library with several sheets of paper that showed the floorplans of the castle's wings and various floors, including basements and attics in some parts. The building was even more complex than Lola realised, with multiple backstairs, including those of the spiral variety. She hated heights and had once had an embarrassing experience coming down the steep stone spiral stairs of the Wallace Monument in Stirling. She hoped to avoid using any in the castle tonight.

'It will make more sense once you've had the tour,' Catherine said, as if she'd read Lola's mind. 'William will take you round whenever you like. He's in the dining room with the others. William is very good at his job, but he's a wee bit morose, I'm afraid. It's not personal.'

A tiny knock sounded from the door. Catherine eyed Lola as if for permission. Lola nodded.

'Come in,' Catherine called.

It was Senga from the kitchen pulling a trolley with coffee and cups on it and what looked like a selection of biscuits on a plate, complete with doily.

'Where do you want it, Ms Ballantyne?' the wee woman asked in a whisper.

Catherine looked to Lola.

'Down by the long table, please,' Lola said, smiling.

A nod, but no eye contact.

Senga came the length of the room, pulling the trolley after her.

When she'd crept away, Lola explained her plan to Catherine.

'I'll sit at the table. You stay by the door, just inside, and greet people when they arrive, then let them bring their notes to me individually. I'll want to ask some of them a few specific questions, so if you could keep the others at bay while I do that?'

'Of course.' Catherine looked about. 'I'll sit here, right by the door.'

Lola poured coffee for them both then took a seat at the table. It was warm in here, but the weather outside sounded worse than ever, the wind screaming and shaking the windowpanes as if it was trying to get inside.

She checked the time and estimated that she would probably have everyone's notes within the hour. In that time she intended to ask some searching questions of Grace Miller and Dr Abbott, both of whom, along with Lola herself, had been near-witnesses of the murder. She would then combine the information they gave her with the notes of everyone else's whereabouts and attempt to narrow down the suspects. In addition, she needed to speak to the guests. She briefly wondered if they could wait till morning, but then rejected the idea. What if one of them had important information? No, it must be tonight.

She groaned. It was going to be a long night.

She sipped her black coffee and turned her attention to the yellow card wallet from Sister Yorke's wardrobe.

Wearing a fresh pair of disposable gloves, she made three piles of the contents. The first, envelopes — standard white office ones with a pre-sealed flap with a pull-off strip. The second, blank, white A4 paper — the kind you found in any printer, same as that used for the anonymous letters that had plagued this place for the past few months. The third, sheets of paper with type already printed on them. There were four of these and she studied them first, steeling herself for the vitriol printed there:

*MURDERER.
THINK WE DONT KNOW?
WE KNOW! I KNOW! I SPOKEN TO POEPLE.*

*CHARLATTAN. FRAUD.
NO DOCTOR I WOULD EVER GOTO.
CHEAT AND LIAR CHEAT AND MOLSTER.
I HAVE EVIDENES + PLENTY OF IT.*

*WHY HAVE YOU NOT ACTED?
WHY ARE YOU PROTTECTING A KILLER?
WHY WAIT?
DO YOU WANT ME TO GO TO THE NEWSPAPERS???*

THIS IS YOUR LAST WARNING FOOLSIH MAN.
PROTECT THE MURDERER + PAY THE PRICE.

She heard voices and looked up. Catherine was talking to someone at the door.

'It's Frankie,' Catherine called down the library to her. 'Can you see her now?'

'Yes, okay,' Lola called back.

She shovelled the papers and envelopes back into the wallet and put it down on a chair beside her, where it would be hidden from view by the table, then stripped off the gloves.

Frankie came down the library while Catherine slipped out into the great hallway. Lola got up.

'Oh God, Lola,' Frankie cried as she hurried the last few metres. 'Oh God, what must you be thinking!' She threw herself on Lola. 'I never thought anything like this might happen! That poor woman's *dead* and you're het for it. I'm so sorry.'

'It's hardly your fault, is it?' Lola said, pulling out of the embrace. 'Unless you pushed her to her death.' She widened her eyes. 'Did you?'

'What?' Frankie looked appalled, then sheepish. 'Guess I'm a suspect like all the others.'

'Strictly speaking,' Lola murmured. She pulled out a chair. 'Sit down and tell me what people are saying.'

Frankie sat. 'Margot Kerr thinks Sister Yorke was sending the anonymous letters,' she said. 'She thinks Izzy McManus wrote some of them too, then Sister Yorke joined in, using the letters to attack certain individuals. She said she's not the only one who thinks that.'

'Oh?'

'Margot says Dr Stenqvist was on the verge of confronting Sister Yorke. Apparently Amy had a thing against Dr Stenqvist because he touched her breasts "accidentally" on more than one occasion. That's why he got so many letters, Margot reckons. He gives me the creeps, if I'm honest.' She gave a theatrical shiver.

'Have you written down your movements?' Lola asked now.

'Such as they are.' She took out a folded sheet of paper from her bag. 'I got to the orangery the same time as you, then I went in to dinner. I went to the loo once, in between.' She shrugged. 'Here you go.'

Lola glanced over the paper.

'Oh, and by the way,' Frankie said, 'I've said to Catherine I'd like to stay here tonight as well. She's going to give us rooms next door to each other on the third floor — right next door to the Kades' suite. Imagine sleeping in the next room to Maya McArthur. She's so nice, by the way. Fragile, if you ask me. Shaking like a leaf after you gave us your talk. I was going to drive to the cottage to get some stuff, but . . . well, I've had quite a bit to drink . . . What will we do?'

'Wait,' Lola said. 'I'll drive us both in an hour or so. You go back to the others and see what you can pick up.'

'That's me recruited to your task force?' Frankie asked mildly.

'It's all hands on deck, I'm afraid.'

Over Frankie's shoulder Lola saw the library door open a crack. Catherine peered in.

'What is it?' she called.

'Shuna wants a word.'

'Okay,' Lola called back.

'I'll go,' Frankie said, getting up. 'Bye, sis. And I am sorry. I shouldn't have got you here under false pretences like this. I know that now. Bit late though, eh?'

'It's okay,' Lola said.

She watched Frankie retreating down the library.

It *was* okay. More than okay, in fact. She wouldn't be admitting it to Frankie any time soon, but her sister had done her a favour. Lola was doing what she did best, investigating, solving problems, finding answers.

Back in her element, in other words.

What that meant for her big career decision . . . well, that was a question for another day.

* * *

12.21 a.m.

'I've written it all down, like a good girl,' Shuna said, taking a seat and sliding a folded A4 sheet across to Lola.

Lola took a glance then laid it face down on top of Frankie's.

'Not going to interrogate me about it?' Shuna asked with a smirk.

'I'll look later. I'm more interested in what you were going to tell me when we were interrupted earlier.'

'Yes, where were we . . . ? Oh yes, my research into Vivien. Well, after Amy Yorke contacted me, I started doing my own digging about Grace Miller, a.k.a. Vivien Wray. I was interested, see. Anyway, one of my Aussie contacts came up trumps.'

'Oh?'

'Grace Miller is writing a book.'

Lola stared. 'Is she?'

'It's not been announced, but she's writing a memoir of the death of the wee boy, the trial that followed and her life afterwards. For a *very hefty* advance. She's got an agent and everything — in New York. One of the big publishers has offered two hundred thousand US dollars for *Vivien Wray: My True Story*. Can you believe it?'

'Jeezo.'

'The US publisher has the worldwide English language rights, but the agent's already flogged translations to *twelve other countries*. There are TV rights in the offing too. Put it this way, I doubt Grace Miller will be coordinating anyone's well-being for much longer.'

'That's . . . very interesting,' Lola said.

'Isn't it?' The journalist gave Lola one of her feline smiles. 'I wonder if Amy Yorke found out.'

'Quite possibly,' Lola said, then frowned. 'But so what if she did? At most, she could expose Grace's past as someone who was tried for murder but acquitted. It might be embarrassing for her, especially with the patients here — sorry, "guests". But why would she give two figs about that if she's pocketing hundreds of thousands of pounds for her memoirs?'

Shuna shrugged. 'We could talk to Grace,' she suggested, eyes gleaming. 'See how she reacts.'

'Or *I* could,' Lola pointed out. '*On my own*.'

Shuna's eyes narrowed and the smirk was back. 'You're no fun, Lola Harris.'

'You're right.' Lola returned the smirk. 'I'm no fun at all.'

***

12.34 a.m.

Grace Miller was Lola's next visitor. She crept down the library, a folded sheet of paper in hand, and took a seat meekly at the table.

'I know what Catherine's told you,' she said, eyes down. 'You know about my past. My real name. Everything that happened.'

'Yes.'

The woman lifted her chin. 'God knows what you're thinking.'

'I'm not thinking anything.'

'Aren't you?' She held Lola's gaze with her very wide, pale-blue eyes. 'Aren't you wondering just a little bit — *did she kill Alex Grimshaw after all?*' The big, blue eyes glittered and she swallowed.

'Amy found out, didn't she?' Lola asked.

A steady nod and the eyes dropped again.

'We hadn't been open a week. We had our first two guests. I thought I'd found somewhere I could do my work and make a contribution and be happy, away from the speculation. And then Amy came to find me one afternoon. I was in my flat upstairs. I thought she'd just come to chat, but she was so odd, watching me, studying my face — and then I knew she'd recognised me. "I'm good with faces, Grace," she said. I said, "Are you?" She held out her phone, and there was a photo of Vivien Wray — me — going into court, aged nineteen. She said, "Don't try to deny it."'

Grace sighed and studied her bone-white hands, folded in her lap.

'"Why would I deny it?" I said. "I've nothing to be ashamed of." And she said, "Then why change your name?" "So I can try to live a normal life!" I said. And do you know what she did? She smiled. A big friendly smile. "It's okay, Grace," she said, "it can be our little secret." But then she went away and started to do her research.'

Grace paused and eyed Lola carefully, as if wondering if she could truly trust her. 'She found chatrooms, forums, all the horrible stuff about me online. *Did she do it? Where is she now?* She found me one afternoon, in my office. She said she wanted proof I was innocent, for her own "peace of mind". I said, "I was found innocent by a jury. The judge said the case should never have come to court. I won't be tried all over again, and certainly not by a bully like you." She didn't like that. She went to Catherine and told her. Catherine came to see me right away and, do you know, she couldn't have been nicer! Amy wasn't happy about that. Not a bit. Next she went to Tom — Dr Abbott.' She allowed herself a rueful smile. 'Except Tom already knew everything.' She eyed Lola. 'Tom and I are in a relationship,' she said. 'But I think you've already worked that out, haven't you?'

Lola said nothing.

'Everything came flooding back to me. The pain of the trial — and the aftermath. The impact on my family, on my poor parents and sister. You know I was physically attacked one time? A man and a woman — not even connected to the case — they saw me out shopping one day and came for me.'

'I think I did know that,' Lola said.

Grace lifted her left hand and showed Lola her pinkie finger. It was just a stump. 'A constant reminder,' she said bitterly. 'As if I need it.'

'I'm very sorry,' Lola said, and meant it.

'I began to hate her. I told Tom I wanted to leave. He said not to. That that would be giving in to her. He spoke to Amy and told her to stop what she was doing. He told her if it continued she would be the one to lose her job, not me. And she did back off, for a while.'

'But only for a while?' Lola prompted.

'Some of us had had letters,' Grace said now. 'Nasty, anonymous ones. It was . . . unpleasant. Frightening. A kind of madness in the shadows. But the letters didn't *know* things, if that makes sense. They were just rude. As if someone was having a spiteful little game. But Catherine and Tom had had enough.

'They held a meeting of all the staff. They showed a couple of the letters on a projector and watched everyone's reactions. I think they hoped someone would reveal their guilt. Maybe confess there and then. But no one did. And then the letters came thicker and faster than ever. Only this time they did know things. They knew things about me. I got two, calling me a killer. A child killer. A murderess. I *knew* it was Amy. I said so to Tom . . .' Her voice cracked. She swallowed and took a few moments to breathe and calm herself. 'I said, "Can't you get rid of her?" He said it wasn't that easy, and what if she started to kick up a fuss? I said I didn't care. I couldn't stand it. He spoke to her. Threatened her, basically.'

'And what happened then?'

'Ha! He got a letter of his own.' She shook her head and rolled her eyes. 'She'd put two and two together. The letter accused him of having an affair with a murderess. You can't imagine how stressful it's been for us. For him as well as me.' She paused and gave a long sigh.

Lola asked, 'Did Amy know about the book too?'

Grace Miller looked surprised, but mildly and only for a moment. 'Ah, so you know about that . . . Yes, she did, as a matter of fact. I don't know how! Nothing's been released to the press, but I suppose word was bound to get out. And that's when I realised what was really going on. It was jealousy, wasn't it? She was jealous of the attention I'd got as a woman on trial for murder; then of my affair with Tom; and finally, she was jealous of the money. She said she didn't think it was right that a child killer should profit from her crime. You know, I didn't even bother defending myself any more. But I'll tell you this: I hated her *so* much.'

She sat up, lifted her chin and gave Lola a long look. 'Go on,' she said, those big blue eyes angry with challenge. 'Ask me the question. "Did I kill Amy?"'

'Did you?' Lola asked.

'No,' she said simply. Then, as if a great pressure had been released, she seemed to relax. 'Is there anything else you'd like to ask me?'

Lola looked over Grace's notes.

'You were in the orangery from approximately six fifteen until just after eight?' she asked.

'That's right. I'd gone to the loo, then I heard the first gong. I was feeling a bit worn out and I didn't fancy going back to the orangery. I thought I'd go to my office for ten minutes, just to be on my own for a while.'

Lola frowned. 'Just after we found Sister Yorke's body, you told me you'd come to your office for your EpiPen. Was that a lie?'

Grace Miller peered at Lola for a moment. 'It was,' she said shyly. 'I'm sorry. I said it on impulse. I do have an EpiPen, but I always keep it with me. I have an allergy to nuts. Even being near them can set me off. The truth is, I'd noticed Tom had left the orangery and I hoped I might find him in his office. We sometimes meet there, you know? I was embarrassed that you'd seen me there, so I made up the excuse about the EpiPen. I'm sorry.'

Lola nodded and returned her attention to the timeline Grace had provided.

'Did you tell anyone you were leaving the orangery?'

'Oh, erm . . . I think I said to Margot I was nipping away.'

'Which toilets did you go to?'

'The ones beside the dining room. Then I used the back corridor to get to the Victorian wing and along to my office.'

'Did you see anyone on your way?'

'No. And the lights were off on the other floors. In any case, I didn't look. I didn't expect to see anyone, so . . .'

'And you went into your office?'

'I knocked on Tom's door first and tried the handle. It was locked, so I went into my own room.'

Lola consulted the notes again.

'The first gong went at five past eight,' she said. 'Dr Abbott and I came along only a minute or two later.'

'That's right. I'd only just gone into my office when I heard you and Tom. I'd left the door open a crack.'

'You spoke to us, then went back into your room?'

'That's right.'

'What did you do next?'

'I sat at my desk. I'd realised something was wrong from the look on Tom's face when he spoke to me. You looked very serious too. I couldn't help wondering what had happened. And then — it was only a few minutes later — I heard Amy's scream and that horrible crash as the vase smashed.' She stopped and took a deep breath. 'It was so horrible.' She put a hand to her mouth.

Lola looked at the notes. 'And that was at eight twenty?'

'I know it was. I'd been keeping an eye on the time. I knew dinner would be at any minute.'

'Tell me exactly what you heard.'

Grace took another deep breath. 'It came out of nowhere. Just a horrible, high-pitched scream. A woman's scream. Distant at first, then . . . closer. A loud smash followed. I was on my feet in a flash and out of the door. I didn't know what I expected to find,' she said, her voice rising with stress. 'I thought maybe a window — something to do with the storm. I was confused, but then I saw Amy in the middle of the floor and pottery shards everywhere. And then, a second later, you and Tom were there.'

'What do you think happened to Amy, Grace?'

The woman blinked and took her time. Then she said, 'I think someone killed her. I think she pushed someone too far, so they gave her a big push of their own in return.'

'What was she doing up there on the high landing?'

'I've no idea.'

They watched each other for a few moments.
'Is that everything?' Grace asked.
'I think so,' Lola said.

* * *

12.45 a.m.

'Grace said she told you everything,' Dr Tom Abbott said. 'I thought you might want to talk to me yourself.'

'Thank you,' Lola said.

The man sat opposite her, his long frame hunched, adding to a look of utter defeat. His skin was grey and eyes hollow. Lola had offered him coffee but he'd refused, saying he needed sleep, not caffeine.

Don't we all?

Catherine had left them alone, saying she would wait in the great hallway to intercept any newcomers.

He'd brought a note of his movements during the evening and Lola cast an eye over it before folding the page and setting it on one side.

'You've no idea what it's been like here,' Abbott was saying. 'All those letters, and it got worse after we confronted the staff about them. Poor Grace has been very miserable.' He peered at Lola sheepishly. 'We realised early on it was Amy writing the letters — the later ones, I mean.'

'Did you?'

'They were so specific, you see — the things the writer knew about Grace. The letters made the same accusations Amy had made to Grace in person — and to me. You see, after Amy threatened Grace and Grace didn't leave, Amy came to me, as clinical director. She told me she'd found out about Grace's past and that she'd "pieced together" all this random evidence she'd collected from various online forums. She said I should sack her.' He gave a small dark smile. 'She had no idea then that Grace and I were lovers.'

'When was this?'

'Before Christmas.'

'What did you say to her?'

'I played along, pretended to be surprised. I said I would speak to Grace. Grace and I discussed what course of action to take. I called Amy in to my office and told her Grace's past was her own business, that she was proved innocent in a court of law, and that she had every right to her privacy. I warned her not to harass or persecute Grace in any way, and I also reminded her of her duty to Ardaig Castle and the Kade Foundation as her employer. She wasn't happy but she went on her way. She became very quiet and sly. Meanwhile, the anonymous letters continued to arrive. Catherine consulted the police, but they could offer very little assistance without being here on the spot, and we couldn't have that. Catherine and I spoke to the staff — and then a new spate of letters began, these much more specific, containing detailed grievances. Grace received some. I did too, threatening to expose me for protecting a killer. I destroyed them. Grace destroyed hers too.'

'You believe Amy wrote them.'

'I know she did. You see, one night in the middle of January I stayed up late, deliberately. I dressed very warmly, made a hot-water bottle and a flask of strong coffee, and took a deck chair to the edge of the woods, right across from the front of the castle, a distance of maybe two hundred yards. I set up camp just inside the trees, binoculars at the ready. And just before four o'clock, I saw her. I saw Amy appear round the left-hand side of the castle. She was wearing a long black coat and she had a hat on, pulled low, but I knew it was her. I watched her through the binoculars. She hurried along the front of the castle, head down, then took something white and rectangular out of one of her coat pockets as she entered the portico. A moment later she was out again going back the way she'd come. I waited five minutes then I crossed the lawn. I was shaking with anticipation. And there it was: a single envelope left in the usual spot, on a stone ledge by the door.

It was addressed to me! I opened it there and then and read it by the light of my phone.'

'What did it say?'

'Horrible stuff. I was "enabling a child killer". She'd discovered we were . . . romantically involved. I would pay for it. My reputation would be in tatters. I'd been warned, et cetera, et cetera.'

He stopped, closed his eyes and let out a long, anguished breath.

'I spoke to Grace the next day. I said I was going to threaten Amy with the police. Grace didn't want me to. She's writing a book — I know she told you that too. She had an idea Amy was unhappy and needed to get things out of her system. She said, let's leave it a month or two then decide whether to leave — the two of us, I mean. We'd talked about moving away from here, maybe to Italy or the south of France. Amy's book was going to bring in a lot of money. The translation rights have brought in almost half a million. Neither of us would need to work any more. Except . . . it seemed so unfair to me. Why should Grace — or I — be drummed out of our jobs by one person's spite?'

'But Grace did nothing wrong,' Lola said. 'As you say, it was proven in court. What harm could it really do if Amy had spoken out?'

'The reputational kind,' Abbott said. 'For the Foundation, I mean. Stefan Kade is trying to build something here. He has political ambitions, a vision for humanity, linked to the genetic research he's so committed to.' He sat up, resolute. 'No, we decided to let her continue her little campaign, to ignore the letters — for two more months.'

'Why two months?' Lola asked.

'Because at the end of March, Grace's American publisher is putting out its announcement about the book. At that point the two of us will resign our posts here. Everyone will know about the book then, and about our relationship.' He allowed himself a small smile of pleasure.

'I see,' Lola said, and made a note.

But *did* she see? Did she really buy their story? Wouldn't a clinical director, faced with a spurious blackmail demand, not have called the blackmailer's bluff and sent her packing? Lola would have, for sure. In fact, she'd have gone nuclear.

'Did you tell anyone else you'd seen Amy leaving that letter in the portico? That you believed she was the writer?'

'Only Grace.'

She sat with her thoughts for a minute or two, while Abbott's eyelids drooped.

'If that's everything . . .' he murmured, eyes on her face.

'Not quite.' She sat up and reached for his page of notes. She scanned down.

'You were with Stefan Kade and Ms McArthur from six fifteen until seven fifteen, then you brought them to the orangery and stayed for drinks and a chat?'

'Yes. Those times are approximate, I'm afraid. Oh, and I went to the bathroom after I brought the Kades to the orangery. I was only gone a few minutes. Sorry, I forgot to note that.'

'You say you stepped out of the orangery at seven thirty to check the dining room and see how Senga McCall was coping.'

'That's right. She was in the kitchen. You get to it via a door and a passage behind the dining room. She seemed to be managing fine, so I left her alone.'

'And a few minutes after that,' Lola went on, 'at approximately seven thirty-five, you saw Catherine passing through the dining room. She asked you if you'd seen Amy.'

'That's correct.'

'How did you answer her?'

He frowned. 'I said I didn't think so. Catherine said she'd checked everywhere. Then I said, what about the attics?'

'The attics?'

'Yes. I said, what about the old nursery in the Victorian wing.'

'Why did you suggest there?'

'Why did I—?' He seemed momentarily taken aback. 'I — I don't know. It just seemed a place she might be.'

'Did Amy go there, to your knowledge?'

'I'd seen her up there once,' he said. 'Or rather, I'd seen her coming down from the third floor. I was on the second floor with Catherine one time. We'd been doing an inventory of the bedrooms there. There's quite a lot of work to be done. We came out of a room and we were on the second-floor landing when we saw Amy coming down from the top floor. Catherine got a fright and asked her what she was doing up there. Amy said she'd been exploring, that was all. She didn't say more than that. Just put her nose in the air and carried on down the stairs.' He lowered his voice. 'Amy could be very superior like that.'

'And you don't know what she was doing up there?'

'No. She had a habit of delving. She was always so curious.'

Lola returned to the timeline Dr Abbott had provided.

'After you spoke to Catherine in the dining room, you headed back to the orangery.'

'That's right.'

'And then you went to Catherine's office and found Catherine and myself in there. And that was at seven fifty-five.' She studied Abbott's face. 'Why did you go there?'

'I was concerned,' he said. 'I thought Amy might be about to stage some kind of . . . *incident*.'

'What do you mean?'

'Earlier in the day she'd made a beeline for Stefan Kade. Catherine stopped her, but I suspected it would only be a matter of time before she tried to talk to him again. When Catherine told me Amy had apparently vanished, I couldn't help wondering if this was a trick of some kind. It was nearly dinnertime, so I went to Catherine's office to see if she'd had any luck searching for Amy.'

Lola nodded.

'Wind forward to when you and I were in your office,' she said. 'When we heard the cry. Talk me through what you heard.'

He studied her for a moment. 'That's just it. A horrible cry. A woman's cry. Then a thud and the vase smashing. I didn't know it was a vase, of course.'

Lola watched him for another few seconds. 'What do you think happened to Sister Yorke, Dr Abbott?'

He lifted his chin. 'I think she was pushed to her death by someone she was harassing with those poison pen letters of hers — someone other than Grace Miller.'

'Who do you think it was?'

The chin rose a little higher. 'I have no idea.'

* * *

1.25 a.m.

'Four more sets of notes,' Catherine told Lola when Abbott was gone and it was the two of them alone in the library once more. 'I know you asked people to bring them to you in person, but you were busy and everyone seemed so tired, so I took charge of them.' She handed them over at arm's length, as if they might be contaminated.

'Thank you, Catherine.' Lola put them with the other notes she'd received.

'And I haven't looked at them,' Catherine said quickly. 'They're none of my business. A few people have gone to bed. Margot and Ms McArthur. Rory and Izzy McManus are still up. Oh, and Frankie's gone up to her room, though she hasn't got any of her things from the cottage. I think she's waiting for you to take her. Anyway, she wanted to rest, so William Rix got her a key and Margot took her up. I hope that was all right. William's in the dining room, still waiting to give you your guided tour. Mr Kade is waiting up with him and Dr Stenqvist. I'm afraid Dr Stenqvist is rather agitating for you to go and speak to the guests in their sitting room. They're all still managing to stay awake, though only just. I'm afraid their medication makes them sleepy.' She bit her lip, embarrassed.

'Florien feels it's stressful to keep them in the dark like this. Mr Kade seems to agree.'

Lola tried to process the information, but her head was swimming. She had the beginnings of a headache.

'I'll speak to the guests,' she said. 'Then William can take me round the castle. After that, I think everyone needs some rest — including you and me. Let me just check if I have everyone's notes.'

She picked up the sheaf of pages.

'Here are the ones we've got,' she said. 'Tell me if anyone's missing. Dr Abbott, Dr Stenqvist, Catherine Ballantyne, Frankie Harris, Grace Miller, Shuna Frain, Mr Kade, Maya McArthur, Rory McManus and Izzy McManus, Senga McCall, William Rix.' She glanced up at Catherine.

'I'm fairly sure that's everyone,' Catherine said. 'You'll want to know the guests' movements too.'

'Of course. I'll be asking them for their notes.'

Lola took a deep breath and released it, feeling her head swim once more.

'I'll go find Dr Stenqvist in a minute,' she said. 'He can take me to the guests. I won't keep them long.' She paused. 'How much alcohol have you had this evening, Catherine?'

'Alcohol?' She stared, almost offended. 'But I don't drink at all.'

'Then would you drive Frankie to Rose Cottage? I can't see when I'll get a chance. Ask her to put some of my things in a bag too.'

'That's no problem,' Catherine said with a smile. 'I'll go find Frankie right now.'

CHAPTER FIFTEEN

1.30 a.m.

Lola went looking for Dr Stenqvist and spotted Izzy McManus tidying up in the orangery.

'Hello, Izzy,' she said.

The woman jumped and nearly dropped a glass.

'What do you want?' Her features were contorted with panic.

'A wee word, if that's all right. We can sit down if you like.'

'Prefer to stand.' Izzy's bottom lip came out.

'That's fine.' Lola took a breath, wondering whether her tack would even work. 'You didn't like Sister Yorke, did you?'

Izzy gaped at her, then looked away, her puffy, pale cheeks reddening. 'I didn't hurt her.'

'I didn't say you did. But you didn't like her. I could see that when you served her at the bar.'

Izzy said nothing but looked away. Her lank hair hid her eyes.

'I saw you with her in the bin shed too. She was saying something to you. What was it?'

Izzy wrinkled her nose.

'She's dead,' Lola said quietly. 'She can't hurt you.'

Izzy's chest heaved. 'She had me spying, didn't she?'

'Did she?'

A tiny nod.

'She said she'd complain to Catherine about me if I didn't do what she wanted. She reckoned she could get Catherine to sack me.' She sniffed.

'How horrible,' Lola said. 'Who did she want you to spy on, Izzy?'

'Grace.' It was a tiny whisper. 'I go in the rooms with the cleaning girls, see? She wanted me to go in Grace's room. Look for stuff. Any papers, letters. I never found nothing, though, and I told Amy. Except she kept on at me.'

'Oh dear,' Lola said. 'How long had this been going on?'

'Since before Christmas.'

'Did you tell anyone?'

'I told Rory.'

'Your husband?'

A nod.

'And what did he think?'

'Said I should go to Catherine direct, or to Dr Abbott. But I didn't want to. I just wanted her to leave me alone.'

Lola heard footsteps and turned to see Rory McManus towering in the archway entrance to the orangery, eyes wide with caution.

'It's okay,' she called to him. 'Come in.'

He crept towards them.

'Izzy's just told me what Sister Yorke was doing to her,' Lola said.

'She was a cruel cow,' McManus said, his face flushing, his jaw moving as if he was grinding his teeth.

'Did you tell her to back off?' Lola asked him.

He shook his head and the pink deepened to red. 'Izzy said not to. She was a devil.'

Lola considered the pair, trying to imagine either — or both — murdering Amy Yorke.

'You got a lot of horrible letters,' she said to Izzy now. 'That must have been upsetting.'

Izzy nodded. 'I wasn't the only one, though.'

'No, I know that.' Lola smiled to reassure her. She wondered if Izzy could possibly know that of everyone at the castle, she'd received the highest number in that pre-Christmas period. 'Who do you think sent them?'

'Don't know.'

'Really?'

Rory McManus made a snorting noise.

'Rory?' Lola said. 'What's your view?'

He shook his head.

'You must suspect someone,' she said, looking back at Izzy. 'Someone you've clashed with. Someone you don't get on with.'

'Senga doesn't like her,' Rory said. 'Neither does that Margot, but she's so bloody prim. Catherine looks down her nose at Izzy too.'

'It doesn't matter,' Izzy protested. 'Just leave it.'

Lola studied the unhappy woman, then her weak, unhappy husband.

A man's voice called through the archway, 'You are looking for me?'

It was Dr Stenqvist.

'I am,' Lola replied. She turned back to the pair. 'You know where I am,' she said.

* * *

1.39 a.m.

'I happen to know Angus Wilde,' Lola told Dr Stenqvist as they made their way to the castle's Edwardian wing.

'Oh?' He stopped at the bottom of a staircase and turned to observe her. 'Of course,' the little man said, 'he was a policeman. But he is retired, no?'

'We didn't work closely together, but our paths did cross.'

He narrowed his eyes and peered closely. 'And this was not a cordial working relationship, I take it?'

'I'm afraid not,' Lola said. 'Though we patched things up latterly.'

A cunning smile curved Stenqvist's lips and a pudgy, hairy hand came up to tug on his black beard. 'How intriguing... So this encounter will be uncomfortable for both of you?'

'For him, perhaps. I suggest I have a word with Angus before I speak to the guests together. Would that be possible?'

'Everything is possible,' Dr Stenqvist said, eyes twinkling. 'You can wait in the passage while I go retrieve the gentleman. How does that sound?'

'Sensible,' Lola said.

Stenqvist turned and they both made for the stairs.

Halfway up the second flight she touched the doctor's arm, stopped him in his tracks. He turned.

She said, 'Angus Wilde's wife was very ill last year. Do you happen to know if...'

'The lady passed away,' Stenqvist said. 'Her death contributed to Mr Wilde's current state of ill health. Along with... other factors.'

'Oh dear.' Stenqvist continued to climb. Lola climbed after him, groaning inwardly.

The castle's four guests were in a sitting room on the first floor. Stenqvist led Lola along a carpeted hallway, then stopped outside the door. 'Wait here, please,' he said with a small bow.

Lola lingered while Stenqvist went in. She could hear voices. A minute later Stenqvist re-emerged, followed by a creeping, hunched figure Lola would not have recognised in the street.

Retired Detective Superintendent Angus Wilde looked deathly. He'd lost a lot of weight and his grey hair had thinned. His face, once round and ruddy — often ruddy due to rage — was now drawn and grey. His eyes were watery and glassy.

'Lola Harris,' he said in a thin, croaking voice as he drew near and peered at her. 'You remember me, do you?'

'Hello, Angus,' Lola said, managing a smile. She turned to Dr Stenqvist. 'Give us a couple of minutes, would you?'

'Of course!' Stenqvist said, and went back into the room, closing the door softly behind him.

There was an alcove by a window where two low chairs flanked a small round table. 'Have a seat for a minute,' she said gently and waited while the frail man, only a few years Lola's senior, shuffled towards the chair and lowered himself painfully into it. Lola waited until he was settled before sitting herself.

Angus Wilde closed his eyes and Lola half wondered if he was dozing, but then he opened them again and gazed at her.

'I'm sorry to find you here, Angus,' she said gently. 'I hope they're helping you.'

He frowned, seeming to take several seconds to process her words, then he gave a little nod. 'Dr Stenqvist is doing what he can.' His voice was cracked, broken.

'Good.' Lola let more seconds pass. 'And I'm so sorry to hear about Cynthia.'

He nodded and sniffed.

She said, very gently, 'Everything that happened between us is in the distant past. I want you to know that.'

'I know.' He glanced up and studied her briefly with those weak, watery eyes. 'You've always been very kind.' His brow creased. 'But why are you here?'

'Now, that's a long story.' She smiled. 'And I'm not here officially. But we're cut off by the storm and a woman's died in suspicious circumstances, so I'm doing what I can to help.'

He nodded, then asked wryly, 'I hope you're not planning to second me to any investigation. I'm in no fit state, let me assure you. These pills — they make me so drowsy.'

'I'm not planning anything of the kind. I'm going to have a word with you and the other guests just now, then, as far as I'm concerned, everyone can head to bed. What have they told you so far?' she asked now.

'About the business here? Very little. A woman's dead. It might be an accident or it might not.' The watery eyes glinted somewhat. 'They haven't told us who it is.'

'It was Sister Yorke. Did you know her?'

'Oh dear. I'm sorry to hear that.' His eyes travelled across the hallway and the frown was back. 'A very silent creature. Secretive, I would say.' He focused back on Lola's face. 'Did someone kill her?'

She breathed. 'I don't know. I think possibly, yes. Is there anything you can tell me, Angus? Anything you've heard?'

His eyebrows went up but he shook his head. 'I saw her most days. She was professional. Officious, even. Was there something in particular?'

'Maybe. Shall we go see the others?' she asked, getting up. 'I'll explain how you and they can help me.'

He nodded then started to get up but failed, falling weakly back into the chair. She gave him her arm and lifted him to his feet.

Stenqvist met them at the door and brought them into the guests' sitting room. It was homely and plushly furnished. A log burner glowed in one corner. Stenqvist helped Angus Wilde to a chair as Lola came forward, conscious of curious eyes watching her.

'Finally, someone to explain what the hell is going on,' a man sneered.

Still standing, Lola turned her attention on him. 'Mr Fox?' she enquired pleasantly.

'That's right.' He jumped up and came to her. His blue-eyed stare was a challenge. 'Cooped up for hours.' He folded his arms and huffed. 'Meanwhile, the Russians are busying away with their 5G plans. What? Don't tell me that's news to you.'

Lola recognised him from the TV. Kieran Fox was thirty-something with voluminous red hair that made him look more like a human flame than a fox. He was a politician for the biggest party at Holyrood, and recently the government's education minister — until he began talking manically about being bugged during a meeting about changes to school examinations policy.

She kept her smiling gaze on him until he began to look uncomfortable, then she turned her attention to the two women in the room, who were sharing a sofa. These were the pair Lola had seen in the orangery during the cocktail hour. One was the dowdy sub-postmistress — Heidi Bryce, according to the list of names Catherine had provided. The other was the reality TV star Josette Daniels, who'd changed out of her shiny purple jumpsuit and chunky heels and was now wearing giant white trainers and a yellow kaftan covered in gold sequins. She was admiring her acrylic nails.

'We wanna know what's going on,' Josette said, pointing the file at Lola. 'I'm knackered as it is — and I'm bloody starving. I can't be up this late on the rations I get here.'

Heidi shot her an admonitory glance. Josette rolled her eyes.

'Thank you for staying up,' Lola said, standing by the log burner.

'Oh, do tell us what's happened,' the sub-postmistress said, nervous hands fluttering to her face. 'We know so little!'

'I'm a detective chief inspector with Police Scotland,' Lola said and saw eyes widen with surprise. 'My name is Lola Harris. I am not here in any official capacity, but I have a duty of care to take charge of an unfortunate and tragic situation that has developed here.'

'Someone's dead,' Fox said. 'We know.'

'That is correct,' Lola said, calmly refusing to be knocked off her stride. 'I'm afraid it's Sister Amy Yorke.' A gasp from Heidi. 'She died after falling from a balcony in the Victorian part of the castle.'

'She *fell*?' the sub-postmistress cried, hand to her mouth. She looked to her glamorous companion, who laid a hand on her arm in comfort. 'Oh, how awful!'

'What happened to her?' Fox asked.

Lola hesitated a moment, then reminded herself there was some information you couldn't — and shouldn't — soften.

'I believe someone pushed her.'

Three faces gawped. Angus remained very still in his armchair, eyes down. Beside him, sitting on a hard-backed chair drawn out from a desk, Dr Stenqvist listened in silence.

'The top of the Victorian wing?' Heidi checked.

'That's right.'

'There are attics up there.'

'Yes.' Lola waited for a further question, but none came. She saw Heidi glance at Angus, then look sharply away, frowning.

'How can you know that?' Fox demanded, eyes darting from one to another of his fellow guests. 'How can you know someone pushed her? I mean, you're on your own here. No experts or anything.'

'I know enough, Mr Fox,' Lola said calmly. 'I have found certain evidence.'

'What evidence?' Fox demanded.

Lola ignored him.

'But who would do such a thing?' Heidi cried in a rising sob. 'That poor young girl. Was it a man?'

'I don't know,' Lola said. 'But I want to assure you that help is on its way. Colleagues are looking to find a way to reach the estate in spite of the difficulties caused by the storm. They should be here with us tomorrow during the day, if not sooner.'

'And meantime, we're stuck here with a murderer,' Fox said.

'*So*,' Lola went quickly on, 'it would be helpful if, before you retire for the night, you could tell me if you saw *anything* that seemed in any way odd during the evening. I'd like you to write a note of your movements from six o'clock this evening onwards.'

'Mine's easy,' Fox said before she could hand out the paper and pens. 'In my room all evening. The kitchen sent up a tray at six. I watched TV and I didn't go out. Not once.' He folded his arms and sat back looking pleased with himself.

'Same for me,' Angus said. 'Though I didn't eat. I was out of sorts and slept most of the evening. I woke when Dr Abbott came to check on me — that could have been around nine, I'm not sure. I get so disorientated.'

'I was with everyone else,' Josette said, a complacent smile pursing her lips. 'You and me sat together, didn't we, Heidi?' She added bitterly, 'I'm sure various members of staff were watching what I ate. I've lost four kilos since I got here!' she told Lola now. 'Still, it's not enough. It's my metabolism, I keep telling them, but they don't believe me.' She shot a narrow-eyed glance at Dr Stenqvist, who said nothing.

'I'm happy to write down where I was,' Heidi said. 'Anything to help.' She smiled at the thought.

Lola presented them with sheets of paper and a couple of pens.

'I — or my colleagues — will want to talk to each of you tomorrow,' she said. 'Meantime, I'll be staying in the castle tonight. I have a room on the third floor of the main building. I'll pin a note to the door with my name on. If anyone knows anything, or remembers something they think is important, *please* come and find me — at any time.'

* * *

2.10 a.m.

William Rix led Lola gloomily about the castle, head down, barely speaking.

'Just a quick tour,' she'd told him. 'No history, just an overview so I understand how the different parts fit together.'

He'd grunted and done as she asked, almost flying along corridor after corridor, holding doors open impatiently until she caught up.

Within fifteen minutes she had a good sense of how the main building and the two wings connected: essentially via the ground and first floors only. She peered into three sets of service stairs, including a dreaded spiral staircase or two. She saw locked doors — a padlocked door, in one case — that Rix told her led to attics.

There was a secret passage too, that connected the library and the dining room via a dog-leg passage. In the library, a bookcase functioned as a hidden door.

'Not the only one in the castle, neither,' Rix told her.

'Who knows about this?' she asked.

Rix pushed out his bottom lip and shrugged. 'Me, Miss Ballantyne maybe. Don't know about the others. Tell you this, though, the passage doesn't show on any plans of the place.'

'Mr Rix,' she said as they made their way along a corridor at the back of the castle, 'you spent more than one night watching the portico to see who was delivering the anonymous letters, didn't you?'

She saw his back muscles tense at the question.

'That's right.' He didn't look round at her.

'Where did you sit?'

'Flower bed,' he said. 'Not that there were any flowers. Dead of winter, wasn't it? Ground as hard as stone. I sat there on a fishing stool, all in black, with my binoculars and a pile of rugs over me.'

'And saw nothing?'

'Not a soul.'

'But no letters were left during that time?'

He stopped dead and turned, his brow creased into a cross frown. 'Who told you that?'

Lola's skin tingled. 'Well, I—'

'Miss Ballantyne, was it?'

'Possibly. I may have picked her up wrong. Are you telling me letters were delivered during that time?'

'That's right. The first of the three nights I kept a watch. Two envelopes.'

'And this was in December?'

'That's right.'

December meant the letters were the work of the original writer.

'But you didn't see anyone?'

'No.'

Lola struggled to think what to ask next. 'From where you sat, could you see the way into the portico?'

'Obviously.'

'And you could see the door?'

'Just, but enough. Besides, that thing's impossible to close quietly.'

'I see.' She fell quiet.

'You going to accuse me of dereliction of duty, are you?' he demanded gruffly. 'Or do you think maybe I put the letters there myself? Or that I turned a blind eye to whoever did?'

'Nothing of the kind,' Lola said, reading the anger on the man's face and seeing it was genuine.

'That's what Catherine thought — that I fell asleep or something. But I didn't.'

'Then how do you account for the letters being there next morning?'

'I don't. I can't.'

He glowered some more. Lola smiled to mollify him. 'Shall we keep going?'

They left the Victorian wing till last but Lola didn't want Rix going too far into it.

'Stay here,' she told him. 'I'll be a minute.'

Turning on lights with a gloved hand, she stood on her own and gazed once more at Amy Yorke's twisted corpse, half on stone, half on a rug, and at the countless white pottery shards that lay around her like a frozen starburst.

She'd spent the last few hours asking others what they'd seen and heard that evening, including the two people who were the closest she had to witnesses: Dr Abbott and Grace Miller. Now she took a minute to recall what she herself had heard, sitting in Dr Abbott's office.

The long, squealing scream had seemed to come from nowhere. Lola closed her eyes and heard again that clear sound of terror, cut off so sharply, so violently. Then the smash, more of a clank followed by the sound of dozens of pieces of porcelain scattering.

Had she heard the body hit the floor? She wasn't sure. She took a step forward and peered up to the balustrade of the top landing, at the empty plinth. Would the pot have hit the ground after Sister Yorke if they'd fallen at the same time? Did the fact it had sounded *just after* the scream ceased indicate it had fallen after her? Did that mean someone had thrown it down once Sister Yorke had gone over the edge? If so, why?

Behind her in the passage, Rix cleared his throat pointedly.

'I'll be two minutes,' she called over her shoulder, another thought having occurred to her.

She eyed the scene before her: the sofas, the rugs, the body and the shards. But also the little tables that sat about, some with lamps on.

Earlier, she'd stood right here with Catherine, and Catherine had seemed to be troubled by something at the far side of the hallway, beyond the mess in the middle. Lola had questioned her but she'd said it was nothing.

She made a quick note — one to attend to in the morning — and followed her surly tour guide back into the main building of Ardaig Castle.

* * *

2.35 a.m.

Margot Kerr had stayed up so she could show Lola to her room. Lola asked her to wait a minute while she hurried to the general office and unlocked the safe to retrieve everyone's notes and the yellow folder of stationery and drafts of letters.

'Frankie's retired for the night,' Margot told her, as she bustled ahead up the stairs a few minutes later. 'She and Catherine went to the cottage. I believe Frankie left things for you on the bed. Catherine's away to bed too, by the way, and I think I'll retire myself. You must be exhausted.'

'I am,' Lola agreed.

By the time they reached the third floor, her head was swimming with tiredness.

'Just through here,' Margot said cheerfully, and now she had a key in her hand. You're in the Red Bedroom, Frankie's next door in the Blue. And down there—' she pointed — 'is Mr and Mrs Kade's suite. I'm sure you'll sleep very well. Well, here you are!'

She handed over the key and Lola said goodnight, before unlocking the room and going in.

And there were her things: a bag of clothes and her washbag, on the bed.

She threw the papers down on a desk in the corner of the room and looked about at the red walls and furnishings. Hardly the most soothing colour.

And then she saw something else. Two somethings, in fact. A pair of envelopes lay on the floor, a few centimetres from the door. She'd stepped right over them.

She opened the first and found a bundle of folded pages. A handwritten note read: *Our guests kindly noted their movements during the evening. F. Stenqvist.* Lola leafed through the four sheets, finding notes in four different hands.

Then she turned her attention to the second envelope—

And her heart jumped into her mouth. The envelope bore a typed name in capitals: *MISS L. HARRIS*.

She had one last pair of disposable gloves and she snapped them on.

She peeled the flap open — feeling suddenly, horribly, more awake — and took out the single sheet of white A4 paper that was inside.

She read the words written there.

GOOD LUCK FINDING WHO KILLED AMY.

I KNOW BUT IM NOT TELLING NO ONE.

SPECIALLY NOT AN INTERFERRING COW LIKE YOU.

So this was how it felt to receive an anonymous letter. To hold in your hands words specially chosen for you, with the intention of causing distress.

She read and reread it, suddenly feeling very alone, with only the noise of the storm to keep her company.

Her first impulse had been to dash out into the corridor after Margot Kerr, to tell the kind and practical woman what had happened and seek some kind of comfort, maybe even a few minutes' company.

But no. Visceral panic was exactly what the letter writer hoped for.

She could always knock on Frankie's door, wake her up and offload some of her shock. But again, what was the point?

What she really wanted was to call Sandy using the emergency phone, to tell him what had happened, to talk through the steps she'd taken. To hear his comforting words spoken in his warm, laid-back voice.

But it would mean waking him and that wasn't fair. He was busy and deserved his rest.

She sat on her bed and waited for the surge of adrenaline to subside.

It was so late and she knew she should sleep, but what hope had she of falling asleep while her mind was in turmoil?

She had one way to use the next few hours: by studying in close detail the notes every staff member and guest had provided, to try and identify who could have killed Amy Yorke.

But first, a cup of tea, as strong as she could make it.

CHAPTER SIXTEEN

3.42 a.m.

Three cups in, and Lola felt she'd made some progress.

Going through the notes, she'd quickly realised she had little chance of working out who could have vandalised Catherine's office in that lengthy window between 6.10 and 7.40 p.m. Almost everyone had spent time unaccompanied during the preparations for dinner.

She decided to focus instead on the ten-minute window she'd identified, five minutes either side of Sister Yorke's death: 8.15 to 8.25 p.m.

Kieran Fox had written in his notes that Sister Yorke had come by his room to check his medication at around 7.50 p.m. He and Angus Wilde had planned to spend the evening in their rooms. She checked Angus Wilde's notes, but he didn't mention a visit from Amy. Instead, he'd slept heavily for a couple of hours, from, he estimated, around 7 p.m. until Dr Abbott came to check on him around 9 p.m. — though these times were approximate.

The first of two dinner gongs had sounded at 8.05 p.m., and people's movements in the period that followed were detailed, as if they'd become more aware of their actions and whereabouts as dinnertime approached.

According to her analysis, and going by individuals' uncorroborated accounts alone, seven people appeared to have strong alibis. They included Lola, Dr Abbott and Grace Miller. Frankie and Shuna Frain had sat together, sipping cocktails and talking in the orangery for a good half-hour, they both claimed. Josette Daniel and Heidi Bryce, too, had stayed in the orangery in one another's company.

Three further individuals had alibis almost as strong. Stefan Kade and Maya McArthur had been in the orangery for most of the time, apart from a five-minute period — around 8.10 p.m., Stefan Kade thought, though his wife was less certain. Ms McArthur had 'needed fresh air', according to the couple's notes, and Mr Kade had gone with her out the front of the castle, where they'd sheltered from the rain in the portico. Mr Kade had smoked a cigar. He suggested the butt might be in the portico still.

Which left everyone else.

Senga McCall, Izzy and Rory McManus and Margot Kerr all had periods when they'd been on their own or only briefly with others. Their timings were vague.

Then there were five people with no alibi at all.

First, Angus Wilde, second Kieran Fox, both in their rooms.

Next, William Rix, who had been outside the castle, taking his time to circle the building as part of his security routine. He did this several times each evening, no matter the weather, he wrote. He'd gone back to the gatehouse once — around 8.15 p.m., he thought, but he couldn't be sure.

Dr Stenqvist lacked an alibi. He'd had too much to drink, he noted, and following the first gong he'd gone to his room to lie down before dinner. He'd detected disapproval from Margot and from Catherine and decided to take a break. It rang true to Lola, going by the doctor's increasingly drunken behaviour in the orangery.

Then there was Catherine Ballantyne. After the first dinner gong, she'd left Lola and Dr Abbott to go to her flat for the spare key to her office. She'd then, several minutes later, got the urgent call from Dr Abbott over the walkie talkie to come to the Victorian wing. What had she been doing all that time?

Surely not Catherine, of all people . . .

Nine possibilities then: Catherine, Dr Stenqvist, William Rix, the two male guests — Angus Wilde and Kieran Fox — then Margot Kerr, the McManuses and Senga McCall.

Could one of these people really be a murderer?

Of course, all of this information would have to be checked and corroboration sought. An alibi that looked strong on paper might prove weak in reality, and vice versa.

She was glad of one thing. She knew the killer couldn't be Grace Miller. Lola herself could attest to her alibi: there was simply no way she could have made it down from the highest landing to the hallway floor in time to be standing there only seconds after that scream and the smash of the vase.

She liked Grace. Felt sorry for her. She'd lived through so much, so young, only to be persecuted once more as a professional adult woman. The idea of being wrongly accused of murder twice in one lifetime was unthinkably cruel.

She stood up from the desk and stretched and yawned, her eyes on the big, inviting bed, with its beautiful, fluffy white duvet and piles of pillows — like something from the grandest suite in an upmarket hotel. And yet she knew she wouldn't sleep.

She reached for the kettle, ready to fill it in the bathroom once again, when she heard footsteps in the corridor outside the room, light and fast.

Kettle still in hand, Lola was across the room and had the door open in a flash.

The fire door at the end of the corridor was swinging, as if someone had just passed through. Back in the room, Lola relinquished the kettle and snatched up the set of keys she was amassing. Then she took off down the corridor, through the doors and out onto the third landing, but found no one there. She listened hard, but the wind was loud around the glass lantern that capped the castle's great hallway. She peered over the wooden balustrade, and caught a glimpse of an arm — a hand and a dark sleeve — as someone hurried down the stairs to the ground floor.

'Hello?' she called, loudly.

She saw the arm recoil into the gloom.

Who could it be? Someone staying in a room on the top floor? A woman, she thought, going by the lightness of the tread — so that meant either Frankie or Maya McArthur. No other woman was staying on that floor, to her knowledge. Or had it been someone from another part of the castle? Someone only visiting the third-floor corridor . . . for the purposes of delivering letters, perhaps?

Lola ran down the stairs, descending flight after flight until she too was on the ground floor. She looked about, holding her breath as she listened. But there was only the moan of the wind. She saw doors that were closed, and archways into passages full of still shadows.

She should check the Victorian wing. Make sure the doors were still locked, that the crime scene remained undisturbed.

She hurried through the archway to the right of the staircase and followed the dog-leg to the rear of the main building, then turned off into the Victorian wing, and was pleased to find the door on this level locked. She returned to the great hall and climbed to the first floor, then followed a dark passage round to where the main building joined the wing on this level, and found this door locked as well.

Relieved, she turned to retrace her steps down the long, shadowy passage, finally feeling a weariness that hinted at sleep — then froze.

A figure stood at the passage's far end, silhouetted against the dim light behind it.

'Who's there?' she shouted, pleased at how angry she sounded.

The figure came forward into the passage — and Lola recognised the swaggering walk.

'Wee Willie Winkie, is it?' Shuna Frain called merrily.

'Shuna! You scared me half to death!'

'Gave me quite the fright yourself,' Shuna said, coming closer now.

Lola saw she was in a black tracksuit and trainers. Her hair was tied back.

'Out for a pre-dawn run, were you?' Who'd have thought the sight of Shuna Frain would be a comfort.

'Hardly.' She cocked her head. 'A certain *something* came under the door of my room about fifteen minutes ago — for me to find first thing in the morning, I expect. Only, I was awake and writing.'

'What "something"?' Lola asked.

'A letter.' She was smirking now. 'Get one too, did you?'

'I did, as it happens.'

'What did it say?'

'Oh, something and nothing. "You won't catch me" and so on. Yours?'

'That I was a "nosy bitch" and should fuck off before I got myself into serious trouble — words to that effect.'

'Did you see who left it?'

'Wasn't quick enough. My room's out in the mews, along with the kitchen and domestic staff. The door opens into a courtyard, motel-style. Whoever it was had scarpered. You see anything?'

'Maybe.'

Shuna's eyebrows rose.

'I heard running feet and I think I saw her flying down the stairs — unless that was you . . . ?'

'Not me. I've been prowling the ground floor. What makes you think it was a "her"?'

'The steps were very fast and there was something in the way she was going down the stairs. I saw her arm.'

'That narrows the field,' Shuna murmured.

'It certainly does.'

'Can't be Catherine or Margot — I reckon both their running days are far behind them. So, who does that leave?'

Lola sighed. She was deeply uncomfortable conferring with Shuna like this, but the extra brain might help. That and the moral support.

'It leaves Izzy McManus,' she said quietly, eyes checking either end of the passage to check they were indeed alone. 'Senga McCall too.'

'The grumpy barmaid and the wee serving woman?'

'There is another possibility,' Lola pointed out. 'Maya McArthur.'

'*Maya?*'

'Why not?'

'Because she's only just arrived here. The letter writer's been at work for months.'

'That's true.'

She looked at Shuna, frowning now. 'If your room is out in the mews, how did you get into the main building? Have you got a key?'

'Yes.' She went into a pocket and brought out a simple Yale key. 'It's for a side door beside the kitchen. It leads into a gun room, though there aren't any guns now. Why are you asking?'

'I'm just interested in who has access to which parts of the castle. It seems everyone can just go everywhere.'

'What are you thinking?' Shuna peered at her curiously.

'I'm wondering why the letters were pushed under our doors. Previously they were left on a kind of stone sill in the portico around the front door.'

Shuna shrugged. 'Maybe the writer got scared. She knows there's a copper in the building. And who knows, maybe there's a bundle of letters waiting there right now.'

Lola studied the key still in Shuna's hand. 'Fancy making a wee recce outside?'

'Aye, why not? The gun room's this way.'

Shuna led the way along the passage at the rear of the main building, past the archway that led to the orangery and then along to the dining room. Beside the dining room door, another passage ran off to the right. They passed the kitchen and then went through a couple of doors until they were in a stone-flagged, green-painted room with gun mounts on the walls but, as Shuna had already said, no guns. A door rattled in the wind. Shuna turned the Yale lock and went first into a cobbled yard.

It wasn't raining but the wind took Lola's breath away.

'This way,' she shouted to Shuna and stepped carefully over slippery cobbles, passing the bin shed where she had seen Izzy McManus smoking, and through the little parking area to the front of the castle. Decorative streetlamps lit the area in front of the building, but the great stone portico was in shadows.

'Stay with me,' Lola said, so Shuna would be able to corroborate anything she found there.

She stepped into the portico and turned her phone's torch on — and there, on a stone shelf, to one side of the door, were three white envelopes.

'I see the postie's been,' Shuna said.

Lola shushed her.

She had no gloves with her, so photographed the envelopes in situ.

'How did she get them here?' Shuna wanted to know.

'I don't know. It must have been before she delivered ours, anyway. This door's heavy and loud. I'd have heard it closing, I'm sure.'

She shone her torch around the inside of the portico. To the right of the door, just above the stone shelf there was a tall slit of a window, no more than ten centimetres across. It was glazed with leaded panes.

'What are you thinking?' Shuna asked.

'Nothing yet.'

'Liar.'

'All right. I'm wondering if that window opens, if you must know.'

'Good question. Want to go back inside and see?'

'I think so,' Lola said.

'And what about the letters?'

'Leave them here for now. I'll need to get some gloves from somewhere.'

'Right,' Shuna said smartly, 'back the way we came?' She set off. 'This is fun, isn't it?' she said over her shoulder as they hurried back round the side of the castle to the gun room door. 'We're a kind of Cagney and Lacey, you and me. The perfect team, I'd say.'

* * *

4.10 a.m.

They entered the great hallway to find Catherine standing at the bottom of the stairs, fully dressed, in jumper and trousers. She was staring into the middle distance. Lola said her name and she jumped and let out a little scream.

'What are you . . .' She stared at Lola and Shuna.

'Sorry,' Lola said. 'Neither of us could sleep.'

Catherine breathed and seemed to relax. 'Nor me.' Her breaths came in short, stressful gasps. 'I thought I was alone but then I heard footsteps. Was it you?'

'It wasn't, no. Lola and I both received letters in the night,' Shuna said, pleased as Punch to deliver the bad news.

'What? Oh no . . .' Catherine put a hand to her mouth. 'This is so horrible. So soon after Amy's death. She's started again, then, hasn't she?'

'It looks like it,' Lola said, and rubbed Catherine's back. 'When did you think you heard footsteps?'

'A few minutes ago. I was sitting in the orangery.' She saw Lola's surprise. 'I go there sometimes when I can't sleep. I like the space and the sound of the fountains. I just have to remember to put a jumper on.' She smiled thinly. 'I felt tired finally, so I came back into the main building. I heard a door close. It gave me such a fright, then I heard footsteps in the passage along towards the Victorian wing. I called out, "Who's there?" and whoever it was began to run.'

'Did you see them?'

'No. Well, I saw a shadow.' She gave Lola a sheepish look now. 'For a second I thought it was the ghost again.'

'The ghost?' Shuna asked.

'The castle has two ghosts,' Catherine said. She pursed her lips and her nostrils flared. 'I've seen one of them. I don't care if you think I'm mad.' She turned back to Lola. 'I pulled myself together and tried to follow. But I'm no match for a fast person. I arrived here just before you. I'm sorry. I make an awful witness, don't I?'

'Not at all,' Lola said.

'What were you doing outside?' Catherine asked now, looking between Lola and Shuna.

'We went to check the ledge in the portico,' Lola said. 'There are letters there.'

Catherine stared in dismay. 'It's like a bad dream, isn't it?'

Lola's eyes stole across the great hallway to the front door, specifically to the space to the left of it, where something didn't add up . . . though the walls of the castle were clearly thick.

'Catherine,' Lola said, seizing the opportunity, 'I spoke to William Rix when he was showing me about earlier. I asked him about the times he staked out the portico. He said that on the first night, letters came even though he was watching.'

'Yes, well he *claims* he was watching. Obviously someone got in there and away and he missed them!'

'There's a window in the portico,' Lola said. 'A tall, narrow window like an arrow slit, but with glass in it. It's to the right of the door and directly over the shelf.'

'That's right,' Catherine said after a moment's thought. 'It's only a dummy, though.'

'A dummy?'

'It's just wall behind it.' She moved to the door and slapped the bare whitewashed wall to the side of it. 'See?' She rubbed her hand over it as if to demonstrate that their eyes weren't deceiving them.

'But the window must have some function,' Lola said. 'I don't know much about architecture, but why would it be there?'

Catherine looked pained.

'That wall's three feet thick, at least,' Shuna said.

Lola stepped forward and hammered the wall with a balled fist. She moved to the left and tried again.

'Hear that?' she said, smiling at her own ingenuity. 'It's hollow.'

'Hollow?' Catherine said. 'Oh! The old stairs.'

'What old stairs?' Lola asked.

'I was shown them once, while the renovations were being completed. We were down in the cellar and shown an old staircase, sort of *inside* the wall. A service stair originally, I expect, but it's blocked up now.' She was frowning hard, eyes roving around the floor as if she was envisaging the foundations of the castle. Then she looked back at the hollow wall. 'That would have been a door, I think. The place is full of passages. It's a maze, really.'

'Can you show us?'

'Yes, I can.' Catherine bit her lip. 'I've a key in my office, if we could stop by there first.'

'And I'll need some more pairs of disposable gloves.'

'We can pick some up from the general office. Oh, now — the lighting in the cellars is patchy at best, so we'll need torches. We keep some in the gun room.'

'I'll go for them,' Shuna said, clearly expecting to be invited along on the subterranean adventure.

'Bring three,' Lola told her, earning herself a wink. She turned to Catherine. 'Let's go get the key.'

* * *

4.28 a.m.

The entrance to the cellars was beside the kitchen. The ordinary-looking door opened to reveal the top of a stone spiral staircase. Clammy air came out to meet them, smelling like churned soil. Catherine leaned into the opening and pressed a switch. A bulb came on at the top of the stairs. Lola saw cobwebs everywhere.

'Is it far down?' she asked, as she contemplated the steep curling steps down to darkness.

'A dozen or so steps, I think,' Catherine said. 'I was only down here once, during one of the site visits before the castle opened. There's a wine store that our first chef began to stock, but apart from that it's just a warren of tunnels and empty rooms.'

Catherine seemed happy to go first. Lola stood aside so Shuna could go next, then took a deep breath and followed, her left hand gripping the cold, rough central pillar, dislodging dirt and getting cobwebs caught round her fingers as she descended. At one point she felt a spider land on her hair and skitter away. She managed not to yelp.

At last they were at the bottom, in a low, brick-lined corridor that led off in two directions.

'Now, let me see,' Catherine murmured, peering into the darkness at both ends. 'I think it's this way.'

They moved along the passage towards shadows. Catherine flicked another switch and more bulbs came on. They were at a T-junction now, and Lola saw doors in the walls on both sides. Some of the doorways were barred, like cells, with solid darkness beyond. She shivered and turned on her torch to try and keep the shadows at bay.

'Now, the wine cellar is that way, towards the back,' Catherine said. 'We're going this way.'

She led them into a wide space with an uneven, earthy floor. The air seemed stagnant and unhealthy. Another single bulb fought a losing battle against the darkness. Catherine and

Shuna turned their torches on, and immediately the space had more definition.

'If I'm right, then we're standing directly under the great hallway. And that means the steps should be over here,' Catherine said. 'Careful where you're standing, there are puddles, no doubt from the storm.'

There was a sudden flapping over their heads and two or more bats whirled about in a panic.

Some relaxing weekend away this turned out to be . . .

'More Famous Five than Cagney and Lacey, wouldn't you say?' Shuna murmured.

Lola was about to answer when Catherine cried, 'Yes, it's here!'

She'd brought them to a gap in the wall that contained the foot of another spiral staircase, this one leading up.

Lola shone her torch on a rickety-looking table at one side of the alcove. There was a bucket on it with what looked like fingers creeping over the rim.

'Do you want to go first this time?' Catherine asked Lola.

'Yes, but just give me a second.'

She stepped up to the table and shone her torch down into the bucket. The fingers belonged to a pair of pink Marigold washing-up gloves. There was a pair of extendable tongs too.

'What is it?' Shuna asked.

'Not sure,' Lola lied. 'Right, I'll go up. You two stay down here.'

'But—' Shuna began.

'No buts,' Lola said tersely.

Shuna made a face and rolled her eyes.

Lola paused to snap on the fresh pair of disposable gloves she'd got from the medicine cabinet in the general office, then stepped into the alcove and onto the first step, torch in her other hand this time as she prepared to climb clockwise.

She went up slowly, heart in her mouth, until at last she was at the top, finding herself in a sort of stone cupboard, only a metre or so square. In front of her was a door, which must be blocked up now on the other side.

And there to her left was the tall, narrow window, with its murky, leaded glass, there as a source of dim light for the staircase, she assumed. She stood close to the window and tried to see through, but the torch's beam only reflected off the glass. There was a curling metal handle. She turned it — and the window came smoothly, silently open. She shone her beam through the ten-centimetre gap and saw what she had expected to see: the inside of the portico, and the shelf where the letters had been left, apparently by an invisible hand.

CHAPTER SEVENTEEN

6.55 a.m.

'That's so creepy,' Frankie said when Lola told her about the letter — and about discovering the letter writer's means of delivery.

They were in Frankie's room, next door to Lola's. Frankie was sitting up in bed drinking tea. Lola had already showered and changed into the fresh clothes that Frankie had fetched from Rose Cottage last night.

'No wonder you look all in,' Frankie said now, smoothing down her top.

'Do I?' Lola asked, not caring much.

'Did you get any sleep at all?'

'A couple of hours.'

'Well, I suppose that's better than nothing,' Frankie said sheepishly. 'I slept like the dead. Don't suppose you want to hear that, do you? So . . . what next?'

'Try to get an update from the council's resilience people,' Lola said, lifting the emergency phone. 'The lines are still down and there's zero Wi-Fi or 4G apart from on this thing. That wind sounds like it's dying down a bit though. Anyway, with luck they'll get through and someone else can take over this mess.'

'I'm proud of you, sis,' Frankie said.

'Aye, well,' Lola agreed wearily, 'I suppose it's what I do best. Then, whatever the resilience guys say, I think I should phone Elaine and make her aware of what's going on here.'

Superintendent Elaine Walsh was still Lola's line manager, even during her secondment to the fraud investigation. The call would be more than a courtesy, though. She wanted Elaine's permission for something.

'Who did it, Lola?' Frankie asked now, eyeing her from the bed. 'Who killed that poor woman?'

'I don't know,' Lola told her honestly. 'I've narrowed down the possibilities, but the question is motive.'

'Someone who hated her, you mean?'

'Possibly. Or more likely . . . someone who thought she knew a very unpleasant fact about them. Someone who'd already murdered once, and got away with it.'

Frankie's face darkened. 'You mean Grace Miller, don't you?'

'You know about her, do you?'

Frankie nodded. 'Margot Kerr told me. It's hardly a secret. Everyone seems to know. She was found not guilty, though. You'd hardly kill someone for threatening to expose you for being found *innocent* of a crime!'

'It isn't Grace,' Lola said. 'She has a motive, but it's a thin one, and she simply *can't* have done it.'

'I'm glad about that,' Frankie said. 'I like her. So you think there's someone else here with a secret they'd kill to protect?'

'That's exactly what I think.'

'Tell me who it could be.'

'No.' She checked the time on the emergency phone. 'It's past seven now. I'm going to start making some calls.'

'There must be a way I can help you,' Frankie said.

Lola thought about it.

'What?' Frankie urged.

'I'm going to talk to everyone at breakfast,' Lola said. 'I'm going to lay it on the line. You can watch people for me — especially when I'm not in the room.'

'Watch them for what?'

'Reactions, nerves, panic. Then report back. Right, see you downstairs in half an hour?'

There was a sudden aggressive banging on Frankie's bedroom door.

'Who the—' Frankie began, but Lola was already across the room.

She yanked the door open, ready for anyone.

'They said you were in the Red Room,' Stefan Kade snapped. 'But clearly you aren't!'

'Good morning, Mr Kade,' Lola said, fixing what she hoped was a tight smile. 'Now you've found me.'

He peered past her and wrinkled his nose when he spotted Frankie sitting up in bed.

'What's the latest?' he scowled.

'I don't know. I'm only just up. I was about to make some calls.'

Kade's dead grey eyes were on Frankie again, then he squinted back at Lola. 'A word in private, please.'

'Certainly.' She stepped into the corridor with him.

'A letter came in the night,' he said, and Lola detected a tremor of anger in his voice. 'Pushed under the door of our suite, addressed to my wife.'

'Ah!' Lola waited.

'The *most unpleasant* personal remarks. Luckily I spotted it before Maya was even awake.'

'I see. Do you still have it?'

'No. I couldn't risk her seeing it. She's . . . fragile. I tore it into pieces and put them down the lavatory.' His face darkened and the scowl was back. 'This *has* to stop,' he said now. 'I want you to find out who is doing this and *deal* with them.'

'I'll do what I can, Mr Kade. But I'm one woman.'

'Then I'll help you. Well, come on — there must be something I can do.'

'Maybe there is,' she said. 'Make sure everyone — I mean, *everyone*, guests included — is in the dining room by seven forty-five.'

He eyed her. 'Very well,' he said, then turned heel and marched back down the corridor to his suite.

* * *

7.07 a.m.

Neil Forbes, of the local authority's resilience team, had been up all night. Lola could hear it in his voice when she called him from her own room.

'That was one storm,' he said with good-humoured strain. 'Worst I ever saw since I looked after this area. We're looking at a lull for a few hours. Might give us a chance at shoring up the road. Phone lines will be down for a few more days, I reckon.'

'Someone was going to try to make it out here on foot,' Lola reminded him.

'Two of my men made a valiant effort,' Forbes said. 'Gave up when one of them twisted his ankle. A whole banking has collapsed, trees down, the lot.'

Lola shut her eyes and willed her heart not to sink any further.

'You said there's a lull due,' she said.

'Aye, a couple of hours. Zebedee's on his way north-east, but Storm Ailsa's coming in from the Atlantic.'

'Please, I really need you to prioritise reopening that road.'

'I'm sure you do. But we've got a group of walkers lost up past Crianlarich. Due back at base yesterday morning. They're taking priority.' He heard Lola's groan. 'You've got a roof over your heads. Think of me and the lads out here!'

She rang Sandy next.

'My God,' he said, when she'd finished her minute-long monologue of horrors.

'My thoughts exactly.'

'And you're still cut off there?'

'Aye. Fancy pulling on your hiking boots and trying to rescue us — well, *me* at least? And no, I'm not being serious.'

'At least you've got Frankie there.'

'S'pose.'

He offered to help. To do anything at all.

'Keep your phone with you,' she said. 'I might need you later, but first I'm going to ring Elaine and fill her in.' She swallowed. 'Love you, Sand.'

'Love you too, Lola. Be careful, won't you? And when this is over we'll book a break somewhere, shall we? Somewhere without any anonymous letters or murders.'

* * *

7.15 a.m.

'No, I'm up and about,' Elaine said when Lola apologised for calling so early. 'Just give me a mo to step into my study.'

Lola imagined her boss in her cosy study at the back of the old manse just outside Lennoxtown, perhaps cradling a steaming coffee in one of her own pottery mugs. She heard a door softly close.

'That's me. But aren't you supposed to be enjoying a weekend away from it all?'

'It didn't quite work out the way I hoped,' Lola told her.

'Oh? Well, I'm sitting down.'

Lola explained what had happened, including the fact Frankie had got her to the castle under false pretences.

'I'll do what I can to help,' Elaine said. 'But you need to be talking to the local DCI.'

'I am,' Lola said. 'He's fully aware and I'm about to call him again. But the thing is . . .'

'What?' Elaine's voice darkened.

'I'm hoping you'll let me use Anna Vaughan to research some stuff. That's the kind of task she excels at.'

'DI Vaughan is tied up on a major case,' Elaine said. 'She's working all hours, but today's her day off — I know that because I instructed her to take it.'

'Please, boss. I'm on my own here. I've barely slept. There's a murderer here, not to mention a lunatic letter writer.'

'Why can't you ask the local DCI to organise this?'

'Because he wants me to keep things together, not progress things.'

'Then do as he asks.' She could almost hear Elaine's eye roll.

'But I can work out who did this with a bit of assistance. I know I can do it.'

Elaine went quiet. At last she sighed. 'It'd have to be off the record, Lola, and only—'

'Thanks, boss.'

Before Elaine could say another word, Lola rang off.

She called Anna, who was up and seemed receptive. The DI listened calmly while Lola explained the situation in a rush. 'I need you to do some things for me,' she finished. 'I'm sorry to ask, but I'm desperate.'

'Just tell me what you need. I only wish I could get out there and join you.'

'Aye, well, you and me both. Now, I need you to look up some names for me on the system. See if anything comes up — any involvement with crime of any kind, including anonymous letters. And I want you to contact a family in Australia called the Grimshaws to check if Amy Yorke was ever in touch with them and, if so, what she said.'

'Let me get a pad, boss, and I'll be right with you.'

It might be tiredness, but in the moments while she waited for Anna to return, Lola could have wept. This was what she'd been missing the last several weeks — the thrill of the chase and the support of dedicated and truly loyal colleagues.

CHAPTER EIGHTEEN

7.32 a.m.

'Ah, you're there,' a reedy man's voice called across the great hallway as Lola made her way downstairs.

It was her former colleague Angus Wilde, up and about in trousers and a sweater, but with slippers on his feet. He came painfully to the foot of the stairs to meet her.

'Good morning, Angus,' she said.

'How are things?' he asked, leaning in confidentially.

'No further on, I'm afraid.'

'Only, there's something I thought to tell you. I remembered it in the night. You don't have a few minutes now, do you?'

'A couple, yes,' she said.

The library was unlocked and she went in ahead of Angus, then closed the door and waved him to a couple of chairs nearby. He lowered himself painfully into one of them.

'Sister Yorke asked me for advice, a few weeks ago now. I should have remembered sooner. I'm afraid I'm taking rather a lot of medication. My brain — it's not working quite as it used to.'

'That's okay. Tell me what she said.'

'She asked me about the law, whether someone could be prosecuted for the same crime twice — in this or other countries. I said you could in Scotland if new evidence was strong enough — the law on that changed recently. She said it wasn't Scotland. She said it was in Australia. I asked her if she could share any details. She said no. But she did say one thing.'

'Go on.'

'She said, "Lightning never really struck twice, did it?" I said, "What are you talking about?" She said that if a rare accident happened twice then it was more likely to be deliberate than a coincidence. I'm afraid that's it. As I say, I should have remembered sooner. I'm sorry.'

'Don't be,' Lola said. 'That's very helpful of you.'

'She said — yes, that was it — that she was planning to go to the top. Right the way up.'

Lola tried not to let her surprise show. 'To the top?'

'That's right.'

'Or "up to the top"?'

He stared. 'I — I'm not sure.'

'What do you think she meant by that?'

He looked off into the room, then shook his head. 'I've no idea. To Dr Abbott, perhaps — he's the most senior person here.'

'Right . . . Thank you, Angus. Oh, and there's one more thing, while you're here.'

'Yes?'

'You said in your notes that you were asleep most of yesterday evening.'

'Yes. I was overcome by weariness, I'm afraid. Out like a light.'

'You don't remember Sister Yorke calling in on you during that time?'

'No, I'm sorry. She usually did in the evening, before eight. She must have found me asleep and gone on her way. Young Fox may have seen her.'

'He did.' She smiled. 'If you remember anything else, you will come and find me, won't you? And please, don't tell anyone what you've just told me about Sister Yorke — about lightning striking twice.'

'Right you are.'

Catherine was crossing the great hallway as they came out of the library. She looked ashen with fatigue but was pleasant to Angus, directing him to the dining room for coffee and breakfast. He went on his way.

'How are you?' Catherine asked Lola, looking pained.

'I'm fine.'

'Have you decided what to do about what we found during the night?'

'Yes, but whether it'll work is another question. You haven't said anything to anyone, have you?'

'Not a soul.'

Shuna had sworn on her life as well, not that that meant very much, coming from her.

'Do you have five minutes just now?' Lola asked Catherine.

'Of course.'

Lola led the way to the back of the main building, then off into the Victorian wing, where she unlocked the door so they could pass through into the open hallway.

Lola sensed Catherine's acute tension at being back there. 'You don't need to go right the way in,' she said. 'But I'd like you to look about and try to tell me what bothered you last night.'

'What bothered me?' Catherine looked mystified.

'You stood here and looked that way, as though something wasn't right. I asked you about it, but you shook it off.'

'Oh, but I'm sure that was nothing.'

'Nevertheless, I'd like you to tell me what you saw.'

'Well . . . See over there, the console table behind the green sofa? There's usually a green Tiffany-style lamp on it, that's all. You know the kind, very art nouveau, a sort of mosaic of glass with jewels and dragonflies. Spectacularly beautiful. Quite a broad shade, with two chains hanging down, one for each bulb. Well, it's not there now. I love it and I always admire it. Well, of course, last night, I wasn't interested in admiring any lamps, but I noticed it was missing. It's very trivial, I'm sure.'

Lola stared at the table. There was a crocheted mat on it, drooping down the sides.

'Stay here a minute,' she said to Catherine, and went into the hallway to inspect the table.

She peered beneath it and saw the part-open flap of an electrical outlet in the floor, half hidden by the back of the sofa.

'I hope it didn't get broken,' Catherine called out.

Lola didn't reply, but prowled about the space, outside the square made by the sofas, looking everywhere a lamp might have been hidden. But there was nothing there.

'Rory McManus would probably know,' Catherine suggested now. 'He looks after the facilities.'

'Yes,' Lola said, returning to her side. 'I'll ask him. Thank you. We'd better head to the dining room.'

* * *

7.46 a.m.

Stefan Kade was a man of his word. Everyone resident at the castle, including the four guests, was present in the dining room, many of them sitting at the long table, while others stood about. Coffee was being drunk at a healthy rate.

'Mr McManus,' Lola said, approaching the tall, hook-nosed facilities manager, who was lingering at the back of the room with his gloomy wife Izzy. 'A quick word.'

Rory McManus followed her out into the corridor. He seemed shifty, eyes sliding about, as if he was trying to spot an escape route.

She asked him about the green Tiffany lamp.

'I know it,' he said, eyes still away off to the side. 'I didn't move it. No one said nothing to me about it.'

'That's okay,' she said, and smiled. He skulked off back into the dining room.

Next she leaned in through the door and waved for Frankie to step out. She caught Shuna's eye and beckoned her over as well.

'Fancy helping me catch a poison letter writer?' she asked.

'What?' Frankie goggled.

'I'm in,' Shuna said, beaming.

'I'm about to tell everyone what we found in the night, and that the bucket, the gloves and the tongs are locked away in my room until I can get them forensically examined.'

'Isn't that a risk?' Frankie asked.

'Not at all. Here.' She took out her room key and passed it to Frankie. 'Right, this is what I want you both to do.'

* * *

A few minutes later, Lola re-entered the dining room.

Kade wanted to talk to her, but Lola ignored him. She wanted to make her address. He could say his piece after that.

'Good morning, everybody.'

All heads turned. She studied their expressions, which ran from weary resignation to intense anxiety.

'I've spoken to the local authority's resilience team this morning, and I'm afraid we're likely to be cut off here for another few hours at least. The storm has passed but another is on its way.'

A gloomy murmur rode about the room.

'As you know, last night Sister Amy Yorke fell to her death. I believe she was pushed. I believe that happened at 8.20 p.m. I have analysed the notes you gave me of your movements and the time window I'm interested in is from 8.15 to 8.25 p.m. Some of you have alibis for that time. Some of you don't.'

She paused to watch resigned expressions become worried ones, while one or two anxious faces appeared to relax.

'This morning I plan to talk to a number of you, one to one. And this time I'm interested in who had a motive for killing Amy.'

A few voices rumbled quietly.

'I want to make it clear that Grace Miller,' Lola said, 'could *not* have killed Sister Yorke. I am her alibi. Those of you who know Grace's past need to cease any speculation that she was responsible for this in any way.'

She looked at Grace, who sat at the table, Dr Abbott at her side. The woman's eyes were closed but she held her head high.

'It's my belief that Amy was writing anonymous letters to various people here at the castle.' She heard a gasp or two. 'One letter she sent accused the senior management of employing a killer. I think she probably meant Grace Miller, but I also believe she inadvertently panicked someone here who has a secret of their own.'

Eyes widened. She let the words sink in. Shuna looked avid with glee.

'I believe someone here in this room killed Sister Yorke to shut her up.'

'My God,' a woman's voice cried.

She didn't see who it was, but kept going, her momentum deliberate to ram the point home.

'Amy only wrote some of the letters, starting in January. A different writer was at work before that, but stopped when the castle's management made it clear they weren't going to tolerate that behaviour. That's when Sister Yorke took over, to air grievances of her own. But last night, a few letters were posted under people's doors. I got one. And three envelopes were left on a shelf in the portico outside the front door of the castle.'

The news caused further astonishment.

'I know how those letters were put there,' she said, then fell silent. Every pair of eyes was on her now. 'They were delivered to the shelf through a narrow window beside the front door, which is reached via a spiral staircase from the cellars. The person who delivers them wears rubber gloves — the kind you use for washing up — and a pair of tongs. I found these. They're in my room now, locked away, ready for forensic examination.'

'This is *incredible*,' Dr Stenqvist piped up. He looked around the room in amazement.

'I want to know who wrote and delivered those letters last night,' Lola said.

She paused to take in as many faces as she could. Just then a woman's thin cry went up at the back of the room. Tiny, bonnet-wearing Senga McCall had risen from her seat and was across the room, now scrabbling at the door to get out.

Lola let her go.

'A last question for you to think about. A green Tiffany-style lamp is missing from the hallway in the Victorian wing. I want to know where it is. Let me reiterate,' she went on loudly over the buzz of voices, 'and most importantly of all, *I want to know who killed Amy Yorke*. If anyone knows *anything*, you need to find me and tell me.'

She paused again, feeling her heart racing in her chest.

'Now, I'd advise you to eat some breakfast. It's going to be a long day.'

CHAPTER NINETEEN

8.03 a.m.

Catherine led Lola over wet cobbles to the mews where Senga McCall had a small cottage. She rapped on the door.

'Senga, it's Catherine. Could you open up for me?'

She peered at Lola, unhappy at the duplicity.

A reedy voice piped up from inside. 'I'm not well.'

'I'm worried about you,' Catherine said. 'Come on, Senga. Let me in.'

'Please go away.' Her voice was close now, as if she was on the other side of the door.

'Come on, Senga,' Lola called. 'We need to talk.'

A strangled cry from inside the cottage.

'I just don't understand it. Senga, of all people,' Catherine murmured.

Lola leaned in and knocked loudly. 'We just need to talk, Senga,' she called. 'To understand. To try to help.'

She could hear tiny sobs.

Lola said more gently, 'There's nothing worse than being upset and on your own. Why don't you let us in — or just me, if you prefer. You can make us a cup of tea.'

Catherine eyed her miserably during the seconds that followed.

Then there was a scrabbling, the turning of a key, and the door swung stiffly open.

'Thank you,' Lola said, and stepped up into the dim hallway. Senga stood back against the wall, head down, hands up under her chin like a tiny animal.

'Would you like Catherine here?' Lola asked.

A miserable nod.

Catherine came in, then turned and closed the door.

'This is cosy,' Lola said, going ahead into a box of a living room. It was very warm and smelled strongly of air freshener — and another smell just under the artificial floral scent: alcohol.

At the back of the room a doorway revealed a kitchen. Lola glimpsed empty bottles by the sink before Senga scurried over and shut the door.

Lola sat at one end of a small sofa, while Catherine remained on her feet.

'Come and sit down,' Lola said to Senga.

She kept deliberately still as Senga McCall edged herself into an armchair.

Lola gave a nodding signal to Catherine to sit too. It was important they were all relaxed, or appeared to be. Senga's head drooped on her chest like a martyr's, resigned to her doom.

'It was you in the night, wasn't it?' Lola asked gently. 'You delivered letters in envelopes to a number of rooms, including mine. Then you went down to the cellar to leave more envelopes in the portico.'

Nothing, then a shaky, frightened nod.

Lola glanced at Catherine, who looked aghast.

'Why did you do it, Senga?' Lola asked now.

Her answer was muttered, indistinct.

'Sorry — you "had no choice"?'

Another nod.

Catherine asked, 'Do you hate us so much?'

Senga looked horrified and gave a violent shake of the head. 'No . . . No!'

Catherine was about to speak again until Lola quieted her with a hand.

'I know that you're a good person, Senga,' Lola said. 'I know you like to help people and do the right thing. And I know from everything I've heard about you that you like to tell the truth.'

'Yes,' she said miserably.

'I also know — from experience — that it feels *horrible* to say things that aren't true. It feels so much nicer to tell the truth. Did you write the letters?'

Nothing for a second or two — then Senga shook her head.

'Or print them?'

Another shake.

Lola could feel Catherine's shocked gaze on her and deliberately didn't turn to meet it.

'You just delivered them?'

A nod.

'Have you delivered them before?'

Another nod.

'But—' Catherine broke out, before Lola shut her up with a look.

'Someone else writes the letters,' Lola went calmly on, 'and makes you deliver them?'

'Yes,' the tiny woman admitted in a gasping whisper. 'I didn't write any of them.'

Beside her, Catherine's fists were balls on her knees. Lola could almost feel the tension emanating from her.

'Would you mind leaving us?' she asked Catherine.

Catherine stared open-mouthed, her eyes flitting to Senga.

'Please, Catherine.'

Catherine bridled then rose, blinking fast. 'Very well,' she said. She shot one last look at Senga, then stepped out of the living room and out of the cottage.

Lola heard footsteps on the cobbles outside.

'You can tell me anything,' Lola said, now they were alone. 'And I'll do my best to protect you.'

'I can't.'

'Whoever has made you do this is a cruel, controlling bully and I can stop her.' She peered into the woman's face. 'It is a "her", isn't it?'

Senga looked up at her, her face tight with fear and emotion. Lola waited.

The strain of the huge and frightening decision contorted Senga's pinched face. Her lips twitched, her eyelids too. Her skin tightened and her teeth appeared in a pained rictus.

'Say her name, Senga. Just say it. I'll make sure you're safe and protected.'

The eyes widened and seemed to bulge, as if the pressure was almost too much.

'I can't,' she said, then the lips clamped together.

Lola watched her, curious. 'Why?'

The mouth became pinched, the decision not to tell made.

'Is it . . . Is it Catherine?'

She looked shocked at that. 'What? *Catherine?* No!'

'Izzy McManus, then.'

'Please don't,' she whimpered.

Senga McCall eyed her.

'I've told you what I did. I'm not proud. I promise I won't do it again. But I can't say more than that.'

'Then I can't help you,' Lola said, rising and looking down at the woman in the armchair.

'I don't need help.'

'Oh, I think you might,' Lola said.

The eyes grew wide.

'You see, you're dangerous now, Senga.'

She'd meant to shock her, and it had worked.

'What do you mean?'

'You know who's doing this — I'm sure of it — and you're on the verge of telling me. That makes you a threat to the person who's the real criminal here. A woman died here last night. Do you understand what I'm saying?'

'Don't threaten me.'

'I'm *not*. I'm *warning* you.'

'Please,' she said. 'Just go. Leave me alone.'

'Very well.' Lola made for the door.

Senga was up now. 'I'm not the only one with secrets,' she said, making Lola stop and turn.

Senga's face was resentful and bitter.

'I'm not the only one who lies.'

'Who else lies, Senga?'

The little woman breathed for a few moments. Then she cocked her head on one side and said, 'That Grace Miller. And Dr Abbott.'

'How have they lied?' Lola asked, suspecting she was about to hear about Grace Miller's past and perhaps her relationship with Dr Abbott.

'An Australian man came here three weeks ago,' she said. 'Came to the gates. He told William he was here to see Grace Miller, only Grace refused to see him. So he asked to see Dr Abbott instead. And Dr Abbott went. They had an argument. William overheard them.' A smirk tilted her lips. 'Nasty things were said, and the man went on his way.'

'What sort of "nasty things", Senga?'

'Don't know. You'll not get anything out of Grace or Dr Abbott. William knows, though. He knows everything that goes on around here. Go ask him.'

'I shall,' Lola said.

'Good.' A haughty sniff. 'And now, leave me be!'

* * *

8.47 a.m.

Catherine was waiting fretfully for her in the corridor outside the gun room.

'She wouldn't tell me,' Lola said.

'I can't believe Senga would do such a thing. She's such a mouse.'

'That's exactly why she was chosen, I expect,' Lola said. 'Now, I need to talk to William Rix.'

'William? I haven't seen him. Was there something—'

But Lola was already on her way to the dining room.

A few people sat about the table, a couple eating, the rest drinking tea or coffee. Voices fell away and people turned to face her.

'Has anyone seen William Rix?' she asked the room.

They looked at one another, then back at Lola, blank or perplexed.

'If you see him, will you say I'm looking for him?'

'Erm . . .' a woman's voice said.

Lola turned. Heidi Bryce, the sub-postmistress, had her hand in the air. She was sitting with Josette Daniels.

'Might I have a word?'

'Yes, of course,' Lola said, distractedly. 'We can go to the library.'

It was warm in the library, but dark, so Lola went about turning on lamps, while Heidi fussed about, choosing a seat then changing her mind, finally settling on a leather bench and smoothing her skirts.

'I'm all ears,' Lola said, sitting opposite her in a low armchair.

'Sister Yorke was in one of the attics before she died, wasn't she?'

'We think so, yes.'

'Angus Wilde liked to go there. He was certainly up there a few weeks ago. And a few people weren't too happy about it.'

Lola frowned. 'How do you know this?'

'He told me! He'd taken himself on a wander around the castle and he found the place. It was an old nursery. There was an old rocking horse in there, and a train set. He was like a child, talking about it. He'd had a train set like it as a boy. He thought he could get it going again.'

Lola waited for the point to materialise.

'He told Kieran and me about it. Then he asked Dr Stenqvist about whether we might try to "upcycle" the toys for a local school. But Dr Stenqvist seemed unimpressed. He said not to go wandering about. That it wasn't safe up there. He said he would tell Dr Abbott to make sure the door was kept locked. Angus wasn't happy about that. He couldn't see the harm and wanted to know why we couldn't go exactly where we liked. Dr Stenqvist got shirty and Angus was *most* put out. But he didn't listen.'

'Didn't he?'

'No! He didn't like being told off like a naughty child, I can tell you.' She lowered her voice. 'I can understand why they were worried, if I'm honest. Angus gets confused, and he's not very stable on his feet.'

Lola let the information sink in, wondering how to store it along with the other information in her mind.

Heidi leaned forward. 'I happen to know he's been back there since.' She peered at Lola.

'Has he?'

'Kieran told me.' She pursed her lips. 'He said something about Sister Yorke planning to read Angus the riot act. Only, then he thought better of it and asked me to forget he'd said anything. He didn't want to get Angus into trouble — because, of course, there's no chance poor Angus could have been behind what happened to Sister Yorke. Though, of course, it's possible he saw something . . . Oh, now I hadn't thought of that before.'

'Heidi . . . ?'

'Yes, sorry?'

'When did Kieran tell you this?'

'Oh, last night. We got to talking, what with all the sitting about and waiting. I told Kieran he ought to say something, but he just pooh-poohed the idea. Anyway, I thought you ought to know. Talk to Kieran if you're interested.'

***

9.04 a.m.

'Still no sign of William, I'm afraid,' Catherine said, when Lola bumped into her on the way back to the dining room.

'It's imperative I speak to him,' Lola said. 'Make sure everyone knows I'm looking.'

'Very well.'

She found Kieran Fox in the dining room, shovelling bacon into his mouth.

'Can't it wait?' he asked her through a mouthful of food when she told him she wanted a word.

'Not really. You can bring that with you if you like.'

He did: his plate and a mug of coffee. Lola opened doors for him on the way to the library, then invited him to sit. If he was nervous, he didn't show it, and went on tucking into his breakfast.

'Last night you told Heidi Bryce that Angus Wilde had been up in the attic nursery.'

He stopped eating and stared at her, then threw down his knife and fork. 'Bloody woman,' he grumbled. 'Knew I shouldn't have told her.' He seemed to silently curse himself, screwing up his eyes and shaking his head. 'Fuck it.'

'You said Sister Yorke "read the riot act" to him about it.'

He peered at her crossly, then seemed to resign himself. 'She was planning to. I don't know if she did.'

'When was this, Mr Fox? When was Angus Wilde in the old nursery?'

'Last night.'

She tried not to look surprised.

'But that doesn't mean he harmed her. Angus is a softy. He liked to go there, that's all. I say, what was the harm? Sister Yorke got a call on that walkie-talkie thing saying he was up there and could she come.'

Lola wet her lips. 'Who was it, do you know?'

'It was crackly. A woman's voice. I couldn't say who it was. Yes, definitely a woman. And Sister Yorke seemed to know who it was, the way she spoke to her.'

Lola leaned forward. 'And this was last night, you say?'

He stared. 'Isn't that what we're talking about?'

'Mr Fox — Kieran,' she said, trying not to sound irritated, 'can you tell me everything that happened, with timings?'

'I wrote it down, didn't I?' he said, miffed. 'It's in the notes.'

She strained to remember. 'You wrote that Sister Yorke came by your room to check your medication, yes.'

'Well, that's when it was! She'd just come into my room and she said Angus wasn't in his room, did I know where he was? I said, "No, why would I?" Then the thing buzzed and she said, "Yes, who is it?" and a voice said, could she talk. She said yes, sort of impatiently, even though I was there. The person said Mr Wilde had got into the old nursery again, that he wasn't cooperating. Something like that. This would have been before the first gong went off for dinner — about ten to eight, say. Sister Yorke sort of sighed and said she'd be right up, and off she went.'

'Did she say anything to you when she'd finished on the radio?'

'She said she had to go and that I should ring if I needed anything. I said, "Naughty Angus in trouble, is he?" and she said, "I'll be reading him the riot act," but jokingly. She and I used to flirt a bit, you know? Nice-looking girl, really.' He smiled, pleased with himself. 'Shame.'

'Thank you, Mr Fox.'

His face darkened at her tone.

'Don't be trying to pin this on Angus,' he said, a little snippily. 'He wouldn't hurt a fly.'

A knock at the library door. Lola called out to come in.

It was Margot Kerr, looking flushed and excitable.

'Oh, sorry!' she cried when she saw Lola was with someone.

'I'm just going,' Fox said, getting up, eyes on Lola to check it was okay.

Lola gave him a nod and he went.

'Was there something . . . ?' she asked Margot.

'I just wanted to check if you needed anything,' the woman said. 'You looked so worn down when you spoke to us at breakfast. If there's anything I can do. A drink perhaps?'

'Actually, that would be lovely. A coffee would go down a treat — black, please.'

'And something to eat?'

'Not just now.'

'Give me ten minutes. Will you be in here?'

'I expect so. For the next hour or so, at least.'

CHAPTER TWENTY

9.10 a.m.

While Lola was talking to Kieran Fox in the library, Frankie was upstairs, sitting on the floor of Lola's bedroom, her back to the radiator, staring into space and an abyss of guilt.

Lola had been on her knees, worn down by her job and emotionally wrung out trying to decide what change to make. And Frankie had responded by pretending to take her away for a weekend's relaxation. Of course, Frankie had never expected it to turn out like this. She'd envisaged a weekend that was ninety-five percent a break, and that Lola might even take some pleasure from advising Catherine about the letters — and forgive her sister for the duplicity. She'd expected Lola to be peeved but knew ultimately she wouldn't really mind; that they might even have a laugh about it, and what a cheeky cow Frankie was. And then they'd drink some wine.

But now look . . .

'Fuck it,' Shuna Frain snapped on her right.

Shuna sat against the same wall, but in a low chair. For the hour they'd been lying in wait, she'd been tapping away at her laptop, muttering to herself and occasionally swearing as she mistyped a word.

'You're battering the hell out of that keyboard,' Frankie hissed.

'Am I?' She looked surprised.

'Someone'll hear you.'

Shuna began to type more softly, but the muttering and swearing continued unabated and got louder over time.

'You're not nervous, are you?' Shuna asked quietly, studying Frankie sidelong.

'No.' It sounded defensive. 'Well, a wee bit.' She smiled, but it was a struggle. In truth she was nervous as hell.

Shuna dropped her a wink. 'Me too. But I keep reminding myself that this is going to make one hell of a story.' She began tapping again.

'Do you think someone will come?' Frankie asked.

'Maybe. I mean, if it's someone really barking mad writing those letters — and let's face it, it must be — then why wouldn't they have a pop at breaking in to retrieve the incriminating evidence?'

The evidence — the bucket, gloves and tongs — was actually in a knotted bin bag in the locked wardrobe of Frankie's room next door, but the letter writer wouldn't know that. And so the two of them were here, waiting, phones at the ready so they could record themselves telling the writer that the game was up.

'Your sister's some woman,' Shuna said now.

Frankie turned to stare, momentarily speechless.

'She can turn her hand to any situation,' Shuna said, 'and she's a match for the worst of people.' She smirked. 'Me included — and don't pretend she hasn't moaned about me. We've clashed a number of times.'

'You should tell her,' Frankie said, eyeing the woman she had indeed heard Lola moan about at length and on multiple occasions.

'Nah. She might not respect me as much if I did.'

'On the contrary, I think she would. Why do you say that?'

'Because I'd respect her less if she ever said anything so mushy.'

The pair of them laughed, then froze in tandem when they heard footsteps in the corridor.

'Is that—' Shuna began but Frankie shushed her.

The door was to their right, hinged on this side, so that someone entering wouldn't see either of them until they were fully in the room.

Frankie unlocked her phone and went into the camera app. Shuna was doing the same when they heard a key slide into the lock.

Frankie felt her arms and shoulders lock. She suppressed an urge to squeal as the door handle began to turn.

She pushed herself into a crouching position, but keeping close to the wall. Shuna remained with her back to the wall, knees up to her chest.

The door came slowly, silently open . . .

CHAPTER TWENTY-ONE

9.18 a.m.

As soon as Fox had gone on his way, Lola had called Anna for an update. She and DC Kirstie Campbell had already done a huge amount of research on Lola's behalf.

'I'll put you on handsfree,' Anna said. 'There. Now tell me when you've got a pen.'

'That's me,' Lola said, putting the emergency phone on speaker beside her pad.

'Right. Might be best to start with names of staff where we found nothing sinister.'

'Go on.'

'The following are all clean: Tom Abbott, Catherine Ballantyne, Isabelle McManus and Senga McCall.'

'Okay.'

'Dr Florien Stenqvist, clinical psychologist, trained in Stockholm. Investigated for malpractice by his professional body in Sweden, *and* by Stockholm police in relation to the alleged molestation of two young female patients. Didn't get to court. Parents of one of the patients, a sixteen-year-old girl, tried to sue him in the civil court. Case was thrown out.

Stenqvist left Sweden a year later, set up a private practice in Russia. He's a fluent speaker, apparently. Left there under a cloud we can't get info on, though Kirstie's going to keep trying. There's a rumour a patient might have died under his care. Something to do with an experimental treatment.'

'Jeezo.'

'Nothing proved, no convictions. After that he moved to Brazil and got into psychiatric eugenics.'

'Psychiatric *eugenics*? Which is what precisely?'

'According to what Kirstie found, it's something to do with "controlling nature and engineering nurture", with a focus on "inferiority in genetic lines related to madness". It was through that he met your Stefan Kade, by the way. Kade's Foundation bankrolled a conference.'

Lola's skin crawled. 'Did it, now?'

'Kade's got a reputation for donating to a number of slightly... well, I'd call them "questionable" causes. Eugenics is one. Unethical drug testing on poor communities in West Africa is another.'

'Why doesn't any of this surprise me?' Lola murmured. 'Go on, who's next?'

'Rory McManus. Arrested after attacking a colleague at work. He worked at a factory then. There was teasing, which got out of hand. He got drunk one lunchtime, then came after the colleague with a claw hammer. Got a suspended sentence. That was ten years ago.'

Lola said nothing, but her thoughts were on the claw hammer currently in Catherine's safe.

'Now we get to the really interesting stuff.'

'Oh?'

'Grace Miller. When we spoke earlier you said you knew about her past, about the trial? Well, there's more than a little chat online, and in the occasional newspaper column, suggesting she *was* guilty of shaking that baby to death. And — get this — *that she'd shaken a baby before*, in a different Australian state. The baby survived but had injuries. It seems the first family didn't want to put themselves through a prosecution.'

'My God.' What had Amy said to Angus Wilde about lightning never striking twice?

'There's word that a couple of journalists are working on an investigation to try and piece things together. I'm going to keep looking into it. Meantime, I've got a contact for Edward Grimshaw, the father of the child Vivien Wray went on trial for killing. I've left a message and I'm waiting for a call back. I'll ask him if Yorke had been in touch with the family.'

'Thanks.'

Lola felt more disheartened than horrified at the news. She'd liked Grace Miller, had felt pity for her. This was hard to hear. But still, it wasn't motive for Amy's murder — not if rumours were already out there. Unless, of course, the rumours might lead to the cancellation of the lucrative book deal . . . But even then, why kill Amy?

Besides, Grace simply couldn't have killed Yorke, could she? She'd been only metres away from Lola in the next office.

'What else?' she asked.

'Biggie for you,' Anna said. 'William Rix might have murdered his mother.'

'*What?*'

'Yep. Five years ago in Dunfermline. His older sister accused him of withholding the old woman's heart medicine and even her oxygen.'

'And the mother died?'

'Yep. The sister had suspected William of mistreating the old lady for some time and laid a trap. Police investigated but the Crown Office decided there was circumstantial evidence but they couldn't make a strong enough case.'

Lola fell silent, circling Rix's name on her pad.

'Boss . . . ?'

'Rix has done a vanishing act,' Lola said quietly. 'Just when I needed to ask him about a mystery visitor who came to the castle a few weeks ago. There's a chance he took fright at an announcement I made earlier.'

'Be careful, boss.'

'Oh, I will.'

'There's more . . .'

'Go on.'

'Maya McArthur, Kade's wife.'

'What about her?'

'A history of manic behaviour and a diagnosis of several personality disorders.'

'Oh dear.'

'Which brings me to my last piece of info for now. It's a goodie.'

'Go on.'

'A case of poison pen letters at a clinic in the Borders three years ago. Several anonymous notes distributed among the staff by a colleague with no apparent motive other than spite. The writer was identified and a confession extracted by the management. It was a private clinic, the kind the wealthy send their kids to in order to dry out. Not in anyone's interest to make it public. It's a nasty story. She was manipulating a junior member of staff, young girl with learning difficulties who worked in the kitchen, into delivering the notes.'

'You've got a name?'

'I have. It was the art therapist. A Margaret Brazier. Brazier was her married name but she's divorced now. And she calls herself Margot. She's Margot Kerr.'

CHAPTER TWENTY-TWO

9.21 a.m.

'Oh, goodness me!' Margot Kerr yelped when she saw Frankie and Shuna, then panted as she recovered herself. 'You did give me a fright.'

'I bet,' Shuna said.

'What are you doing here, Margot?' Frankie asked, pleasantly enough, relieved she sounded less nervous — and shocked — than she felt.

'I was—' Margot's eyes roved the bedroom as if searching for an excuse — 'looking to see if Lola was here.' She beamed. 'In case she wanted a cup of tea or anything to eat. I know how hard she's working.'

'She's not here,' Shuna said. 'But you knew that, didn't you?'

The smile vanished but was back a split second later.

'I don't know what you mean.' She gave a tinkling laugh but her eyes betrayed her. The way they darted about.

Shuna stepped over to the door and shut it.

'Tell us why you're really here,' Shuna said, and folded her arms.

Margot watched her, then seemed to wither in the face of the journalist's implacable stance. She turned to Frankie and pinned on that warm smile again. 'Frankie?' she implored. 'Please . . .'

Frankie gazed at Margot Kerr with a kind of confused wonder. This kind, bustling woman couldn't be the letter writer who'd tormented the castle's staff all these months — could she? The thought that it was her fingers tapping out line after line of spite to send to her colleagues was astonishing. Those colleagues who seemed to like and respect her . . .

Frankie swallowed. '"Please" what?'

The smile faded and her breathing now came in panting little gasps. 'Oh dear . . . Oh, dearie me.'

'Game's up, Margot,' Shuna said.

Margot's face crumpled and tears began to bubble. She stood there, arms by her side and sobbed, snivelling, her whole body racked as her misery seemed to manifest itself.

'Why did you do it, Margot?' Frankie asked. 'Why did you write the letters?'

Still sobbing, she slowly shook her head.

'You don't know?' Frankie checked.

'Make you feel better, did it?' Shuna prompted. 'Kind of a release?'

She nodded now, eyes closed.

'A release,' she said, 'but also a means of correction.'

'Of correction?' Shuna said. 'Meaning what?'

'Of discipline. Of *standards*. To make people buck up and do their jobs as they should. So many lazy, useless so-called professionals. And our guests need them to do their jobs well. They need proper care, such as the care *I* give them!'

'I see,' Frankie said, curious.

'I've tried in the past, you know? I've given people advice, I've even reported them — to managers or the regulatory bodies — but nothing good comes of it.'

'So you're a kind of standards warrior?' Shuna asked. 'Intriguing. And an innovative way of doing it. Didn't you mind that your colleagues were frightened by these letters?'

'Pah,' Margot said. 'I rather hoped they were!'

'What about their mental health, Margot?' Frankie asked. 'Weren't you concerned about harming them?'

'Harming them?' She frowned, thinking about it, then began to sway alarmingly.

'Sit down,' Frankie said, jumping forward and taking Margot's arm.

For a moment, Margot allowed herself to be led, but then she snapped, yanking her arm away and rearing round, lips curled back.

'Get your filthy hands off me, slut.'

'I beg your pardon?' Frankie was genuinely shocked.

'You and that Lola aren't sisters, are you? Pair of lesbians.'

'Woah!' Shuna cried, laughing.

'And *you*!' Margot spat in Shuna's direction. 'You're a bully and a bitch!'

'Right . . .' Shuna said, eyes wide, clearly enjoying this eruption of madness.

'Margot, do you think you might need some help?' Frankie tried, kindly.

'Help?' She reared up, as if ready to fight. 'The kind of help where you sit in a room with some disgusting hairy pig of a doctor like Florien Stenqvist? Where you tell him your innermost thoughts while he's fantasising about *doing it* to you. Of *fucking* you. Or the kind of help where they pour drugs into you till you're a zombie? Like they did to my poor sister?' The snarl was back. 'You *fucking idiot.*'

She began to look about, eyes roving the room.

'Where are they anyway?'

'The gloves and tongs?' Shuna asked.

'In here, are they?' She made for the wardrobe but found it empty but for a few jangling hangers.

'They're not in this room, Margot,' Frankie said.

'It was a trap,' Shuna added. 'One you fell right into!'

'But I need them back,' Margot insisted, momentarily reasonable again. 'I've got to have them.'

'You can't,' Shuna said.

Margot stared, then seemed to sag. Tears began to flow again.

She looked tragic, sitting there, deflated and depressed.

'Did you write all the letters?' Shuna asked.

Margot shook her head. 'Not all of them.'

'Oh?'

'Amy did some of them.'

'Did she know you'd started them?'

Margot shook her head and a tiny smirk of delight pursed her lips. 'I decided to stop when they spoke to the staff. I knew they were rattled and taking it seriously, so I thought I'd better take a break. Then new letters started to come. I got a couple. I mean, I'd always sent them to myself, as a cover, you know? It was interesting to receive letters from another writer. She was sloppy though. Didn't take care when she left them in the portico. She'd go there in the middle of the night, leaving by the side door and running round to the front of the castle. I kept watch one night. Silly girl didn't see me.' She smirked. 'So I let her carry on and enjoyed everyone's reactions. Then, when she died last night, I thought it was important to pick up the reins again — so many people need to improve!'

She tittered.

Shuna said. 'Did you kill Amy?'

Margot gazed up at her, mouth open.

'Did you, Margot?'

She frowned and sneered at the very idea. 'Of course not! *No!* I'd never — how could you even—'

'Then who did?'

'What—? I don't know.' She looked to Frankie as if for help. 'How could I know that?'

'But you know so many things,' Shuna went on. 'You know everything that goes on here, don't you? Everybody's secrets.'

'I don't know *that*.' She gawped, horrified, at her two captors.

'You didn't like Amy, did you?'

'I didn't like her, no. I don't *like* any of them, apart from the guests. I didn't kill Amy.'

The sound of shouting came from outside the castle: a man yelling urgently.

Frankie went to the window and saw a small crowd had gathered on the lawn, looking up at the castle. She saw Dr Abbott, pointing, Dr Stenqvist beside him.

'What is it?' asked Shuna.

'I've no idea,' Frankie said. 'Whatever it is, I don't think it's good.'

CHAPTER TWENTY-THREE

9.48 a.m.

'You need to come!' Catherine blurted when Lola opened the library door in response to her knocking. 'Up on the roof — now.'

'On the roof?'

'Follow me, quickly.'

She paused only to lock the library door before crossing the great hallway for the open front door of the castle.

It was dry and the wind was light, barely ruffling the lawn. She saw the two doctors and Rory McManus standing on the grass, all looking skyward.

Lola joined them and lifted her gaze. There, on the edge of the castle roof, was a tall figure wearing what looked like a dark cloak, complete with a cowl that hid its face.

'Who is it?' she demanded of the men.

Just then a woman screamed, making them all start. Izzy McManus had appeared and now stared up in horror, hands clamped over her mouth. Catherine crossed the grass to comfort her.

'Rix,' Abbott said. 'It's William Rix. He's been walking up and down the parapet. The man must have lost his mind.'

Lola looked up again. The figure had turned and was slowly pacing along the edge of the roof, beside the battlements.

'How long has he been up there?'

'Ten minutes,' Abbott said. 'Maybe more. Florien saw him with the habit on and tried to talk to him, but Rix pushed him out of the way — literally pushed him with both hands. He went off, talking to himself, heading upstairs. Florien came to find me.'

'We need to reach him,' Lola said quietly. 'How can I get up there?'

Abbott gawped at her. 'Are you mad? Rix is deeply unstable. He's liable to take you over with him.'

She ignored him and said to Rory McManus, 'Rory — do you know how to get out onto the roof?'

He stared at her, bewildered for a second, then seemed to pull himself together. He nodded.

To Abbott she said, 'Get everyone inside. An audience won't help.' To Rory McManus she said, 'Show me the way.'

* * *

10.02 a.m.

The stairs from the third floor up to the roof were spiral — they would be. McManus's boots kicked up dust as he went before Lola. She tried not to breathe in, nor flinch as cobwebs caught in her hair.

The door at the top was ajar, banging slightly in what remained of the wind.

'Let me go first,' Lola said, and McManus stood aside.

They'd come up at the back of the main building and before her were the roofs of Ardaig Castle, shallow slopes of slate, shining wet, and chimneys and the occasional turret. To her left was a worryingly low parapet, with jagged battlements. She could see treetops through the mist and the thought of the three-storey drop to gravel below made her head swim and adrenaline crackle in her chest.

Calm and steady. You're not going to fall over.

Three steep steps led down from the doorway to a flat narrow strip between the tiles and the parapet. This extended several metres away, then took a ninety-degree turn to the right, to where Rix might still be pacing, currently out of sight.

'It'll be slippery,' McManus said behind her.

'I know. You stay here.'

'Keep your centre of gravity low and watch out for any sudden blasts of wind.'

She descended the steps, knees bent, arms out to help her balance. Then she was on the narrow strip beside the parapet, which was only knee-high.

A gust caught her, lifting her hair and making her cry out as she fought panic. Every cell was urging her to get down, to crawl back to the safety of that doorway, and descend the spiral stairs as quickly as she could. She fought and carried on, panting, and in a minute she was at the corner of the roof, with a dizzying view of the castle's front lawn, including the H of the helipad. She looked along the parapet — and there was Rix, or the person assumed to be Rix, standing at the far end, at the next corner round. He stood very still, facing outward, looking out over the trees.

You're fine. Nice and calm. A few more steps, then you'll be near enough for him to hear you.

She pushed on, knees bent, keeping low, hands out to steady herself, eyes fixed on that dark, cowled figure against the white-clouded sky.

'Hello, William,' she called when she was further along.

She detected a tensing of the shoulders, but he didn't turn.

'It's Lola Harris. I'm worried about you.'

Nothing now. Still looking out over the woods.

'Can I come a bit closer?' she called. 'Gonnae make myself hoarse shouting like this.'

Nothing.

She took another few steps, eyes never leaving his back.

'William? I want to talk to you, but the truth is, I'm scared to death of heights. Can you help me a wee bit?'

Still nothing. She thought for a moment, weighing her options. Weighing the risks.

'This is about your mum, isn't it? Amy found out, didn't she? Sent you one of her horrible letters. Then I guess I gave you a fright this morning in the dining room, talking about people who might have — well, done something bad in the past. I didn't mean to upset you. All I want is to talk.'

The figure moved, ever so slightly.

'How would that be? A chat. Just you and me — but please, not here. Somewhere I'm not fearing for my life, eh?'

The figure began to move, to walk towards the rear of the castle.

Oh God . . .

Lola followed, crouching as she went, cursing the situation she'd found herself in.

The figure stopped at the back of the roof of the main building. Lola approached and had a glimpse of a wood-and-glass structure extending away below. The figure was right over the orangery.

'William, please,' she cried out, as another blast of wind lifted her hair.

Very slowly, the figure turned, until it faced her — except the face was in shadows.

Lola remembered Catherine's story of the ghostly monk, and how she'd claimed to have seen him one day, tearing across the lawn before vanishing into the trees. A chill ran through her.

She waited, steadying herself as a gust of wind threatened to knock her off balance.

'How about it, William?'

Thin, bone-white hands came up and pulled back the cowl, dropping it so his skeletal face showed, devoid of any emotion.

'That's better,' she said, though it wasn't particularly. 'Now, how about it? Fancy following me back down those stairs? We can get a cup of tea and talk about what happened here.'

'I didn't kill Amy!' he shouted suddenly, his voice high and reedy. 'I know you think I did, but I didn't!'

She nodded. 'Okay. But I'd like to understand why you came up here. You must be feeling out of sorts. Come on, William. Come down with me.'

'It's a trap, isn't it?' he called. 'You'll take me down there then you'll trick me and then I'll be under arrest.'

Another gust of wind, this one stronger. She had to suppress the urge to cry out, to squat beneath the top of the parapet.

'I actually just want to get off this roof. I don't care if that stuff with your mum is true. I don't actually care about Amy Yorke. She sounds like a nasty cow, if you ask me. Everything that's happened here these past few days — that's someone else's job to clear up. But while I'm here I'm cursed to try and keep everything and everyone together. To stop anything else bad from happening. Because imagine how that will look for me! They'll know I was here. If they hear I didn't try to help you off this bloody roof, they'll be gunning for me. It's called a duty of care and it's a real burden, I tell you.'

A frown creased his forehead. He blinked.

'What do you say, William?'

He said something indistinct, then cleared his throat.

'What was that?'

'I said — I killed her.' He closed his eyes.

'I see . . . Amy, you mean?'

He opened his eyes again and the frown was back. 'My mother. Like my sister said I did. I — I lived with her for years. I just — I couldn't do it any more. She made my life a living hell.'

His eyes were shut again and he began to sway.

'Look at me, William,' Lola called. 'Come on, open your eyes now.'

But they remained closed.

'She destroyed every chance I ever had of being happy. It was too late. That's what she kept saying to me. "It's too late,

William. It's too late for you. No woman will ever want you. Not at your age. Not the way you are."'

'Let's talk about this downstairs, eh?'

'She threw her lunch across the living room. Said she'd never wanted what I'd made her. That my cooking made her physically sick. And so I decided it was time. I'd already been giving her fewer heart tablets. I waited until she became breathless one morning and just didn't give her any oxygen.' He smiled sadly. 'She died in her chair by the fire. The day I found her there was the happiest in all my life.'

He opened his eyes.

'And Amy worked it out. Don't know how. Of course you think I killed her too. Motive, no alibi. I know how it works. Keeps things tidy, doesn't it?'

'That's *not* how it works at all. Come on now.' She took a step towards him. 'Take my hand if you like. We can work our way back round to the stairs.'

'Stop!'

She did.

'Stay where you are.'

He reached inside the habit with his right hand — and brought out a knife. A thin-bladed, lethal-looking thing with a black handle. He showed her it, turning it. She could see its serrated edge even from here.

'William—'

'A monk slit his wrists here once,' he told her. 'Ran round the estate with his hands in the air, screaming as he went. People still see him. He'd gone mad, they say. I know how he felt.'

'Put the blade down, William.'

'Too late for that.' He threw both arms in the air so the sleeves of the habit fell down his arms, exposing his bone-like wrists.

Then in a violent spasm he began to cut his left wrist, sawing urgently as red began to spurt.

Lola darted forward, keeping low. He cried in pain but kept on cutting. She heard the blade squeak as it ground against his bones.

Lola tackled him, falling on him so that he'd collapse onto the slope of the roof.

He fought her, scrabbling. Blood was everywhere. A hand flopped uselessly on its wrist. She was down but he was up, over her, stabbing now at his throat, swiping and cutting — and swaying.

He staggered, tripped and fell, letting out a strangled cry as his body plummeted through glass.

CHAPTER TWENTY-FOUR

10.37 a.m.

Lola half-crawled back the way she'd come, legs like jelly as she tried not to think about the drop to one side. Her heart hammered and she had to fight the urge to vomit. But she made it, and four minutes later she was down three floors and in the orangery.

Tom Abbott had got there first and stood over Rix's crumpled, bleeding body.

A huddle of onlookers — Dr Stenqvist, and Rory and Izzy McManus — stood at the entrance. Catherine arrived at the same time as Lola and cried, 'Oh dear God!'

'Keep away,' Lola ordered them breathlessly.

She went into the orangery, stepping between glinting shards of glass, and joined Dr Abbott.

'He's dead,' he said to her, his lips drawn back. He looked pale with shock.

Rix lay half in, half out of a fountain. The water foamed pink.

'Should we move him?' Abbott asked between panicked breaths.

'No,' Lola said. 'Turn off the fountain. Help will be here today. We need to seal this whole area, then get out.'

He seemed relieved, and went behind the fountain to find the electric switch for the pump.

The plume of pink water fell away.

'So Rix killed Amy?' he asked her quietly in the silence that followed.

She looked at him. 'I'm not so sure.'

* * *

11.01 a.m.

'Everything I've worked for — everything the Foundation has tried to achieve — now in tatters.'

Stefan Kade's usually smooth features were contorted with rage. He jabbed repeatedly at her with a finger.

'You must be very upset,' Lola said, not much concerned about whether it sounded genuine or not.

Lola sat in the library hugging a hot-water bottle, as provided by Izzy McManus. Her bones were frozen from being on the roof, her muscles locked tight around them. She'd called the local DCI and told him about Rix's suicide, then Kade had come to root her out. He remained standing, fists clenching and unclenching. She let him get on with it.

'You drove him to this with your threats this morning.'

'I didn't make any threats. William Rix took his own life, and he meant to do it.'

'And what did you do to stop him? Nothing! Instead, you went capering about up there like King Kong.'

She raised her eyebrows in surprise.

'You think you're really something, don't you?' he said now. 'In fact, you have zero authority here. You're an agent of chaos. I wish you'd just leave well alone. Instead, this place and my foundation are going to be all over the papers. Who in their right minds — what *senior political leaders* in their right minds would want to come here for a retreat? It's going to be a scandal. God knows where it will end.'

'As it happens, I think it'll end quite soon,' she said placidly.

'What do you mean?'

'I know who killed Amy.'

'Do you?' He bridled, seeming almost offended that she could be so confident. 'Well, go on then! *Who?*'

'Can't say just yet,' she said. 'I'm hoping to gather some more evidence before I air my thoughts.'

'Can't say? Yes you can! I own this place! Tell me now.'

She squinted at him, realising she was quite enjoying the man's rage. 'No,' she said. She raised her chin so she could look down her nose at him. 'You can wait, like everyone else.'

* * *

11.15 a.m.

'But I thought that's why he killed himself!' Dr Abbott said. He'd come to the library shortly after Kade had stormed out. 'Why else do something so . . . final?'

Lola said, 'He killed himself because he murdered his mother. That's what he told me, up there on the roof. The police investigated her death at the time but lacked evidence to bring it to court.'

Abbott gaped at her across the table.

'Didn't you know? It's my belief that Amy had written one of her letters to Rix, which upset him badly. Possibly she knew about his mother's death, or maybe she didn't. Either way, he thought he was going to be exposed and had a sort of breakdown.'

'None of that means he didn't kill Amy.'

'He denied it when I asked him. Why would he do that when he had nothing to lose?'

Abbott slumped down in his seat.

'Anyway, what did you want to see me about?' he asked gruffly.

'A few weeks ago, a man came to the castle. He stopped at the gatehouse and asked to speak to Grace Miller but she refused. So he asked to speak to you instead. You went to see him and had an argument.'

He stared, but she could tell from a flicker of his eyelids that he was rattled.

'Who was he, Dr Abbott?'

'What did Rix tell you?'

Nothing. I didn't get the chance to ask. 'I want to hear your version.'

He licked his lips and his breathing grew quick and shallow. 'I don't know his name. He was after a story. Gossip.'

'About what?'

'About Grace. About her past.'

'Talk me through what happened.'

He frowned. 'Why would I? After all—' his top lip curled in a small sneer — 'you have no authority here, do you? And I *certainly* have no legal representation.'

She watched him for a moment and drew on her well of weary irritation. 'You can refuse to talk to me, but it won't look good for you.'

His eyes narrowed and she could tell he was weighing options. The mask was off now. No more the genial, helpful Dr Abbott.

'What did the visitor want, Doctor?'

More seconds passed, then he spoke. 'He was investigating Grace's past. By what he was saying, he'd been lapping up internet rumours that she was really guilty of killing that child. Worse: that she'd harmed another baby too. I sent him packing.'

'He was an investigator, you say?'

'I said he was *investigating*. I don't know who for, or why.'

'A journalist, was he, or . . . ?'

'No idea.'

'He didn't tell you?'

'If he did, I don't remember.'

'And his name — did he tell you that?'

'Possibly.' The tiniest smirk touched his lips. 'As I say, I sent him packing.'

'Where did this conversation take place?'

'By the gates.'

'In earshot of William Rix?'

'I — I'm not sure. I made him walk away down the lane with me, away from the gatehouse.' His eyes narrowed unpleasantly. 'You can hardly ask Rix about it, can you?'

She ignored the jibe. 'How long did you talk for?'

He stared. 'Not long.'

'Approximately?'

'Three or four minutes.'

'What was he like, this man? Age, colour, hair, accent — that sort of thing.'

'He didn't make any impression on me.'

She considered whether to go a little further, just to see his face.

'William Rix did hear the conversation,' she said, eyeing him. 'He told someone about it.'

The smile vanished but he said nothing.

'Not a lot,' she admitted, 'but it could be enough.'

'Enough for what?'

'To identify the man.'

He raised his eyebrows. 'Good luck with that.'

'Like the fact the man had an Australian accent.'

He couldn't conceal the alarm in his eyes.

'Grace didn't hurt those babies,' he said now, low and gruff. 'She couldn't hurt anyone. I shouted at him. I wanted him to understand he couldn't persecute her any more. That she'd been through enough!'

She considered his words, eyes on his face, on his trembling jaw.

'Grace suffered tremendously,' he said. '*Tremendously*. You know she was attacked — physically assaulted — a year after that damned trial. A man and a woman attacked her while she was out and about, minding her own business. Left her traumatised and injured and determined to leave Australia for good.'

She nodded.

'And now,' he said, stretching his back and beginning to rise, 'we've all had quite a morning, and I'd like to make sure Grace is all right. Everything that's been happening here — it's triggered a kind of post-traumatic reaction. She's anxious and frightened. She had a panic attack in the night.'

'I'm sorry to hear that.'

'Yes, well . . .'

* * *

11.44 a.m.

Anna had sent a text to the emergency phone, asking Lola to ring her ASAP.

'I spoke to Nathan Grimshaw, the father of the baby Vivien Wray was accused of killing,' she told Lola.

'Oh?'

'Sister Yorke had been in touch with him and his wife. She sent emails — several, in fact. He's kept them in a special folder on his computer. He's forwarding them to me. He thought she sounded crazy, as if she had a personal vendetta against Grace Miller. She'd send reports about her daily activities, and she kept forwarding content from conspiracy sites about the child's death. He asked her to stop — and it seems she did.'

'When was she last in touch with him?'

'A matter of weeks ago. Latterly, she claimed she had proof that Grace Miller, or Vivien Wray, had shaken and injured another child. That she'd been speaking to a writer of true-crime books who was investigating the cases—'

'What writer?' Lola interrupted.

'She didn't say, but a true-crime writer *had* been in touch with the family separately, and I do have a name for him.'

'Go one.'

'He's a Benedict Wilton. I looked him up while I was waiting for you to call me back. He's done a couple of books — big sellers, by the look of them — on cold-case crimes. He's based in Sydney.'

'Get in touch with him, Anna. And I think I'd like to talk to him myself. Try to get a number for him.'

'Will do, boss. Everything all right there?'

'Not really. A man committed suicide before my eyes this morning.'

'My God!'

'I'm managing things. I just hope to God they open the road to the castle before long. Oh, and Anna, there's another thing I'd like you to check on.'

'Anything, boss. Fire away.'

'Someone attacked Vivien Wray a couple of years after her trial. A man and a woman. Can you find what happened and what their names were?'

'Sure thing. Leave it with me.'

* * *

12.05 p.m.

Catherine knocked just as Lola was coming off the phone from Anna. She relayed details about lunch. Nothing fancy, a cold platter: bread, meat, cheese, some salad. No alcohol. Izzy was laying it out in the dining room right now. People could come and go as they pleased.

'How are things?' she asked quietly, once she'd delivered her information.

'Interesting,' Lola said. 'What's being said?'

'Dr Abbott is in a bit of a state. Your name was mentioned.'

'Oh dear.'

'He's away in his room. I think Grace is with him. Senga is hiding out in her cottage. She liked William. Oh, not like that! They were friends. An odd pair. I can't imagine what they talked about. She's like a mouse and he was . . . so odd. She's very upset about his death. And then—' she lowered her voice, for no apparent reason — '*there's Margot.*'

'Yes,' Lola said. 'There's Margot. Have you spoken to her?'

'I tried. She's still in her room. Won't open the door. I can hear her wailing in there.' Catherine closed her eyes and shook her head. 'I still can't believe it.'

'I'll try to talk to her later,' Lola said.

She'd tried, briefly, after Rix's suicide, banging on Margot's bedroom door and telling her, bluntly, that enough was enough. Frankie and Shuna were all for following her in, like a pair of excited kids. She'd made them wait at the end of the corridor.

'Friendly, helpful Margot,' Catherine went on. 'But all this time, writing horrible, *horrible* letters to every one of us. So much spite. Why? What made her hate us so much?'

'I don't think it was personal,' Lola said. 'She'd done it at this other place. I'm sure Dr Stenqvist has a view, but it seems to me to be more of a compulsion, a sort of bloodletting on paper.'

'I can understand that, I suppose — writing down all your negative feelings. But to deliver the letters, then go about your business, all cheerful, and "good morning" and "how are you this lovely morning" to everyone, knowing they've read your vile words . . . It's pure madness, isn't it?'

'I'll go talk to Senga,' Lola murmured to herself. 'Oh, and would you check where Angus Wilde is? I need a word with him.'

* * *

12.18 p.m.

Senga was drunk, that much was clear. She banged into a low table and nearly fell as Lola followed her into her tiny living room.

'I'm sorry about your friend,' Lola said, breathing in alcohol fumes.

'Oh, William . . .' Senga said, collapsing back into the chair she'd been occupying, judging by the vodka and rum bottles on the table beside it. 'A lonely man but a kind man.'

She began to weep.

Lola perched on the edge of the little sofa. 'Margot Kerr has admitted to writing poison pen letters to her colleagues,' she said, then waited for the words to sink in.

'Oh!' Frowning, Senga peered at Lola, then her pinched little face brightened. 'So it's over . . .'

'Hopefully,' Lola said.

'Good. I told her it was wicked.'

'Did you?'

A tiny nod. 'Oh, yes. But she never forgave me for catching her. I saw her late one night — very late — printing in the general office, with just one lamp on. I made her jump and she lost hold of some papers and one fluttered down and I saw it. It looked just like the letter I'd received. I said, "It's you!" and she laughed. I said, "It's wicked, what you're doing." She said . . .' Senga took a few gasps of air. 'She said . . . oh dear . . .' She swallowed and eyeballed Lola, then bit her lip.

'She had something on you, didn't she?' Lola asked.

Another tiny nod.

'What was it, Senga? It can't be that bad.'

'Don't tell Catherine,' the woman whispered. 'It's such a small thing but she wouldn't like it.' She sniffed.

'Go on.'

'I helped myself to a bottle or two from time to time. From the wine store in the cellar and once from behind the bar in the orangery. I took Izzy's key and helped myself. I thought — well, I thought I deserved it. I work hard.'

'Margot knew, didn't she?'

'She was nice about it — at first. She saw me. She made me sit down and was very kind. Even let me keep the bottle. She said it would be our secret but to try not to do it again. All smiles. And then . . .'

'And then you caught her and she used it.'

A nod.

'And she made you her accomplice. Did she threaten you?'

Another nod.

'She said she'd tell Catherine and Dr Abbott. That they'd sack me. That they'd never believe someone of her character would write nasty letters. She showed me how she put the letters into the portico. It was horrible down there. Then, once or twice a week, she'd come to the cottage with a fresh batch and make me go down there and poke the letters through that window. Oh, I was so frightened! I've been . . . so, so frightened.'

'It *was* wicked of her,' Lola agreed. 'Coercive and cruel, and possibly criminal.'

That shocked Senga. 'Oh, I can't go to court! Please don't make me give evidence. I just . . . I just want Margot Kerr to go away from here.'

Lola smiled. 'I don't think you've anything to fear there,' she said.

* * *

12.46 p.m.

Lola went wearily to the dining room and, without making eye contact with the handful of people sitting about, piled a plate high with cheese, turkey and salad, including some impressive-looking heritage tomatoes. She poured a glass of fizzy water and looked around.

'Sit here,' Dr Stenqvist called to her.

He was at one end of the table, sitting with Heidi Bryce.

'Maybe they'll open the road again soon,' Heidi said.

'Maybe.'

Lola assembled the ingredients between two bits of bread and began to eat.

'There she is,' a familiar ironic voice called.

It was Shuna, with Frankie on her heel.

Lola swallowed her mouthful. 'You two best pals now?'

'I think we make a good team,' Shuna said, wrinkling her nose at Frankie.

'We're going to meet up from time to time,' Frankie said. 'When this is all over.'

'Is that right?' Lola asked, eyeing Shuna. 'I'll have to watch what I confide in Frankie in future, then.'

They went to get food.

Catherine came in, with Stefan Kade behind her. He looked pissed off — all the more so when he saw Lola sitting eating.

'Taking a break?' he enquired unpleasantly.

'What about it?' she asked him, nice and loud. 'I'm not exactly on the payroll, am I?'

He didn't like that. She could see him bristling and it warmed her heart. He turned heel and headed to the table of food.

Lola waved to Catherine, then rose to talk to her. 'Any sign of Angus Wilde?' she asked.

'He's in his room. He says to go up whenever suits.'

* * *

1.15 p.m.

'I was asleep the whole time,' Angus Wilde told her. 'That's what I put in my notes, because that's the truth!'

He was sitting in an armchair by the window, dressed but wearing slippers. He kept frowning and peering fretfully out at the damp afternoon as if he was waiting for someone to arrive.

Lola tried a different tack.

'You like to wander round the castle,' she said.

'Yes. It's very interesting. What's wrong with that?'

'Nothing. One day you found the old nursery, in the attic in the Victorian wing.'

'Yes, I did.'

'When was that?'

He frowned. 'Don't ask me. Before Christmas, I think.'

'You suggested you might upcycle some of the toys.'

'That's right. But I was told to mind my own business and keep out of there.'

'Who by?'

'Dr Stenqvist. He said it wasn't safe for me. Organised for the place to be locked up. All those old toys in there, going to waste. Real shame.'

'When did you last go there?'

He looked at her as if she was daft. 'Before Christmas. Like I said!'

'Just that once?'

'Yes.'

'Did you go there last night, Angus?'

'*What?*'

'Did you?'

He opened his mouth then shut it again.

'Angus . . .'

'I was sleeping! I was very tired! I told you this. I wrote it down. I felt unwell in the afternoon. A bit sick, as if I was going to faint. So I went and lay down. I know I get confused. I woke up at one point and didn't even know where I was, but most of the time I was asleep — until well after nine!'

Lola stared. 'You didn't know where you were?'

'What?'

'You just said: "I didn't even know where I was."'

He thought about that. 'The room seemed the wrong way round. I was confused, that was all. But then I woke up in my own room and Dr Abbott was here. And I had this damned headache. What's this all about, anyway? Asking me if I was in the attic? Surely you don't think I killed that poor girl?'

'No, Angus,' Lola said. 'I don't think that.'

'Then—'

The emergency phone began to ring. It was Anna.

* * *

1.48 p.m.

Lola took the call in the corridor outside Angus Wilde's room.

'Boss, I got a number for the chap who writes the true-crime books.'

'And?'

'And I spoke to his wife. Boss, Ben Wilton travelled to the UK three weeks ago to research his next book, about Vivien Wray. He spoke to his wife from a hotel in London the morning of the day he was going to go to the place where Wray now worked, up in Scotland. He said he intended to get some answers. That was the last she heard of him. She reported him missing. I've looked, and there's a missing notice on file. Male, age thirty-eight, mousy hair, small beard. He flew to Glasgow the morning of the thirtieth of January. Not seen or heard from again. Australian police have looked at his phone records. There's a UK mobile number on there. He made repeated calls to it, and it called him. I just rang it, boss. It goes straight to the answering service. A voice says, "Hello, this is Amy Yorke. Please leave a message after the tone."'

'My God.' Lola pondered for a moment. 'Did you get a chance to look up the other thing I asked about?'

'About the attack on Vivien Wray after the trial?'

'Yes.'

'There are three news reports online. The details seem to tally. She was pushed down a flight of concrete stairs outside a shopping centre. Cuts and lacerations and three broken ribs. It was a man and a woman who did it. The woman was some sort of cousin to the mother of Alex Grimshaw. Her name was Clarissa Brown. The man was her boyfriend, a John Summers.'

Lola was silent for several seconds.

'You still there?' Anna asked.

'I'm still here . . .'

'Was there something else?'

'Aye, there was. Find out everything you can about Vivien Wray's sister. I've already seen photos but try to find more close-ups. She went along to the trial with her parents every day.'

CHAPTER TWENTY-FIVE

2.03 p.m.

PC Stephanie Moore was on duty. 'Is it about the road?' she asked. 'Because you're better to talk to the resilience team direct—'

'It's not about the road,' Lola said. 'I'm interested in whether there've been any unidentified bodies found locally in the past few weeks. Male, late thirties, mousy hair, beard.'

'Not that I'm aware . . . What area?'

'Anywhere within, I don't know, ten or fifteen miles of this place.'

'No,' she said, more decisively now. 'But then . . .'

'What?'

'We do find bodies from time to time. People who went missing years ago. The forests are so deep and there are ravines everywhere. Only last year a couple of hikers found the skeleton of a man who went missing in the 1980s. He'd come to the Trossachs looking for a rare dragonfly, believe it or not. No idea if he found it.'

'I see.'

'Sorry I can't help.'

Lola ended the call.

Dragonflies. The man had been looking for dragonflies.

She saw a sudden image in her mind, one so vivid, so electrifying, she jumped to her feet.

But then the phone burst into life again.

* * *

2.27 p.m.

'Vivien Wray's sister was called Janine,' Anna said. Lola was alone in the library now. 'She died four years ago. Killed in a car accident north of Sydney.'

'What do we know about her?'

'Not a lot. She was three years younger than Vivien. She attended the trial with her parents most days. Innocent teenager, taken out of school, wanting to support her big sister. Clever but quiet student, very pretty. Photos show she and Vivien looked quite alike. She was home-schooled after the trial, and there was a mention of musical ambitions that were cut short.'

'Oh?'

'She'd been a talented flute player, but she couldn't play after the age of fifteen thanks to an accident.'

'What accident?'

'Her hand got trapped in a swing door. She lost half her pinkie finger.'

CHAPTER TWENTY-SIX

3.12 p.m.

Lola stood alone in the old nursery in the attic of the castle's Victorian wing. Weak daylight filtered through dirty dormer windows and the two bare bulbs cast little light. She'd brought a torch, not Dr Abbott's this time, but one taken from the gun room. She shone its beam on the pile of cushions and toys against one wall, where stuffed animals were stacked on top of one another, their eyes catching the torch's beam. And there it was, shining back at her, a dragonfly in leaded green glass, half hidden. She went forward and moved a teddy bear with a gloved hand, then a monkey with a curling tail — and revealed a green glass lampshade.

Minutes later she was downstairs, at the bottom of the well of the hallway, amid the mess of pottery shards, beside Amy Yorke's twisted corpse. She imagined what had happened here.

She craned her neck to peer up at the highest landing over her head and at the empty plinth. Then she moved to the table where Catherine had said the Tiffany lamp stood.

She returned to the passage through which she and Abbott had come last night, on their way to his office after surveying the mess of Catherine Ballantyne's office. She studied the angles of the sofas and the planes of sight.

She moved to consider the empty table top, then turned to survey the office doors behind her. She recalled where Grace Miller had stood when Lola and Abbott had come out of his office and found her presiding over the scene of devastation.

And she knew what had happened.

She'd made one mistake, one which might have ramifications later. There was, however, one way to mitigate that error. She needed Amy Yorke's killers to confess.

To do that, she needed to set a trap.

* * *

3.30 p.m.

Lola found Shuna in the dining room, drinking coffee and typing like the wind.

'I need you,' Lola said quietly, landing on the chair beside her.

'Seriously?' Shuna's eyebrows met her hairline.

'Seriously. But I need you to make me two promises.'

'Depends what they are.'

'I need you to keep your trap shut for the duration. And you *cannot* write about it afterwards. What do you say?'

* * *

3.51 p.m.

'I'm going to search the old nursery,' Lola told Catherine in a loud, bright voice.

'Oh?' Catherine stopped and looked at her.

They were by the orangery. There were people about, listening.

'I believe there's something up there that's the key to this business,' Lola said.

Catherine's eyes were everywhere, anxiously assessing who might overhear. 'But what?' she asked, nervous tongue wetting her dry lips.

'I don't want to say,' Lola replied. 'I'm going to go up there in the next hour or so. But before that, I'm going to get myself a good strong coffee.'

She strode off, beaming, in the direction of the dining room.

* * *

4.15 p.m.

The stairs outside the old nursery creaked rhythmically as feet mounted them slowly. Then the creaking paused, as if the person was listening.

Lola was by the attic doorway, concealed behind the folding screen she'd lifted out from behind the mountain of soft toys.

Another creak from floorboards on the landing.

She listened intently, and heard the gentle turn of the doorknob, the click as the door's latch came open, then the quietest squeak of its hinges.

Through a gap in the screen, Lola saw a figure slip into the attic. The door closed behind it. A torch came on in the darkness, and the figure moved forward into the room, now in view.

It approached the train set and the pile of toys and bent to peer close. It took something from a pocket, something dark, that rustled as it unfurled.

Lola rose and stepped neatly out from behind the screen and darted for the light switch and at the same time flicked on her own torch. The attic was lit.

'Looking for something, Dr Abbott?' she asked loudly.

He whirled round, nearly tripping. He stared at her in appalled horror, the black bin bag trailing from his hand.

'I found it earlier today,' she said. 'It's locked away, safe and sound, ready for a fingerprint analysis.'

'I don't know what you mean,' he replied in a strangled cry.

'The lamp, Doctor. The Tiffany lamp. The one you stashed up here.' At that his face fell. 'I remembered I'd seen a dragonfly glinting among the toys when I came up here last night. It caught my torch. Of course, I wasn't looking for it then. I didn't even know it had been moved until Catherine told me. I expect you heard me talking to Catherine downstairs a wee while ago. Took fright and decided to come and retrieve it, did you? Were you going to take it away in that bag?'

He attempted a smile, but failed. He looked panicked and sick. His eyes flitted to the door.

'You can go if you like,' Lola said, theatrically standing to one side. 'But I'd be very interested to hear your side.' She smiled and folded her arms.

'You would, would you?' he asked in a low, dark voice.

He went into a pocket and lifted something to his lips. A radio. 'Come up,' he said tersely. 'Now.' He put it back in his pocket.

'Your accomplice?' Lola asked.

He said nothing.

'That's what she is, isn't she?' Lola went on. 'Or are you hers? Is that how this works? She has the power? The control? You're merely her puppet.'

'I don't know what you mean.'

Lola groaned. 'Oh, cut it out, Doctor. We both know you killed Amy — or conspired to, should I say?'

'You may think that,' he said.

'But you couldn't possibly comment?' she finished.

His eyes were on the door again.

'Coming here, is she? Forewarned and maybe forearmed?'

They watched one another, facing off in the dusty toy-strewn attic, under the eaves, under the moan of the dying storm.

'Waiting till she gets here?' Lola asked. 'Can't be trusted to speak for yourself? Shame.'

He said nothing, just stood there, his blond curls almost touching the apex of the long attic room.

And then Lola heard the creak of the stairs, under fast-approaching, lighter feet this time.

The door started to open.

Grace Miller slipped into the attic and closed the door behind her. Then she saw Lola. 'Oh—!'

'Hello, Grace,' Lola said. 'Answered Dr Abbott's call like a good accomplice, did you?' She looked from one to the other. 'I'm intrigued as to how you got into this wing. So much for me having sealed it up. I assume you have spare keys for the connecting doors.'

Neither said a word, but looked at each other with wide eyes, communicating silently.

'Nothing to say?' Lola asked.

'Tell us what you know,' Abbott said, eyes still on Grace. 'Or what you *think* you know.'

'I *think*,' Lola said, 'the two of you killed Amy Yorke.'

'Do you?' Abbott asked.

Grace Miller said nothing.

'Yes. I think you killed her because she was about to blow the lid on a deception worth hundreds of thousands of pounds. She was going to ask Stefan Kade to help her. She had the evidence she needed but she also had her own agenda and her own way of doing things. She didn't want you merely arrested. She wanted you exposed. You didn't have long to plan it, but I have to say, you killed her in a most ingenious way.'

Neither Abbott nor Miller said a word.

'But first, the motive. Amy believed Vivien Wray was guilty of the death of the Grimshaw child, despite being acquitted. Not only that, she believed Vivien Wray had shaken and injured another child in her care. An incident that had been hushed up. She had been in touch with the Grimshaw family. She was also in touch with a man called Wilton who was writing a book about Vivien Wray. He claimed to have actual evidence of Vivien's guilt.'

'Which allegations Grace denies absolutely,' Abbott said, eyes on Grace, who continued to give nothing away.

'The writer, Mr Wilton, travelled to the UK just over three weeks ago. I believe he was coming to the castle to confront you, Grace, having been invited there by Amy, whose number was in his phone. He had an Australian accent — so William Rix told Senga McCall. He asked to speak to you, Grace, but you refused. Then he asked to speak to Dr Abbott. I assume he knew of your relationship from Amy. You had a shouting match and "sent him packing", so you said, Doctor. The writer, Benedict Wilton, disappeared. He hasn't been seen or heard of since that day. I expect that's because he's dead.'

Abbott shrugged. 'As I've already told you, I sent him on his way. He knew he wasn't going to get anything from us. I can't account for his movements after that.'

Lola waited a few seconds.

'You'd been contracted to write a book,' she said to Grace. 'For a hefty sum. Rights have been sold around the world.'

'What of it?' Grace Miller asked in a small voice.

'It's my guess Amy believed the revelations about the second child would stop the book being published. I believe you killed her to protect that deal.'

'Utter rubbish,' Abbott sneered. 'The allegations aren't proven. And any scandal would only boost sales! You know that. That's what people are like! They'd lap it up. Before you know it, Grace would be getting paid to go on chat shows and appear in documentaries.'

'I agree,' Lola said. 'In itself it would be no motive for murder. No, it's not the allegations about the second child that threatened the deal. It's the possible exposure of another, much bigger secret.'

Grace Miller looked frightened now. Abbott's eyes were steely.

'What you feared might come out — what I believe both the true-crime author and Amy suspected — was that you, Grace, *are not Vivien Wray at all.*'

Grace began to hug herself tightly.

'You didn't lose half a finger in the attack in Australia. In that attack, Vivien received cuts and bruises and a couple of broken ribs. Loss of a finger is serious and would have been reported in any story. Vivien's sister *Janine*, however — she lost half a finger when it was trapped in a door. It stopped her playing the flute.'

Grace's head drooped.

'You're Janine Wray, aren't you, Grace? Vivien's younger sister. It was Vivien who died four years ago. She was living under a new name. I'm sure she died under that new name too, and no one knew the infamous Vivien Wray had passed. You came here to the UK and you met Dr Abbott here. Was it he who had the idea that you should start pretending to be Vivien so you could cash in, or was it you? Either way, you were set to make a fortune from a tell-all memoir, but which was second-hand at best, fiction at worst.'

Abbott muttered what sounded like a curse under his breath.

'Now, I don't think Amy knew that much,' Lola went on, 'but I expect you feared she would eventually work it out — especially if she was working with Wilton. I wonder why she felt the need to pursue you. An inflated sense of moral righteousness, perhaps? Amy came to you, didn't she, Doctor? She told you what she suspected about the second child. She didn't know about your relationship, though, so I expect you gave her some flim-flam and sent her on her way. Next she contacted Shuna Frain, and asked her to write a story. Hence Shuna's presence here this weekend.

'Amy tried to talk to Stefan Kade when he got here, but Catherine and others stopped her. I bet that gave you a fright. I think she'd have tried again later, but then Shuna appeared in the orangery with Catherine and I think she panicked. So she left.

'You acted quickly. One of you drugged Angus Wilde so that he'd fall deeply asleep. I think you moved him to another room. That way, when she went on her evening round, Amy would find him absent. Then you, Grace, contacted Amy on the radio and said Angus was in the old nursery in the attic and behaving erratically. Unfortunately for you, she happened to be with Kieran Fox at that moment and he heard the exchange. That was at about ten to eight.'

Grace Miller's eyes widened with fear at that. She looked at Abbott.

'Amy headed for the Victorian wing and climbed the stairs. I wonder what she found there . . . the nursery door open perhaps? I think you ran at her, Grace, taking her quite by surprise. I think you struck her with the hammer. I think she either stumbled over the balustrade or perhaps you helped her over the edge. She fell, landed on the hallway floor three levels below, breaking her neck and probably dying instantly. You then ran down to the ground floor and hid her body, pulling it behind a sofa or perhaps into a corner, so that when Dr Abbott and I came along the passage a little later — because, yes, that was all pre-arranged too — we wouldn't see that anything was wrong.

'I think that earlier, you'd brought one of the ornamental vases down from the third floor and placed it on the table in the hallway. You — or perhaps Dr Abbott — had moved the Tiffany lamp to this attic to make room for it. Anyone passing that way wouldn't notice an empty table. So the scene was set and you went into your office to wait. Another scene had been set elsewhere in the castle. Dr Abbott, I assume, had gone into Catherine's office and ransacked it, taking the letters as if that was the purpose of the break-in. He wrote a message on the mirror using Catherine's own lipstick, to plant the idea that another killer had been triggered by Amy's letters. The office trashed, he then manipulated Catherine, suggesting she might find Sister Yorke in one of the attics — specifically the old nursery — for which purpose she would need a key. Looking for the key, she found her office in a mess and came to find me. You then "happened along", didn't you, Doctor? You invited me to use the emergency phone, which you kept in your office. And so we went there, bang on cue, only minutes after Amy had plummeted to her death.'

'No one will believe any of this,' Abbott said. But Lola could see he was rattled. Badly. As for Grace, she stood very still, still hugging herself, her eyes screwed shut.

'You heard us coming, Grace, and even popped your head out of your door in a friendly greeting. That way I knew where you were. I followed Dr Abbott into his office and made the call to the local police. Meanwhile, you left your office, Grace, and pulled Amy's body back into the middle of the floor. Then you lifted the vase and threw it as high as you could into the middle of the hallway. They're large, those vases, but they're delicate and quite light, and it landed and smashed to smithereens. As you threw it, you screamed loudly: a squeal that you cut out as the vase smashed. Then you waited, hands to your mouth in horror, as if you'd just emerged from your room to find that a woman had fallen to her death.'

Grace Miller opened her eyes and gazed at Lola, and Lola knew she was right.

'And then I made my mistake,' Lola said. 'You, Doctor, offered to check if she was dead. You pretended to look for a pulse. You said, "She's still warm," or words to that effect. I believed you. I trusted you, because I'd been with you — plus, you were a doctor, so the right person to check for life. If I had checked myself, I think I would have found her body was cooler than it should have been.

'I think that while I was talking to Stefan Kade with Catherine, you then moved Angus Wilde back to his own room,' she said to Abbott. 'He remembers waking briefly and finding you standing over him.'

Abbott said nothing.

'And there you have it.'

Abbott swallowed. 'You won't prove any of this,' he said now.

'You think? I'll prove Grace isn't Vivien Wray. That won't be hard. The publishing deal will be off the table, I'm sure.'

Grace hung her head.

'Is it all you care about?' Lola asked her. 'The money?'

'You won't prove Grace killed Amy,' Abbott said.

'Oh, I think there'll be enough circumstantial evidence,' Lola said. 'Juries like that, you know? All those tiny strands add up to a compelling case.'

'Like what?' he demanded.

'For a start, fingerprints on the smashed vase. There'll be some. I doubt you wore gloves,' she said to Grace. 'There wouldn't have been time to take them off. We flew out of that room when we heard the racket.'

Grace's sharp, panicked look at Abbott told her she was right.

'I expect there'll be some on the Tiffany lamp too. And maybe some DNA on the claw hammer. Then, there's CCTV in Aberfoyle and along the B-road before you get to the castle turn-off. It'll show Benedict Wilton coming out here. I doubt it'll show him returning. Senga's evidence about the row Rix heard will be useful. Then there's Mr Wilton himself. His body will be found, you know. You can't have taken it far. It's coming into spring. Walkers will be out in the forest and in the hills. Someone will find him. Then we'll work out how he died. We'll check for a forensic link between you, Doctor, and him.'

Grace Miller said something that Lola didn't hear.

He gawped at her, then frowned angrily. 'No!' he spat at her.

'Yes!' she snapped back. 'What's the point without the book?'

'No, Grace,' he said to her. 'There's another way.'

Grace's eyes widened. She looked at Lola then back at Abbott.

'Can we do it?' she asked him. She licked her lips. 'Can we really?'

'It's got to be worth the risk,' Abbott said, and his own eyes slid towards Lola.

'You're thinking of sending me over the edge of the balcony too?' Lola asked him. 'Clouting me with a hammer first? You'd really do that? Another murder? The murder of a police detective? You'd *never* get away with it.'

'I think we might,' Abbott said quietly. He nodded once at Grace. 'Now!'

And he ran at Lola, while Grace grabbed her from the other side.

'Stop right there!' Shuna Frain yelled, stepping out from behind the screen.

Grace yelped in shock and fell away, while Abbott's grip on Lola's arm loosened enough for her to yank herself free and step away.

Shuna held up her hand, showing a square, silver object. 'I heard every word you said and so did this thing.'

Grace whimpered. Abbott gazed in abject horror, face drawn, jaw quivering.

'It's over, Doctor,' Lola told him.

The attic door flew open, making all of them start. Catherine stood there, hands to her mouth. Behind her was a man Lola didn't recognise. He gaped in at them.

Lola approached the door. She spotted a woman behind the man, and another man behind her. Catherine moved aside.

'DCI Lola Harris,' she said to the waiting group. 'You'll be local CID, then? It's about bloody time.'

CHAPTER TWENTY-SEVEN

7.34 p.m.

'You're awake,' Frankie said when Lola appeared in the doorway of the kitchen of Rose Cottage.

'Just about,' Lola said.

She was feeling surprisingly serene after three hours' deep, blissful sleep. Ibuprofen had eased the pain in her arm where Abbott had grabbed her, though there'd be bruising. The hour after the police arrived had finished her off. In that time she'd handed the case, and the killers of Amy Yorke, over to a local DI and his DS, plus an operational statement of her own involvement in the case. With Catherine's help, she'd gathered the staff and guests in the dining room and told them as much as she could.

'You're a very impressive young woman,' Heidi Bryce had told her afterwards, catching her in the corridor.

'Not all that young, I'm afraid,' she'd replied.

'You're a force of nature,' Heidi had replied, her eyes twinkling.

'Aye, okay, I'll take that.'

Frankie asked, 'Do you want a tea or a coffee or something to eat, maybe?'

'Tea, please.'

But Frankie didn't move. She was looking at Lola with anxious concern.

'What's wrong?'

'Nothing.' She busied herself filling the kettle.

'No, go on. What were you going to say?'

Frankie turned off the water and put the kettle down. She said, eyes averted, 'I was wondering when you were going to go through me, that's all.'

'Go through you?'

'Aye, well. I feel I deserve some kind of bollocking. So, come on. Let's get on with it.'

Lola watched her sister, amused.

'Frankie . . .'

Frankie winced.

'It's been some weekend,' she went on. 'I mean, there's no denying that.'

'I overstepped, didn't I?'

Lola shrugged. 'Aye, a wee bit. But you never intended me to end up dealing with a murder.'

'I feel bad.'

'Well . . .'

'Well, what?'

'I was going to say, feel bad if it'll make you feel better, but . . . that doesn't sound quite right, does it? Look, it wasn't all bad.'

'Meaning what?' Frankie dared to look up at Lola.

'I was in my element. Doing what I do. Doing it well. Or well enough . . .'

'*Well enough*,' Frankie mocked. 'You did a bit better than that, Lola.'

'It's what I do. It's what I trained for. It's what I'm experienced in.' She frowned as the thought took shape in her mind. 'I think it might be what I'm here for.'

'What you're here for?'

'Here, on earth — not to be grand about it. It's my vocation, isn't it? Solving problems, putting things back together again. Giving people some peace of mind.'

Frankie permitted herself a small smile. 'So . . . you'd let me organise another weekend away some time?'

'Maybe not quite yet,' she demurred. 'I hate my job, Frankie. My new job, I mean. I hate it with a passion. Not that I feel any passion for the job itself — which is the problem.'

'So leave,' Frankie said. 'Tell them you're out of there. A week's notice max. Go back to Elaine Walsh and tell her to take you back or you're quitting the police. Sandy's desperate for you to work together. Go on, get militant. You're good at that.'

Lola breathed. 'I signed up for it,' she said. 'I said I'd do it. I have to do it. It's . . . about duty, I suppose.'

'Sod that, Lola.' Frankie made a dismissive noise. 'Life's too short.'

'Aye, well . . . Hurry up with the tea, will you? I'll go stoke up the stove.'

* * *

8.46 p.m.

'You should come again, in the summer perhaps, or the autumn,' Catherine said. 'Everything will be running smoothly by then, I hope.'

'We'll see,' Lola said.

'Yes, well . . .' Catherine bit her lip. 'I'd understand if you're a little reticent about coming back here.'

Four of them sat round the log burner — Lola, Frankie, Catherine and Shuna — like four friends at the end of an enjoyable weekend away.

Catherine said, 'I'm glad you're staying one more night. Quite honestly, I think I would feel quite abandoned if you left as well as everyone else.'

The Kades' helicopter had come just after five, and whisked Kade and his wife off to London. He'd come to find Lola, to sheepishly thank her. 'You're welcome,' she'd said simply and let him shake her hand, while all the time that sinister word flashed in her head — *eugenics, eugenics, eugenics* — making her want to withdraw her hand fast and scrub it clean.

'When will we know the truth about what Grace was up to?' Catherine asked.

'When she decides to speak,' Lola said. 'If she decides to speak. The injury to her hand suggests very strongly that she is Janine Wray. She can't keep up the deception forever.'

'But why would she pretend to be her own sister?' Frankie asked.

'Attention, the chance to have a tragic past to confide about? I don't know. Remember, in her mind, Vivien was innocent. What was the harm?'

'William Rix's sister contacted me,' Catherine said. 'Strange woman. Wants to know if his belongings can be sent to her immediately. Got quite shirty with me, so I told her to speak to the police and put the phone down. Do you think he really did kill his mother?'

'He claimed he did,' Lola said. 'She was old and ill, I expect. Maybe she'd have died anyway, but he certainly intended her to die.'

'Strange how he wore that monk's habit. It was such a Gothic scene, him walking along the roof like that, like Hamlet's father.' She shuddered. 'And the way he cut his wrists. That's how the ghostly monk was supposed to have died, only he ran around the estate, arms in the air. I wonder now . . .'

'You wonder what?' Frankie asked.

'I thought I saw the ghost once, running along the edge of the trees then vanishing into them. I told a few people — it seemed so real, and yet, at the same time, so bizarre . . . William was always a very odd chap.' Catherine sat up. 'When Tom Abbott wrote that horrible message on the mirror in my office — "How many killers under one roof?" — do you think he knew about William?'

'I doubt it,' Lola said. 'I think he simply wanted to plant the idea that Amy might have stumbled on another killer at the castle — not Grace, in other words — and make everyone look elsewhere for Amy's killer.'

Inside the burner, a log fell, causing a burst of sparks.

'What will happen to Margot Kerr?' Shuna asked.

'I hope she'll leave in the morning,' Catherine said stiffly. 'She was still in her room when I left the castle just now. She hasn't come out all day. I tried to talk to her. I tapped on her door and called through. She told me to "eff off".'

'Can't you charge her with something?' Shuna asked Lola, sounding aggrieved.

'*I* won't be charging her with anything,' Lola pointed out. 'But she could be charged with a Section 38 offence, yes. It's essentially a breach of the peace. She's behaved in a threatening or abusive manner, likely to cause a reasonable person fear or alarm. But as I say, it's not up to me.'

'Back to the day job from tomorrow, then?' Shuna asked, a little pointedly.

Lola caught Frankie's slightly guilty eye and realised she must have filled Shuna in on her current professional misery.

'Aye, back to it,' she said, more cheerfully than she felt.

'Then enjoy the champagne I brought you,' Catherine said, rising. 'Shuna, will you come back to the castle with me now, or . . . ?'

'She'll stay for a glass or two, won't you, Shuna?' Lola said.

'Aye, just a couple,' Shuna said.

CHAPTER TWENTY-EIGHT

Monday 24 February

1.25 p.m.

Detective Superintendent Elaine Walsh told Lola to come in after 1 p.m. By then she'd have finished her meetings and would have some time.

It was strange being back at Helen Street, familiar and alienating at the same time. She'd worked here for several years and now she didn't. She had her own office in a super-secure building twenty miles from here, with her own team. And no job satisfaction — or pals.

Anna was there and jumped up to embrace her, full of concern for what she called Lola's 'ordeal'.

'It wasn't an ordeal,' Lola said. 'I mean, it was. But I was so tired, I just went onto a kind of autopilot.'

'Do you want a coffee or something?'

'No, thanks. I'm here to see Elaine. She's still technically my line manager, so . . .'

A sharp-suited figure swaggered through the office. DS Aidan Pierce stopped when he saw Lola, and his self-satisfied expression darkened.

'Hello, Aidan,' Lola called.

'Mm,' he managed.

'Missing your time at the MIT, I expect,' she said.

He said something indistinct and slunk to his desk.

'Ah, Lola!' Elaine appeared through the doors from the stairwell. 'Are you coming through?'

* * *

'You look fine,' Elaine said when they were in her office. 'Better than that, in fact. I'm most surprised.'

'Thanks, I think.'

'I'd go as far as to say you look . . . strangely *victorious*?'

'Do I?'

'Have a seat.'

Elaine made her recount the whole thing. She did it, without notes, and in under five minutes.

'Of course,' she said when Lola had finished, 'you didn't do what you should have. That is, protected the evidence, checked for threat to others' lives . . . and sat tight.'

'No, boss. I didn't do that.'

'Instead you shook the whole place up, identified not one but two poison pen letter writers and solved a murder — two, if you count William Rix's confession about his mother's death. Not to mention possibly working out what happened to the missing Australian writer. All that in under twenty-four hours.'

'I know, boss.'

'Only you, Lola.'

'Only me?'

'Only you could do that. Then sit there like you've rearranged your kitchen cupboards and are happy with the result.'

'Are you telling me off, boss?'

'Hmm.' Elaine rocked back in her seat and chewed the end of a pen. 'I'm not sure. I expect you enjoyed every minute, didn't you?'

Lola considered the question. 'I didn't enjoy going into that cellar — or up onto that roof. I'm sorry I couldn't stop

William Rix taking his life. But . . . in general terms . . . aye, you might be right.' She allowed herself a smile.

Elaine nodded and rolled her eyes.

'So you're taking today as annual leave,' she said now. 'Back to Gartcosh in the morning?'

'Aye. I'll be there. There's a big meeting. Comms are leading it, worse luck.'

'You hate it, don't you?'

'I'm a detective, boss, not a project manager. And all this analysis the team are doing? I don't care about what it leads to. I don't even care if anyone gets prosecuted. And that's not good, is it?'

'You're more than competent for the role.'

'Maybe. But it's not what I'm here for, is it?'

'When you say "here" . . . ?'

She shrugged and smiled. 'Here. Alive and on earth.'

Elaine's eyebrows rose.

'I know it sounds grand,' Lola went on, 'but if this weekend has taught me anything, it's that I need to do what I'm best at. And I'm best at investigating, sleeves rolled up, calling the shots and, well, catching the bad guys.'

Elaine smiled sadly. 'Your secondment is for six months.'

'I want to come back, boss. I want to work for you again. ASAP.'

Elaine said nothing, just pursed her lips.

'If you'll have me,' she pressed on, but still nothing. 'I guess it's partly out of your hands though, isn't it?'

'You're right about that,' Elaine murmured.

'Please, boss. I need to be here. If I can't, then I'm going to have to resign from the force. I really don't want to do that. Sandy wants me to work with him — for twice the money I get here! But . . .'

'But what?'

'This is where my heart is,' she said. 'In this job, working for you, working with Anna and Kirstie and . . . well . . .'

'Aidan Pierce?'

'Aye. Him an' all.'

Elaine inclined her head. 'Secondments change people,' she said. 'You might not feel the same about this job.'

'Do you think?'

'You might miss the authority you've had, the contact with our most senior leaders, our most senior corporate comms people.'

'Doubt I'd miss any of that, to be frank.'

'On the other hand, you might relish being back,' Elaine went on. She narrowed her eyes. 'You might even decide to toe the line a bit more, to stick to protocols.' She leaned forward and said meaningfully, 'To go through the proper channels from time to time.'

Lola bridled. 'Not sure about that either, boss. That'd be a bit . . . radical, don't you think?'

'Hmm.'

Elaine glanced at her desk phone. She reached for the receiver. 'Let me make a phone call.'

'Thank you, boss.'

'No promises, all right? But I'll try. I'll try my very hardest. Now, you hop it and enjoy the rest of your day off.'

'Thanks, boss.' Lola rose. 'I won't let you down.'

'I know that,' Elaine said.

Lola smiled.

THE END

ACKNOWLEDGEMENTS

Big thanks, as ever, to Chief Inspector Kirsty Lawie of Police Scotland for her assistance with the policing elements of the plot (though this story was slightly different!).

Patrick Hughes advised me on the kind of clinical set-up you might expect to find in such a unique place as Ardaig Castle. I've taken some artistic licence with his advice.

Karen Corbett, who lives in a castle (or part of a castle!) showed me around and helped me think about the layout of Ardaig Castle.

Thanks once more to Simon and Chris for letting me work at their place in the wilds of Kintyre. Thanks, too, to Niall Kinsella, for looking after my website.

My beta readers were immensely helpful — and very speedy, thankfully. Thanks to my mum, Julie, as well as to Astrid Reid, Janice Fraser, Jill Crawford, Fiona Macdonald, Joanne Welding, John and Rowena Gregory, Katharine Bradbury, Linda Mather and Yvonne Boyd.

Emma Grundy Haigh helped shape the outline for the book, before my new editor Siân Heap took over. Thanks to both of them, and to Kate Ballard too.

I really value my wonderful agent, Francesca Riccardi, for keeping me sane and focused — on top of all the agency/contracty stuff. Thanks, Fran!

A big thank you to my other half, Gordon, for his love and support, and to Rasmus for keeping me company.

THE JOFFE BOOKS STORY

We began in 2014 when Jasper agreed to publish his mum's much-rejected romance novel and it became a bestseller.

Since then we've grown into the largest independent publisher in the UK. We're extremely proud to publish some of the very best writers in the world, including Joy Ellis, Faith Martin, Caro Ramsay, Helen Forrester, Simon Brett and Robert Goddard. Everyone at Joffe Books loves reading and we never forget that it all begins with the magic of an author telling a story.

We are proud to publish talented first-time authors, as well as established writers whose books we love introducing to a new generation of readers.

We won Trade Publisher of the Year at the Independent Publishing Awards in 2023 and Best Publisher Award in 2024 at the People's Book Prize. We have been shortlisted for Independent Publisher of the Year at the British Book Awards for the last five years, and were shortlisted for the Diversity and Inclusivity Award at the 2022 Independent Publishing Awards. In 2023 we were shortlisted for Publisher of the Year at the RNA Industry Awards, and in 2024 we were shortlisted at the CWA Daggers for the Best Crime and Mystery Publisher.

We built this company with your help, and we love to hear from you, so please email us about absolutely anything bookish at feedback@joffebooks.com.

If you want to receive free books every Friday and hear about all our new releases, join our mailing list here: www.joffebooks.com/freebooks.

And when you tell your friends about us, just remember: it's pronounced Joffe as in coffee or toffee!